Frightened to Depths

Frightened to Depths

Cruising Sisters Mystery

K.B. Jackson

TULE
PUBLISHING

Frightened to Depths
Copyright© 2024 K.B. Jackson
Tule Publishing First Printing, January 2025

The Tule Publishing, Inc.

ALL RIGHTS RESERVED

First Publication by Tule Publishing 2024

Cover design by ebooklaunch.com

No part of this book may be used or reproduced in any manner whatsoever without written permission except in the case of brief quotations embodied in critical articles and reviews.

This is a work of fiction. Names, characters, places, and incidents are products of the author's imagination or are used fictitiously. Any resemblance to actual events, locales, organizations, or persons, living or dead, is entirely coincidental.

AI was not used to create any part of this book and no part of this book may be used for generative training.

ISBN: 978-1-965640-75-3

Dedication

For my sisters. I'm so glad to have been on this journey of life with you.

"I can't go back to yesterday because
I was a different person then."

Lewis Carroll

Room Assignments

701: Charlotte McLaughlin and Jane Cobb
802: Alexander St. Jacques (Trumpet)
806: Percy Brown (Double bass)
807: Heath Hubbard (Vibraphone)
808: Bancroft Suite—vacant
809: Ophelia Thibodeaux (Singer)
810: Victor Lutz (Piano)
811: Webster Powell (Drums)
812: The Doran suite rented by Professor Emmett Guidry

Chapter One

I SPOTTED THE lifeless figure as soon as I rounded the corner.

"Over here!" I called to whomever could hear me above the roar of the ship's engines.

I rushed toward him, crouching to get a closer look.

Oh no. No!

A memory flashed of Jane and I dancing to his music in my bridal suite as I attempted to shake off my nerves hours before my wedding.

Music that was now forever silenced.

My heartbeat pounded in my ears as I stared into his dark, unblinking eyes, frozen in a state of fright. The only movement I detected came from the whiskers cloaking his face, ruffled by the brisk sea air.

I collapsed onto the ship's deck. My foot kicked a small object. It clanked and rolled a few inches from me. As the full moon emerged from behind the clouds, its glow reflected off the item, a piece of silvery metal lying on the ground beside his limp hirsute hand.

It was a bullet casing. Etched on the side in an old-fashioned scroll font was one word: ROUGAROU.

⚓

48 Hours Earlier

"Isn't this nice?" my sister Jane asked as we walked past Jackson Square in the heart of the French Quarter.

Jane and I were back in New Orleans following a quick jaunt to Baton Rouge for the Louisiana Book Festival. We had one last night in the Big Easy before our residential cruise ship—the *Thalassophile of the Seas*—set sail again. Next stop: Port-au-Prince.

"Isn't what nice? Do you mean the city?" I juggled a garment bag containing a formal ballgown in one hand with a pastry and a large chicory latte in the other.

"That, but also, isn't it nice to be off the ship?" Jane had her own dress slung over her shoulder like a sack of flour.

"Are you already tired of a life at sea?"

"Not at all. It's just a nice change of pace to be on terra firma for a few days. And of course, no murder."

I laughed. "I watched the news last night. New Orleans isn't exactly what I'd call murder free."

"Sure, but we aren't in the middle of those cases trying to solve them. Promise me, Char. No more murder investigations."

I crooked my head to look at her. "You've got something on your face."

Jane brushed her fingers across her mouth. "Powdered sugar is the glitter of the dessert world. One tiny bag of beignets has enough powdered sugar at the bottom to cover the surface of the earth, with enough left over to coat the moon as well."

If she were being honest with herself, the bag of deep-fried donuts from Café Du Monde in the center of the French Market was far from tiny, and three full-sized beignets weren't exactly what I'd call a light snack, especially at nine in the morning.

The bottom of the bag held more superfluous sugar than I'd used in a decade; I'd give her that. As a matter of fact, I had a box of powdered sugar on my pantry shelf left over from the great panic buying of Y2K.

"Don't change the subject." Jane wagged her index finger and then held up her pinkie. "Promise me."

How binding was a pinkie promise? "I'd rather not."

"Charlotte." She jabbed her pinkie at me.

"Fine. I promise." I linked my right little finger with hers.

After all, I'd never seen an episode of *Judge Judy* where the defendant was held to a pinkie promise.

"Char—"

"I said I promise."

"Not that. I just wanted to check in with you. You just passed a major milestone, and we didn't even talk about it."

"Milestone?"

"*Charlotte.*" She looked down her nose at me.

My attempt at obtuse hadn't fooled my sister. She knew me too well.

She meant my husband Gabe's death, of course. The one-year anniversary. It wasn't that I hadn't remembered. I hadn't known what to do with it.

How did one commemorate such a significant, yet complicated, loss?

Kyrie Dawn had put together a makeshift memorial service in the Azure Lounge. She claimed it was important for Quinton to honor his father's memory, despite the fact he was only a toddler. I'd come down with a convenient migraine that day, but Jane had gone in my place and reported back to me.

The program had started with a short slideshow of photos set to *their* song, "Saving All My Love" by Whitney Houston—because, of course it was—but Kyrie Dawn only had the ones taken since she'd met Gabe, and I'd declined to submit any.

Between ten and fifteen people had shown to pay their respects. They'd known Gabe from the many sailings he and Kyrie Dawn had made in their love nest at sea. Most of those people hadn't even known he had a wife until he died.

Of course, I'd only learned about the existence of Gabe's longtime mistress and their son the same day two uniformed officers had shown up on my doorstep to tell me his car had hit a pole following a fatal heart attack.

So, yeah, it was complicated.

Despite the shock of his death, the revelations that he'd been keeping all sorts of things from me, and the added bonus of humiliation over his betrayal, I'd waded through the year of firsts like the stalwart I always tried to be. I'd braced myself against each wave. Thanksgiving had been spent consoling our nephew Andy following the death of his fiancée on their wedding cruise. On Christmas morning,

Jane and I had assisted in serving more than eight hundred of Seattle's less fortunate with an organization called Cozy Connections. On Gabe's birthday, Jane had booked us a full day at the spa. Our anniversary required a bit more alcohol and chocolate, but I'd been prepared.

There was something different about crossing that threshold into year two that I couldn't quite reconcile.

"Have you thought about therapy?" Jane asked.

"I talked to someone."

"I mean ongoing."

"I have you for that."

"Char, I can't be responsible for your mental—"

"Of course, I don't expect you to be. I'm fine, Jane. Really. Good, even. Now, here's the plan. We do brunch at Brennan's, dinner at Commander's Palace, and finish off with drinks and jazz someplace."

"We can put a pin in that conversation, but you need to talk about it, preferably to a professional."

I gave a noncommittal murmur. If I started honestly dealing with my feelings about the situation, there was a good chance I'd drown under them.

Jane sighed and shook her head. "So, your plan is to roll ourselves back up the gangplank tomorrow because we'll have eaten our way across this entire city?"

I smiled at her, relieved she wasn't pressing the issue further. "Exactly."

We turned into Pirate Alley at Royal Street. Navigating the cobblestone in my heeled boots proved challenging. The cast iron lampposts that bordered each side of the path were unlit, and although the sun was attempting to peek through the clouds, the alley itself was appropriately shaded for its reputation as a haunted playground for the wandering spirits of pirates, novelists, priests, and prisoners.

Rumored to have once been the stomping grounds for pirate Jean Lafitte and his cohorts from the marshy islands of Barataria Bay, Pirate Alley was now a prominent stop on any New Orleans ghost tour.

"I read in the guidebook that the ghost of William Faulkner is purported to haunt this alley." Jane shivered for dramatic effect. "That's almost scarier than running into the ghost of a pirate."

"Your disdain for him is as legendary as it is inexplicable." I nodded at a cream-colored building with baby blue doors ahead of us. "Speak of the devil." A small blue-and-gold sign hung above the doorway. FAULKNER HOUSE BOOKS. "Wanna peek inside?"

Jane brushed powdered sugar from her navy-blue sweater. "Not if it's only Faulkner."

"I believe they have rare and collectible books as well. Perhaps we'll see the ghost of old Billy-boy writing at his desk, and you can tell him why you despise his work so much."

"I'm always down for that."

As we entered the store, a young woman greeted us from the counter in the back, which was lighter and brighter than I'd expected for a seller of antiquated books. Usually, those shops smelled like mildew and soot and were dimly lit by incandescent bulbs dating back to the time of Edison flickering their archaic filament's grand finale. This place had fresh paint, polished chandeliers, and gorgeous woodwork.

It was narrow, but meticulously organized shelves reached all the way to the tall ceiling.

I deeply inhaled the scent of my first love: books. "Do you miss it?"

"Do I miss what?" Jane shoved the beignet-less bag into her purse. She caught me staring at her, and she grimaced with embarrassment. "You never know when a spare cup of powdered sugar might come in handy."

"You mean like pocket sand, but instead it's purse sugar?"

She gave a bewildered smile. "What? What does that even mean?"

"You know, like in those old martial arts movies, where they'd keep a handful of sand in their pocket in case they needed to throw it in the eyes of their adversaries for a quick getaway."

"Not a bad idea. I can think of a couple times recently when that would have come in handy. Now what were you asking? Do I miss what?"

"Do you miss the library? The book world? The creak of a hardcover upon its inaugural opening?" I added that last part because I knew it would bug her to no end.

Her horrified expression was comical. "What kind of monster cracks the spine of a book?"

I was that kind of monster. "Tell me again why you can't stand Faulkner."

Jane glanced at the woman behind the counter. "Shh.

You can't disparage Faulkner in front of Faulknerites. They're rabid in their devotion to him, although I can't imagine why."

A man in a tan trench coat and a fedora entered the shop, his head down. He hustled back to the clerk. "*Bon matin*, Angelique. How are you today?"

"Fine as always. I was wondering if I'd see you today. The month is coming to an end and I've only seen you twice."

"I've been fully engrossed in a project, and this is the first I've poked my head out of my office in days."

"Sounds fascinating. How can I help?"

"I'm looking for folklore stories about the Rougarou."

I jerked my thumb toward the counter. "She's otherwise occupied. You're fine. Tell me where this abject hatred of one of America's most significant writers of all time originated."

"I had a professor at UDub who was obsessed with Faulkner, and I was obsessed with the professor, so I read everything I could get my hands on. I didn't get it. I thought I must have accidentally picked up the works of some other guy named William Faulkner. But no, it was him, and it was nothing special. I just think he's overrated. Have you read *Spotted Horses*? There's literally no arc to the story. It's just a bunch of guys at a horse auction. Nothing happens."

"*The Sound and the Fury* is an important novel. You have to admit that."

"I do not. Reading that book reminded me of what happens when parents feed ice cream to their preschoolers before coming to story time at the library. A blathering of nonsense with zero pauses to take breaths, along with a meandering plot." She wandered over to one of the mahogany shelves and ran her finger across the broken spines of several classics. "This is a tragedy."

"They're just well-loved, that's all. The way books are supposed to be."

She snorted her derision. "Blasphemy."

"By the way, what was that professor's name? You've never mentioned him. I wonder if I ever had him."

She sighed the smiling sigh of a schoolgirl's crush as she turned away from the bookshelf. "Emmett Guidr—oh my good gawd!" Her gaze widened.

I whipped my head around to see what she was gaping at.

"It's him!"

"Who? Faulkner's ghost?" I scanned the bookstore but saw no apparitions.

Jane knocked over a display of books, causing both the clerk and the man at the counter to look at her with alarm.

"I can't believe it," she whispered.

A flash of recognition crossed the man's face.

Jane swayed. She placed one trembling hand on the display table for support.

"I can't believe after all these years, it's really him."

Chapter Two

THE MAN LEANED against the counter and stared back at Jane with his head cocked and a curious expression. He stood straight and took a step forward. "I feel as if I know you." He had a lilting Southern accent. "But I can't quite place your face."

I judged him to be in his early-to-mid-60s, with a distinguished Clooney-esque quality I deeply resented in aging men. He was tan with light blue eyes and salt-and-pepper hair that leaned saltier.

"Professor Guidry." Jane touched her freshly French-tipped fingers to her décolletage. "I'm Jane Cobb. I'm not sure if you remember me. I was in your early modern American lit class at the University of Washington, back in the eighties."

The sparkle in his eyes was visible even from across the store. "Jane! Jane Cobb. It *is* you. I can*not* believe it. What are you doing here in New Orleans?"

"My sister Charlotte and I"—she waved her hand in my direction—"live full-time on a cruise ship, and we've been docked here for a few days. We leave again tomorrow. What are you doing here? I mean, not here in Faulkner House. Of course you'd be in Faulkner House, I remember what a fan of Faulkner you were. Or probably still are, considering you're here. At Faulkner House, I mean." Babbling was one of Jane's tells that she was nervous.

She kept her contempt for Faulkner out of her voice as she said his name, and I had every intention of haranguing her about that later.

I hadn't seen her this way in the presence of a man for quite some time. He must have been fresh out of grad school when he was teaching her class, because he didn't look to be more than five years older than her.

As he moved closer to us, Jane took a sharp intake of breath. She was rattled.

"I'm now at Tulane, here in the city, although I'm currently on sabbatical. I'm writing a book about Louisiana folklore."

"How fascinating!" Jane's normally alto speaking voice hit a pitch even a soprano would envy. Another nervous tell.

"What's fascinating is, you live full-time on a cruise ship. How did that come about?" His slow drawl contrasted sharply with Jane's fevered pitch in a comedic way.

"Long story, but basically Char—oh, I should introduce you. Professor Guidry, this is my sister, Charlotte McLaughlin."

"Emmett. Please." He extended his hand. "Nice to meet you."

His skin was the kind of soft that spoke of a life devoid of manual labor, and his flaccid handshake was like that of belles, debutantes, and other members of genteel Southern society. My prejudices against such things judged him untrustworthy, but at least I felt guilty about it.

"Likewise."

"Anyway, Char's dead husband, Gabe, bought a floating condo love nest for rendezvous with his mistress, and we live there now."

Emmett Guidry gave me the same pitying glance I'd become accustomed to whenever my dirty laundry was on display. "My condolences," he murmured.

"Yeah, thanks." It was all I could muster.

Perhaps one day the sting of those expressions of condescending sympathy would abate. Even after a year, it was still too fresh not to get under my skin.

"I overheard you asking the clerk about something called Rougarou. What is that, some type of Cajun dish?" Jane asked.

He chuckled. "Cajun, yes. As for food...well, you're more likely to be the Rougarou's dinner than he is to be yours."

She flashed him a puzzled look. "Pardon?"

"A Rougarou is a werewolf. The term originated in medieval France as *Loup-Garou* but was brought to North America with the Acadians, from whom I am descended. When they migrated from Canada to the Bayou, they brought with them the legends, and over time the name morphed into *Rougarou*."

"Interesting. And you're researching this...Rougarou for your book on local folklore?"

"I am. I figured it was time I pay homage to my ancestors

and accurately record their cultural heritage. Speaking of Cajun dishes, I would love to take you to lunch, Jane." The professor's neatly manicured brows angled in a hopeful—almost boyish—way.

"Oh, I don't know." She turned to me. "We had plans to go to Brennan's for brunch."

She wanted me to let her off the hook. Her weak protest and hopeful expression said as much. If I decided to make a fuss, she'd have to go along with our original plan, but that risked a pouty, resentful Jane.

Still, it was tempting. I didn't want to eat alone, and someone had to keep her from impetuously diving in headfirst with a man she didn't really know.

She fervently blinked her desired response like a distressed boat signaling S.O.S.

I waved her off. "It's fine. I can do Brennan's by myself. I have a good book to read." I held up my shopping bag. "Several, in fact."

Her gaze conveyed her thanks.

"If you prefer, we could do dinner instead," Emmett said. "Jacques-Imo's Café on Oak Street in the Garden District has the most amazing shrimp and alligator sausage cheesecake, but they don't open until five."

Jane's normally pink cheeks took on the pallor of an overripe avocado. Despite her penchant for spontaneity, she wasn't the most adventurous eater I knew. "Mm. Sounds, uh, delicious. But I heard you had to book reservations months in advance for that place."

"I have my ways." The professor winked. "Connections."

Despite the wimpy handshake, I was beginning to see why Jane had been infatuated with him in college. As charming and handsome as he was in his sixties, he must have been smoking hot as a twenty-something teacher.

"Char and I have reservations at Commander's Palace for dinner. Let's stick with lunch."

"Perfect. Let's meet at Liuzza's by the Track at noon." He flashed her a thousand-watt smile.

"See you there." Jane's words were so breathless they were barely audible.

She grabbed me by the arm and hustled me out of the bookstore. She didn't slow down until we'd reached the end of Pirate's Alley at St. Louis Cathedral, at which point she burst into maniacal laughter to the point of nearly hyperventilating.

"Pull yourself together."

She bent over, wheezing, with her hands on her knees. "I can't. This is bonkers. What are the odds?"

"It's a stunning coincidence. No doubt."

She stood upright. "It's not a coincidence. It's fate."

Practical, no-nonsense Jane just labeled something as fate? "You once told me fate was a concept people invented to justify their hearts' desires, especially when they knew they shouldn't be doing it."

She shrugged. "I stand by that assessment for most situations, but how else can you explain it? The moment I'm uttering that man's name after not having spoken of it in more than thirty years, he appears right in front of me?"

"I don't do statistics, so I can't tell you the actual numerical probability, but I think it was skewed by the fact we were in Faulkner's former home—or according to some, his ghost's current home—and Professor Guidry is an ardent Faulkner fan."

"All I know is that for the first time in, I don't even know how long, I think I have a date."

⚓

WE PARTED WAYS at eleven thirty. Jane sported a new top and bright red lipstick for her lunch with Professor Guidry. I had changed into pants with an elastic waistband for my solo brunch at Brennan's.

The exterior of the iconic restaurant was painted a salmon pink color, with white doors and windows accented by black shutters and black wrought iron balconies on the second floor. The dark cloud I had been eyeing warily chose at that moment to open up and begin a torrential downpour. I quickly ducked under the green awning but not in time to avoid a full soaking.

The hostess gave me a sympathetic smile. "Welcome to fall in N'awlins. Do you have a reservation?"

"I do. It's for two people under McLaughlin, but unfortunately, my sister had a change of plans." Was there a touch of bitterness in my tone?

"No problem at all. Follow me."

The dining room featured large marble columns and whimsical murals surrounded by fern-green lattice accent panels. The ceiling was covered in the same green lattice and the floor was a harlequin diamond or checkerboard pattern. The semicircular booths were tufted green leather of a similar hue, but the rattan dining chairs were upholstered in a bright salmon pink leather that coordinated with the shades on each wall sconce.

The theme would aptly be described as indoor French garden party.

"This is the Chanteclair Room. We also have the King's Room, the Queen's Room, which is often used for private parties, and then the Roost Bar." She placed one menu at a four-top table in the center of the room. "Here we are. Your server will be right with you."

She sashayed back to the entrance before I could finish uttering my awed thanks.

I'd heard about Brennan's, but it truly was a special place to behold.

As I perused the menu, I couldn't help but observe the conversations happening on either side of me. At the table to my right, a young man fidgeted with his napkin while the young woman next to him sullenly pushed her food around her plate with her fork. A woman about my own age—but significantly more put together—swigged her mimosa like her life depended on it.

Next to her, a gray-haired man in a dark blue suit, light blue shirt, and an ascot scowled at the young couple seated across from him. "This isn't exactly how I prefer to learn that my daughter is engaged. It's simply not how it's done."

"I understand, sir." The young man could barely look his future father-in-law in the eyes.

To my left, four children—two girls and two boys—about twelve years of age or younger sat alone at their table. Where were their parents? They didn't seem to belong to anyone. Their varied ethnicities indicated they likely didn't belong to the same family, either.

Despite their ages, however, they seemed quite mature and well-behaved.

Of the many things I missed most about being a librarian, the top were all the children's literature programs and events I used to host. Kids were inquisitive and hilarious.

One of the girls of this group seemed to be doing most of the talking. "I just think we should be looking into the Rougarou as well."

Her comment piqued my interest. I'd just learned about the term for Louisiana werewolves.

The boy to her right was on the verge of exasperation. "Jasmine, if we investigate every story of every legendary creature in this area, we'll never get a chance to search for the Honey Island Swamp Monster!"

"Jake's right." The other girl twirled a strand of her dark curly hair around her finger. "We don't want to get sidetracked again, like we did with Nessie and the Big Grey Man of Ben MacDhui. You agree, right, Lanny?"

The small boy who appeared younger than the rest nodded fervently. "I'm with Benny and Jake. It's almost Halloween. There's about to be a full moon. I do not want to come face-to-face with the glowing red eyes of a Rougarou."

I leaned over toward the group. "Excuse me, sorry to interrupt, but are you kids talking about hunting werewolves?"

The girl they called Jasmine exhaled, causing her strawberry-blonde bangs to flutter. "Apparently not. Apparently, we're only allowed to hunt one thing at a time."

The older boy, Jake, handed me a card. The names listed were Jake Nelson, president; Jasmine Davis, vice-president; Laniban Mahajan, administrative assistant; and Bernadette Hathaway, sales and marketing.

Cute.

"Sasquatch Hunters of Washington?" I read aloud.

"Incorporated," added the younger boy, called Lanny.

"I'm originally from Washington State also, but I've never heard of Sasquatch Hunters."

Jake squared his shoulders. "We're a fairly new investigative team looking into sightings of cryptids, particularly those in the Bigfoot family."

"Wow. That must make for quite a lot of great adventures. Nice to meet you all. I'm Charlotte."

"My parents don't allow me to call grownups by their first name," Lanny said.

I smiled. "Understandable. I worked at a library for several years, and many parents had that rule. You can call me Mrs. McLaughlin if it makes you more comfortable. So, I'm curious. What were you talking about when you mentioned the Big Grey Man? Is that a type of Bigfoot?"

Jake's eyes lit up at the question, and I felt a pang in my chest. Even though it hadn't been very long since I'd left my post at the library, I'd already forgotten how impactful it could be when kids felt seen and heard by a grownup. So much of their lives were managed by others—their parents, teachers, coaches—that having an adult stop and pay attention to the things that excited them was often the difference between a kid with confidence and a kid who felt like they didn't matter.

The pang deepened to an ache. I hadn't just left a job. I'd left a place where I'd felt purposeful.

"The Big Grey Man of Ben MacDhui is sort of a Scottish Bigfoot," Jake said.

"We even got to look for him in the mountains of Scotland!" Jasmine said.

"Amazing! Did you find him?"

"Sort of." Jake pressed his lips together.

The four of them exchanged wary glances and eyebrow raises. An understanding passed between them. No telling what secrets they were holding.

"Well, I've never heard of it. Or him." I held up the card. "But I have heard there are all sorts of legendary creatures in the swamps of Louisiana. In fact, I learned about the Rougarou for the first time just this morning."

Jasmine folded her arms. "Apparently, we have to focus on the Honey Island Swamp Monster. Apparently."

Jake nudged her. "*Apparently*, Jasmine has forgotten the purpose of this expedition."

She huffed and jumped to her feet. "We doing this?"

The rest of the kids stood and pulled on their jackets.

"Well, good luck to you all. Don't forget to work together. Teamwork makes the dream work, and all that."

"I like that." Lanny scribbled on a notepad. "Teamwork

makes the dream work."

As they shuffled out of the restaurant, the ache migrated from the center of my chest across my entire upper body. What was wrong with me? Was I getting sick?

The waiter came by, and I ordered eggs Sardou, a creole-style dish with crispy artichokes, creamed spinach, and *choron* sauce, described to me as a tomato-spiked bearnaise.

I pulled out one of my new mystery novels and began reading. By the time I was done with my delicious meal, I was on chapter three and the miserable future in-laws had also left.

I meandered over to the open-air French Market, where I found everything from fresh produce to artisanal soaps and street poets.

"*Cher*, come see what I got," one vendor called to me.

I waved and smiled but kept walking. I wasn't used to exploring a new city by myself, and I was surprised to discover how much I enjoyed it. I wouldn't want to do it by myself all the time, but for an afternoon it was nice.

Overhead, hundreds of bead necklaces hung from tree branches or were draped across power lines like Spanish moss. New Orleans was unlike anyplace I'd ever visited.

It was nearly two when I finally caught a taxi back to Jane's and my hotel in the Garden District. She had yet to return from lunch, which was somewhat surprising.

I texted her asking if she was okay but got no response. Concerning.

By two thirty, I was worried.

By three I was in a full-blown panic.

Chapter Three

"DO YOU HAVE any idea how worried I've been?" I scolded Jane.

"I said I was sorry. I didn't see your text. Emmett and I were in such deep conversation it was like the world around me had faded into the background." She practically floated through the hotel room and flopped herself on one of the beds, her arms splayed.

"Now he's Emmett? What happened to Professor Guidry?"

It was ridiculous. Irrational. I knew it as the words left my mouth. She was a fifty-something-year-old woman, and he was no longer her teacher. He was her peer. Still, she was acting like a smitten teenager with no thought of how her lack of consideration impacted me.

Jane, however, was too giddy to let my chastisement bother her. "Charlotte, we really clicked. I haven't felt such instant chemistry in my entire life. And get this. He's coming onboard."

For a moment, I thought she was referring to the Mississippi Riverboat cruise we'd booked for the next morning. "Wait. You don't mean he's coming on the *Thalassophile*?"

She gave a blissful sigh. "Yep. He said he's been wanting to go to Haiti since there are so many similarities between the two cultures. The French influence, the architecture, the traditions, voodoo. He says it's the perfect opportunity to do research for his book, especially since he's on sabbatical."

I wanted to be happy for her. I was happy for her. Mostly. I was a slow adapter, so I needed time to acclimate to this whirlwind September-October romance. Whether Jane would give me the courtesy of allowing that time remained to be seen.

"So, it was good? Romantic sparks and all?"

"Definite chemistry, although I don't know that he's quite ready to start anything." Her expression turned somber. "Char, he's a widower. His wife died two years ago in some tragic accident."

I felt that twinge of empathy that arose whenever I encountered others who'd experienced the unexpected loss of a spouse.

"I'm sorry to hear that. Was it a car accident?"

"He wasn't too forthcoming with the specifics, but I can tell he's still not over it."

The thing that was difficult to explain to Jane and anyone else who hadn't gone through that type of sudden loss of a partner was, there was no getting over it. Ever. It became a part of who you were, entwined in the fabric of your very existence. You learned to operate in a new reality that included an abiding grief. You became accustomed to the pain, like someone with a chronic condition mostly invisible from an outside perspective.

Professor Guidry—Emmett—had asked about our plans for dinner, and Jane had insisted on including him on our reservation at Commander's Palace. She hadn't asked me, and I probably wouldn't have rejected the idea even though I wasn't keen on it. My goal was to go with the flow for Jane's sake, even though that wasn't my strong suit.

The restaurant wasn't far from our hotel. A landmark since the late 1800s, Commander's Palace was an impossible-to-miss turquoise Victorian building in the Garden District. It had been the top recommendation of every single person we'd spoken to about where to eat while in town. Of course, those were visitors and tourists, not locals. There were probably some amazing places frequented by residents that flew under the radar.

Emmett was waiting outside when we arrived. "Ladies, you look gorgeous tonight."

I murmured my thanks.

"And you look so handsome," Jane gushed.

Who was this tittering woman, and what had she done with my normally unflappable sister?

Emmett wore a taupe silk-blend suit with a satin pocket square and his white pressed shirt open at the collar. His silvery hair crested away from his face in a coiffed wave that looked effortless despite the precision of it. His gleaming white veneers contrasting with his sun- (or spray tan) kissed skin made me wonder if anything about the man's appearance had not been meticulously contrived.

The three of us were seated at a corner table on the second floor of the restaurant. The lighting had been dimmed for ambience, and judging by all the canoodling couples surrounding us, it occurred to me that Jane's and my initial reservation for two might have been misinterpreted. Now, I was playing third wheel on her date with the World's Most Interesting Man.

Despite her reservations, Emmett cajoled Jane into ordering a bowl of minced snapping turtle soup. Her smile was forced as she assented, and her eyes held the horror of a woman who really didn't want to be doing something but was overcome by her irrational desire to be in the good graces of an oblivious man.

At one point, she glanced at me with an expression I read as a plea for help, but the petty, stubborn part of me chose to ignore it. She'd made her bed, and all that.

Of course, I had no one to impress, so it was an easy pass for me.

The server put the finishing touches on Jane and Emmett's soups tableside by adding a splash of aged sherry. I suppressed my smirk as I watched her lift a trembling spoon to her mouth. Her lips were pressed tight like an infant rejecting puréed peas, despite the fact she was attempting to feed herself.

If she got even an ounce of that soup inside her body, I'd have been surprised. She played an old trick we used as kids by doing a lot of stirring and relocating the soup without a lot of consuming.

Emmett also convinced her to order stuffed quail so they

could share plates. I swear I saw a tear silently stream from her left eye as he offered her a taste of some of his chargrilled hog spinalis.

The disparate ratio of meal cost to enjoyment was off the charts. Not that it was the restaurant's fault. Jane should have asserted herself, but she was more focused on impressing her date.

Meanwhile, I thoroughly enjoyed my autumnal salad with pecans and apples tossed in an amazing bacon vinaigrette and my beef filet smothered in a creole mustard demi-glace.

When the final course of our meal arrived—a creole bread pudding soufflé—a look of relief washed across Jane's face.

As we stood in front of the restaurant preparing to hail a taxi back to our hotel, Emmett clapped his hands.

"I say we head to Buddy Dupree's Sugar Club over on Bourbon Street for drinks and jazz. Canailles Nous is opening their reunion tour tonight with Alexander St. Jacques."

Canailles Nous was a bluesy jazz ensemble who shot to the top of the Billboard Hot 100 chart in the early 2000s with their unexpected crossover hit "Lamoreaux." Roughly translated, it meant *the lover*, which proved to be prescient. As fast as their fame skyrocketed, the group blew apart with rumors that trumpet player Alexander had been unfaithful to his fiancée—lead singer Ophelia Thibodeaux—and then signed a solo contract with their record label behind her back. His fellow bandmates weren't happy with him either.

After a year of legal wranglings the group began performing again—sans St. Jacques—but they never again achieved the level of success they had with "Lamoreaux." By 2010 they had completely disbanded. Alexander, however, had gone on to have multiplatinum solo albums and even won a Grammy award. His popularity had waned slightly over the past several years, though, and he hadn't released an album in quite a while.

"Funny you should mention that," I said. "Canailles Nous is headlining the entertainment for the next leg of our cruise."

"Is that so? How marvelous! I'm so looking forward to it." Emmett turned to Jane and squeezed her upper arm. "Shall we go?"

Jane glanced at me uncertainly. "Char?"

"Sure. It could be fun."

If he noticed my lack of enthusiasm, he didn't acknowledge it.

Bourbon Street was impassible due to so many pre-Halloween revelers, so the taxi dropped us off a few blocks from Buddy Dupree's. We passed an alley where a man was selling red SOLO cups filled with hurricane cocktails that he'd scooped out of an industrial trashcan.

"That seems sanitary and not at all likely to lead to hospitalization," I quipped.

Jane, not typically one to hold back her witty observations, was unusually quiet as we weaved our way through hordes of drunk or near-drunk people in costumes ranging from sexy nurse to the Grim Reaper and everything in between. I spotted a *sexy nun* sporting at least six strands of beads, and I shuddered to think of how she'd earned them. Perhaps I was a prude, but when it came to such things as baring my breasts for strangers, a ten-cent necklace didn't seem a worthy reward.

After paying a cover charge, Emmett, Jane, and I squeezed into the foyer of the dimly lit club. It was standing room only, but that didn't matter much considering I had yet to spot a single chair—occupied or not. The venue was set up with a large open dance floor and a stage. The second level featured a full balcony all the way around. It was nearly full with people draped over the railing.

A woman passed us wearing a mesh dress with nothing underneath and, to his credit, Emmett quickly averted his eyes. The two young men standing nearby did not. They whistled and catcalled her, making lurid comments and gestures as she sashayed toward the bar.

Emmett put his hand on one of the guy's shoulders. "Hey now, just because a woman chooses to express her confidence in her body through her clothing does not give you permission to harass her."

The guy shrugged to remove his hand. "Whatever, dude." He scowled at his buddy, and the two of them moved to the other side of the club.

"Thank you for doing that." Jane's admiration was plastered across her face like a Times Square billboard.

"It shouldn't be solely a woman's responsibility to tell men they're out of line. Now, what can I get you ladies to drink?"

Jane and I decided this spot might be a better option for trying a hurricane than out of a trashcan in an alley.

"Isn't he great?" Jane beamed, watching Emmett place our orders with the bartender. "He's so much more evolved than most of the men I've dated. He's the real deal."

I gave a noncommittal murmur. Prior to living on the ship with me, Jane had been a librarian in Turlock, California, where the majority of residents were either college students or retirees, so the dating pool—and her experience in it—was limited, to say the least. Not to mention, Jane had never wanted to be in a position where she was dependent on a man or anyone else. Her relationships tended to have a shorter shelf life than a gallon of milk.

As for being the real deal, I was on the fence about whether Emmett was the real anything at all. Something about him registered to me as false, I just hadn't yet been able to put my finger on what that was.

He approached us holding two tall curvy glasses filled with a tangerine-colored liquid.

I took a sip. "Whoo! That's strong. What's in it?"

"Three types of rum, among other things." Emmett held up his glass. "Cheers, ladies. Here's to a great evening and the next two weeks' adventures at sea."

Jane and I each held up our glasses, clanging against his and each other's.

"Cheers." I took another sip. It went down a little smoother the second time.

A zydeco band called Maque Choux on the Bayou was introduced, and the whole place erupted.

A man in a cowboy hat with an accordion strapped to himself took center stage. He was joined by a man on drums, one on bass guitar, one on electric guitar, and a guy wearing a metal washboard vest called a *froittoir*.

As the strains of the syncopated up-tempo folk music filled the room, I found myself getting lightheaded. Perhaps it was the hurricane. Perhaps it was the jostling crowds stomping their feet to the beat. Perhaps it was the muggy atmosphere. Perhaps it was all of those things.

I leaned toward Jane and whispered in her ear, "I need to get some air. I'll be right back."

She gave me a questioning look. "Huh?"

I raised my voice to be heard above the music. "I said, I'll be right back."

She nodded and then flashed a brilliant smile at Emmett, whose hand had snaked its way around her swaying hip.

I bobbed and weaved my way toward the nearest illuminated exit sign, gasping as I burst into the back alley like I'd surfaced from twenty thousand leagues under the sea with nothing but a snorkel. A man leaning against a lamppost near the door stopped mid-inhale on his cigarette.

I waved my apology. "Didn't mean to disturb you. Just needed to catch my breath."

He gave a head nod and blew out smoke in a slow stream. "It's quite all right. Can be pretty chaotic in there."

The man looked like he'd been transported from a different era where day drinking at business meetings was not only commonplace but expected and women made sixty-three cents on the dollar. His blue satin suit with matching bowtie was appropriately accompanied by a black fedora tilted just right.

"Are you one of the musicians performing tonight?"

He let his cigarette dangle from his mouth and reached out his left hand toward me. "Heath Hubbard. I'm with Canailles Nous."

"Oh, wow. It's an honor to meet you. I'm Charlotte McLaughlin." I shook his hand, making note of his long, thin fingers. "I can't remember. Do you play piano or guitar?"

"Vibraphone, actually."

"That's right. I'm not from around here, but I've never known anyone who played the vibraphone. How did you start playing?"

"My daddy played. He didn't leave me much when he died, but he left this legacy." He blew smoke into the air. "He even gigged with Yardbird once or twice."

"Yardbird?"

"Charlie Parker."

"Wow, that's amazing. Didn't Charlie Parker die young?"

"Yeah, 1955, I believe. He was in his thirties. Just about five years before I was born."

"There's no way you're in your sixties. I thought you were younger than me, and I'm...no longer in my forties."

He gave me a broad smile. "You know what they say."

"What they say about what?"

"Black don't crack."

I laughed. "Apparently."

A door at the other end of the building flung open, smacking loudly against the side of the building. A woman marched into the alley. She was dressed head to toe in black, including her wide-brimmed hat.

A man in a tuxedo followed close behind. He glanced up at the moonlit sky, inhaled sharply, and then turned his gaze back at her. "Don't do this, Fee."

She whipped her body around to face him, her long dark hair following suit. "I'm not doing anything. That's the whole point. Lucky for you, because I literally want to choke you with my bare hands right now."

She was gorgeous, even in her anger. And recognizable. It was Ophelia Thibodeaux, and the man she was threatening to murder was Alexander St. Jacques.

He rubbed the back of his neck. "Look. I'm sorry you don't like the terms of the contract, but it's signed and that's that." His Louisiana accent was melodic.

"I can't believe you did this to me again, Alex. Fool me once…"

"Fee, you signed it. Nobody made you do it. It's not my fault you didn't read it."

Heath dropped his cigarette on the ground, stepped on it with his toe, and blew out a stream of smoke. "Looks like Mom and Dad are fighting again," he muttered.

"I'm not getting on that stupid cruise ship with you," Ophelia sputtered. "You can't make me. Not even an ocean between us is enough space from you as far as I'm concerned."

"Be that as it may, there's a heavy penalty clause for

breaking the contract, and I know for a fact you don't have the money to cover it. That's why you agreed to this reunion in the first place. It obviously wasn't because your hatred of me has thawed over the years. Face it, Fee, you're broke. You need this gig."

"That's low," she growled.

"We're all broke," Heath called to them. "All of us except you, Alex."

Alexander jerked his head in our direction, noticing our presence for the first time. "I know that, Heath, that's why I put this reunion tour together. I'm trying to make amends."

"Then maybe you shouldn't have included that extra 15 percent off the top of our payment into your own pocket in the contract in teeny tiny print." Ophelia put her hands on her hips. "Always thinking of yourself above everyone."

A large, tattooed man with wire-rimmed glasses, a full beard, and his light brown hair combed back in a dramatic pompadour-style popped his torso through the cracked doorway next to me. "Guys, we're on in ten."

Heath nodded at him. "Thanks, man. Be there in a second."

The man took in the scene. "Everything okay out here?"

Alexander inhaled and pursed his lips. "Percy, maybe you can enlighten Fee here about contract law and how damaging it would be to all of us if she doesn't follow through on this tour."

Ah, Percy Brown, double bass. He looked quite different from the early days of the group. He'd never been slim, but he now had the stature of an offensive lineman.

"I'm a production assistant on a reality small claims court show, Alex, not an attorney."

"Still." Alexander's jaw clenched. "Help me out here, man."

Percy sighed the weary exhale of a man used to playing peacemaker against his will. "Fee, we all need this. My mom is in a memory care facility, and that's not cheap. I know that Alex can be a selfish jerk—"

"Hey!"

Percy continued, ignoring Alexander's protest. "We have a second chance here, and I for one don't want to miss it."

Ophelia clucked her tongue. "Fine. But he's not allowed to speak to me offstage for the entirety of the tour."

"That's not—" Alexander shut his mouth as soon as he caught sight of Ophelia's glare. He slumped his shoulders and nodded.

Percy clapped his hands. "All right, kiddos, time to put on a show."

⚓

I WEAVED MY way through the crowd to where Jane and Emmett were awaiting the onstage arrival of Canailles Nous.

"I was starting to worry about you," Jane shouted above the din.

"I was out back getting fresh air. Well, sort of fresh. Someone was smoking. Heath Hubbard, actually."

"Wow, that's cool. Not the smoking, but the fact you saw him."

"Talked to him, actually."

"It's dangerous around here, especially at night." Emmett scowled.

Whoa. "I'm perfectly capable of taking care of myself, particularly when it comes to tipsy college kids."

"I'm not talking about that. I'm talking about the Rougarou."

I snorted. "Werewolves? Roaming Bourbon Street? Come on now, Emmett. Sounds like you've taken your folklore research a bit too seriously."

Jane glared at me.

Emmett's expression darkened. "Yes, Charlotte, I'm quite serious when it comes to werewolves. Maybe someday you'll fully understand why. Until then, just take my word for it. You don't want to walk alone on these streets."

Tension radiated from Emmett, which caused Jane to tense even further, kicking me into mood-lightening mode. It was a deeply ingrained coping mechanism.

"Believe it or not, I actually overheard some kids today at brunch talking about searching for evidence of the Rougarou. They're visiting from Washington State, looking for the Honey Island Swamp Monster. Get this. They've formed a business called Sasquatch Hunters." I chuckled.

Instead of easing the tension, however, my comment seemed to have made Emmett even more perturbed. "Kids have no business wandering the swamps of Louisiana unsupervised looking for monsters."

I held up my hands in mock surrender. "Take it up with their parents."

Thankfully, the MC chose that moment to welcome the members of Canailles Nous to the stage one by one.

First came drummer Webster Powell. He wore a tie-dyed T-shirt and a peach-colored wool flat cap. Next was pianist Victor Lutz, in his black velvet sport coat, purple V-neck, and black felt porkpie hat. They were followed by Heath up to the vibraphone and Percy on his giant double bass. If a double bass were an instrument, it would be Percy Brown.

The energy and excitement of the crowd grew with each addition, and the bandmates looked to be enjoying the ovation.

"Next to the stage we have the beautiful, sensational, the baroness of blues, Ophelia Thibodeaux!"

The place erupted in cheers and applause. Ophelia glided to the microphone with grace and confidence. Her beaming expression gave no hint of the anger I'd witnessed just minutes earlier.

"How're y'all doing tonight?"

More cheers and woops.

"It is my pleasure to introduce to you the man, the legend, Alexander St. Jacques!"

The club sounded like a football stadium following a home team touchdown. Urgent foot stomps on the hardwood floors echoed off the vaulted ceiling.

Alexander sauntered onstage with the swagger of a superstar, the spotlight glinting off his trumpet like a beacon.

Without a word, he lifted the instrument to his mouth and began to play a slow, haunting melody. The crowd hushed immediately.

He riffed for a full minute, the rest of the band motionless, faded into the background.

And then the spotlight shifted to Ophelia. Her eyes were cast downward. As she raised her chin, she opened her mouth and began to sing the opening strains of "Lady Sings the Blues."

Her face contorted with each note, and I felt the pain behind the lyrics course through me in a visceral way.

When she got to the line about wanting the world to understand why she had the blues, she allowed her steely gaze to drift toward Alexander.

I'd never before seen that much vitriol directed from one person to another, and I'd never before seen a more picture-perfect embodiment of the phrase *if looks could kill.*

Chapter Four

JANE SURVEYED THE welcome reception in the *Thalassophile*'s main dining room. "This reminds me of The Pirates of the Caribbean ride at Disneyland. You know, at the beginning, where the boat slowly creeps past the diners at the Blue Bayou Restaurant and the old man is rocking on his porch smoking a pipe while crickets chirp and frogs croak?"

It was an accurate description of the scene in front of us. Located on the ninth level—Mykonos—the dining room's décor typically reflected the theme for whatever the ship's current itinerary or upcoming port of call. This time it was heavily influenced by the culture of New Orleans, which had also been heavily influenced by transplants from Haiti, our next stop.

Hanging from every chandelier, dimmed for ambience, was Spanish moss. Twinkling lights were tacked to the ceiling, presumably to represent fireflies. In the corner of the room, an old, bearded man in a straw hat played the banjo and a woman leaned against a stool playing a mouth harp.

Hawk, one of the newer servers onboard, approached Jane and me holding aloft a tray of cocktails. "Ladies, would you like to try our version of a Sazerac?"

"What's in it?" Jane raised her chin to get a better look. She sneezed. "Excuse me!"

"Gesundheit," Hawk said.

"Is this the Cortesazerac?" I asked. "Cortes made me one on our way to Yokohama. I think he said he replaced the rye whiskey with tequila."

He lowered the tray for our perusal. "Nah, Cortes isn't on this trip. Egan's on his own this time."

Egan was a charming dark-haired Irishman in his mid-to-late twenties who shared bartending duties with Cortes.

"I'll fill in for Egan when he needs me, along with all my other random duties."

"Still no official position?" I took a glass from the tray.

"Nah. It's fine, though. I keep thinking I'm done here, but they keep pulling me back for one more sailing." Under his breath he repeated, "Just one more sailing."

"So what makes this version of the Sazerac special?" I lifted the glass and held it to my lips.

"Egan's making it with Hennessey Paradis Cognac and Beefeater gin, along with the standard absinthe, Peychaud's bitters, and of course a twist of lemon. I've heard some call it a millionaire's cocktail, which seems fitting for this crowd."

Jane took a glass and, after inhaling, flared her nostrils. "Not my thing." She placed it back on the tray and sneezed once more into her sleeve. "Excuse me again! Can you bring me a martini instead?"

"Sure thing. Vodka or gin?"

"Vodka. I'm pretty sure I'm allergic to gin. I get a rash every time I pass a juniper hedge. That's probably why I just sneezed. Oh look, there's Emmett. Emmett!" She waved her hand and joined him at the entrance to the dining room.

Hawk blinked at me. "What does she mean she gets a rash?"

I shook my head. "Don't ask. She's convinced that because juniper makes her skin itch when she brushes against a shrub that means she's allergic to gin because gin is made with juniper berries. Although I've never heard of anyone being so allergic to juniper that sniffing gin causes them to sneeze."

His gaze widened. "Oh. Huh. Dunno."

He wandered back to the bar just as Jane and Emmett arrived arm in arm.

"This ship is just as amazing as you said it would be, Jane." Emmett placed his hand over hers and patted it twice.

"I'm so glad you think so." She beamed.

"How's your room?" I asked him.

"Great. Great. I was able to snag a nice one-bedroom on the eighth floor from the rental website: 812, close to the elevators."

While many of the owners had purchased the exclusive units solely for their own use as a private vacation home, some rented them to carefully vetted guests by the sailing itinerary through a company called Travel the World Experiences and Rental Properties, which Jane so aptly pointed out created the acronym TWERP.

"Oh, 812, that's the Dorans' unit. Their daughter is due to give birth any day back in Pittsburgh. First-time grandparents," Jane said. "Also, FYI, the eighth level is called

Santorini."

The name of the ship—*Thalassophile*—meant *lover of the sea* in Greek, and all the floors also had Greek names. The third level, Marina, was where the crew resided. Floor four was Perseus, home to the theater, the casino, and a couple of restaurants. Five—Capri—housed a few studio units, the medical office, the beauty salon, the marketplace, shopping boutiques, the fitness center, spa, and the solarium with an indoor pool.

Six, seven, and eight were the main residential floors—Aegean, Odyssey, and Santorini—with Jane's and my two-bedroom unit, 701, located on Odyssey. The captain's lounge was on Santorini. In addition to the dining room, Mykonos was where the Azure Lounge, the expedition lounge, the library, and the observation deck were located.

The tenth—and top—level was called Kalispera, which meant good afternoon or evening in Greek. It was the perfect place to observe not only the sunset, but also the sunrise. Closed to passengers during the cooler itineraries, the deck was open for this particular cruise to the Caribbean despite it being autumn.

Also on the fifth level was the security office, run by Xavier Mesnier. I had yet to run into him since boarding the ship that afternoon.

"What are you looking for?" Jane gave me a bemused look.

"Hmm? Nothing. Why?"

She arched her left brow. "Is that so? Then why are you craning your neck like a submarine periscope to scan the crowd?"

"I wasn't. I'm just seeing who's all here. I recognize some of the passengers but not others."

Jane leaned toward Emmett. "She's definitely looking for someone in particular. If I had to guess, it's someone particularly French."

"Do tell." Emmett grinned.

"Do not tell," I snapped.

If Jane recognized my tone of warning, she ignored it. "It's the head of security, Xavier Mesnier. He's *très* handsome."

"Ooh la la," said Emmett. "Should I be jealous?"

"He's not my type, don't worry." Jane patted his arm. "As for Char, well…ooh la la." She gave him a mischievous grin.

It took everything in me not to tell them both where to stick their *ooh la las*. "I'm just surprised we haven't run into him yet, that's all."

"Sure, Char."

I wanted to wipe Jane's smug smile off her face with a similarly juvenile comeback, but the blaring of a singular trumpet note preempted my retort and drew everyone's attention to the entrance. A low C if my high school choir days taught me anything.

Alexander St. Jacques stood in the doorway with his trumpet at his lips, which somehow couldn't hide his self-important smirk. He held the note for quite some time before slowly easing into the next note, an E. Then an F and a G. As he played the familiar strains of "When the Saints

Go Marching In," a gasp of recognition washed across the room, followed by cheers.

He burst into a lively version and began making his way through the crowd, now clapping along and shimmying their shoulders to the irresistible beat. Not necessarily *on* beat, as many of them were lacking in rhythm. Parading behind him with maracas, rhythm sticks, a tambourine, and musical spoons were Victor Lutz, Percy Brown, Webster Powell, and Heath Hubbard.

Bringing up the rear and holding a cordless microphone, Ophelia Thibodeaux started singing. "Oh when the saints…come on, everybody, sing with me! Go marching in…"

She held the mic in the air and the crowd joined in. The energy in the room had gone from sedate to celebratory in an instant.

Hard to believe the last time I'd seen Ophelia she'd just gotten done threatening Alexander's life. They were dancing side by side like the old friends they were, or at least pretended to be.

Once the song was done, adoring fans gathered around the members of Canailles Nous, some clamoring for autographs on cocktail napkins, others asking for photos.

At the center of it all was the charming Alexander St. Jacques. With his boyish good looks, his broad smile, his affable sense of humor, and that lilting New Orleans drawl, it was no wonder he had so many fawning admirers.

That apparently didn't include Emmett, who narrowed his gaze suspiciously at Alexander. "He's crafted quite the persona for himself."

An odd commentary coming from someone I perceived to be very image-conscious, verging on phony.

"Oh look," said Jane. "There's Xavier."

I hesitated. It would be embarrassing to look too eager. I slowly glanced over my shoulder. Even that subtle movement caught his attention.

He was in his standard uniform of khaki slacks and a navy-blue sweater. His arms were crossed in his default mode of intimidation. Speaking of personas, I suspected it was his military and special forces training that had formed that nearly impenetrable shell of his.

He raised his brows in acknowledgment but didn't move from his spot near the bar. It was the perfect location for keeping an eye on the entire room. He was in work mode for sure.

I followed his gaze, and it seemed to be resting on Ophelia Thibodeaux.

Who could blame him? The woman was gorgeous and talented.

It stung, though, because he'd never looked at me that way. Maybe he never would.

⚓

"I HAVEN'T DRESSED up for Halloween in years." Jane adjusted her shoulder-length orange wig and pulled at the collar of her purple dress. "This is itchy. I know it's only supposed to be for one night, but could they at least try to not make costumes out of sandpaper?"

"I look like a potato."

She gave me a once over. "You do not. I told you that I would be Velma and you could be Daphne, but you had to play the martyr."

Martyr? Not quite. The costume shop only had a medium in the Daphne costume and Jane's lithe body was the only one of the two of us who could reasonably make it work. The Velma costume was a roomy extra-large. "At least with this bulky orange turtleneck I can eat as many treats as I'd like tonight."

As if by magic, the dining room had been transformed literally overnight from Louisiana Bayou to haunted house, with a makeshift stage set up in the corner for Canailles Nous to perform. Hawk was executing one of his many roles, this time that of the D.J. Halloween songs blared from speakers positioned around the room, and occasionally he led the crowd in a call and repeat.

"When I say holla, you say ween. Holla!" he called.

"Ween!" the crowd yelled.

"Holla!"

"Ween!"

Jane nodded in Hawk's direction. "You know, I could have sworn I saw Hawk skulking around up on the eighth floor, but when I asked him about it later, he said he never had any reason to go to Santorini and I must have mistaken him for someone else."

"Maybe you did." I shrugged.

She pursed her mouth. "I don't think so."

"Must be his evil twin, then."

She narrowed her gaze into a glare.

"My tail keeps whipping people as I walk past them." Emmett, oblivious to the tension between Jane and me, pulled the offending appendage against his body.

He'd joined us at the costume shop prior to boarding and the decision had been made—more of a declaration by Jane, really—to do a group costume. Surprisingly, when the idea of dressing up as characters from Scooby Doo was raised, Emmett forewent dressing as Fred or Shaggy and instead chose to go as the mystery-solving Great Dane himself.

Between the spooky lighting and costumes, it was difficult to identify the partygoers. Most of the residents and guests were over forty, with the median age around sixty, so there weren't as many *sexy* versions of non-sexy occupations as I'd seen on Bourbon Street two nights earlier. The main exception was Kyrie Dawn, my late husband's paramour and current ship yoga instructor. She wore a skimpy Tinkerbell outfit, and her young son, Quinton, was adorable as Peter Pan.

My animosity toward Kyrie Dawn had thawed over the past several months. It was a slow process, acclimating to having her living on the ship with Gabe's son. I wouldn't say we were friends. We might never be friends. But we were family because of Quinton, and family relationships were messy. Complicated. They were also permanent, while friendships were not.

This crowd tended toward the classics: Frankenstein's

monster, vampires, knights, princesses, various culturally appropriated outfits, and witches.

Throughout the evening, I had also spotted three werewolves. One was Alexander, the other I wasn't sure. The third wasn't just a werewolf, it was Teen Wolf. He was wearing a yellow basketball uniform over his furry bodysuit.

Ophelia had transformed herself into a renaissance maiden, perhaps a nod to her namesake. Unfortunately, the Ophelia of Shakespeare's *Hamlet* was characterized by her inability to manage her own emotions or handle her own distress, which resulted in her untimely demise. In fairness, Hamlet was the instigator of her distress, and I'd always seen him as an antihero.

Alexander would have been more appropriately dressed as Hamlet to Ophelia's... Ophelia, as he was most definitely the instigator of her distress.

Pianist Victor Lutz was aptly fitted as Amadeus Mozart, bassist Percy Brown was Hagrid from Harry Potter, Webster Powell, the group's drummer, had kept to type as a reggae musician, and the always-slick Heath Hubbard was strutting through the room wearing a voodoo priest costume complete with skull-adorned top hat and a skull handle cane.

Emmett jutted his chin toward Alexander. "Takes a lot of nerve."

"How so?" Jane asked.

He shook his head. "Never mind. I'll be back in a bit. I need to use the toilet, and this costume requires a full undressing, so I'm going to my room for privacy."

He said the word *privacy* with a short *i* rather than a long one, like British people and pretentious Americans. Annoying, but I kept my mouth shut for Jane's sake.

"Hurry back!" Her tone was playful verging on childish, but thankfully she didn't add any terms of endearment like boo-boo or sweetie pie.

Calling her out on her simpering seemed like a fruitless endeavor. For whatever reason, she was enamored with him, and it was causing her to regress.

"Our French friend is looking quite fetching tonight."

She nodded, so I glanced over my shoulder. "Hmm," was all I said in response.

Xavier prowled the perimeter of the room in his 1920s gangster costume, complete with pinstripe suit and gray shoe spats. Even his officers—muscly Pike Taylor in his pirate regalia and redheaded Lonnie Irving dressed as a superhero—were more successful at blending into the crowd.

It surprised me that Xavier had worn a costume. He tended to avoid participating in the ship's theme nights. Perhaps he was finally getting into the spirit of things.

Pike, despite being on duty, snuck a kiss from Kyrie Dawn. Their relationship had also evolved over the past few months, and they were now officially a couple.

After about an hour of mixing and mingling, Webster sat at his drum kit and began lightly tapping the high hat. A spotlight shone on the stage.

"Ladies and gentlemen," Maître D' Ulfric Anton announced in his thick German accent. "The moment for which you have all been waiting. The *Thalassophile of the Seas* is pleased to welcome Canailles Nous!"

The audience cheered as members of the group joined Webster onstage, taking their places near their instruments.

Ophelia slinked to the mic stand and purred a sultry, "Happy Halloween, witches!"

The crowd laughed.

"Are you ready to party?"

The crowd cheered.

"In N'awlins we have a saying for nights like this. I want you to repeat after me. *Laissez.*"

"*Laissez,*" we all shouted in response.

"*Les bon temps.*"

"*Les bon temps!*"

"*Laissez les bon temps rouler!*"

This time the response was muddled by the crowd's inability to regurgitate the complete French phrase.

"Ah, nah, not good enough. *Laissez les bon temps rouler!*"

We tried again, with only minimally improved results.

She laughed. "Good enough. As we say in the Big Easy, *laissez les bon temps rouler!* Let the good times roll!"

We cheered again, with the audience whipped into a frenzy of anticipation.

"Put your hands together for Mr. Alexander St. Jacques!"

We all applauded, but Alexander didn't appear.

Ophelia tried again. "Alexander St. Jaaaaaaacques!"

Still, he didn't appear. Ophelia turned to her bandmates, but they all shook their heads. She put her hand to her forehead and peered into the crowd. "Alexander, are you out there?"

A murmur weaved through the audience as people began

to realize something wasn't right.

Xavier reached the stage, and Ophelia whispered in his ear. His already serious expression hardened. He was in *I've got a job* to do mode. He signaled to Pike and Lonnie to join him.

He lowered his head and said something to them under his breath. Each of them nodded and left the room.

He caught me watching him and his brows drew together. His olive skin paled, and his mouth drew taut.

I'd seen that look before. I'd seen it the morning he'd shown up to our suite to tell my nephew his fiancée was dead. I'd seen it when he'd discovered a man lying in the corpse pose in Kyrie Dawn's yoga studio. Something bad had happened once again, and once again it had been on his watch.

Ophelia gave a coy giggle. "Ladies and gentlemen, it seems we have misplaced our bandleader. I do apologize for the delay. We will start as soon as possible. Thank you so much for your patience."

She eyed Hawk and mouthed something. He nodded in return.

"In the meantime, here's an all-time favorite. Get some drinks and start dancing!"

The opening strains of "Thriller" began to play, and squeals of delight filled the room.

It was amusing to see some of the wealthiest people I'd ever met—bankers, CEOs, heirs to family fortunes—excitedly lining up to do a dance they'd learned back in the early 1980s.

There was nothing amused or amusing about Xavier's expression.

It was probably nothing. I chewed my lip. If it were something, I probably shouldn't get involved anyway.

He scanned the crowd for a third pass. Whatever—or whoever—he was looking for, it seemed urgent. Desperate, even.

I'd have been a bad friend if I ignored that he obviously needed help. I squared my shoulders.

CHARLOTTE MCLAUGHLIN: ALWAYS THERE WHEN NEEDED (AND EVEN SOMETIMES WHEN SHE'S NOT)

"What's happening?"

His expression contorted. "Not your concern."

"Come on. Something's clearly wrong. Let me help."

After a moment of obvious conflict, he tipped the brim of his fedora and leaned close. "Ophelia said she saw Alexander leave the party about thirty to forty minutes ago. She's been calling and texting him without response. I have sent Taylor and Irving to his cabin up on Santorini, but I have a bad feeling about this."

"He's probably just lost track of time. Why the concern? Musicians are notoriously flaky."

Xavier pulled at his thin white tie, loosening its grip of his neck. "A threatening note was slipped under his cabin door this afternoon. He suspected it was one of his bandmates. They all claimed innocence. But now this."

"You don't mean—"

He shrugged and tightened his mouth into a straight line.

"You don't think he's actually—"

His nostrils flared.

"Not again."

"I sure hope not."

Jane joined us with Emmett in tow. "How can we help?"

Xavier put his hands on his hips and exhaled as he dropped his chin. He raised it again, shifting his gaze from me to Jane to Emmett. "Emmett Guidry?"

"Yes, but…" Emmett furrowed his brow and looked at his chest, patting it like he was looking for something he'd misplaced. There were no pockets in his Scooby-Doo costume. "How did you know? I'm not wearing a nametag."

"I make it my business to be aware of all new guests."

Emmett nodded. "I see. And you are?"

Xavier reached out his hand. "Xavier Mesnier, head of onboard security."

Emmett responded in kind. "Nice to meet you."

Enough with the pleasantries. "Maybe Alexander's out having a cigarette," I offered. "We can split up and look for him. I'm sure he's fine."

Even I didn't believe the words coming out of my mouth. Xavier never got worried, so his worry, worried me.

"*D'accord.* Let us start with this level and go from there. Taylor and Irving have gone up to Santorini where the members of the group have their suites. If he is upstairs, they will radio me."

Emmett nodded. "My room is on the same floor, but the

opposite side. I believe Alexander is in 802."

We tried to make our exit as subtle as possible, which wasn't that difficult considering much of the attention was on the synchronized zombie dance taking place in the center of the room.

"I will go to the Azure Lounge." Xavier nodded at Emmett. "Monsieur, please accompany Madame Cobb to the expedition lounge and the library."

"I'll check out the observation deck."

Xavier and I parted ways with Jane and Emmett since the Azure Lounge and the observation deck were the opposite direction from the library and expedition lounge. We said nothing as we walked down the hall until we both attempted to break the silence at the same time.

"How was Baton Rouge?" he asked as I said, "I like your costume."

I gave a nervous chuckle and he smiled.

"Thank you," he said.

"Baton Rouge was great, thanks."

He didn't mention my costume. Not the wig, or the orange turtleneck, or the fake horn-rimmed glasses I wore.

He knew it was a costume, right? He had to know.

We reached the entrance to the Azure Lounge. The door to the observation deck was just a bit farther.

He indicated the door. "Alert me if you locate him."

"Will do."

The vibe was awkward, but I didn't have time to think about it.

I pushed the door open. It required extra effort because

the wind from the ship's movement created resistance.

The temperatures had been comfortable in New Orleans, but out in the open air, sailing across the Gulf of Mexico, it was chilly.

The short brown skirt of my Velma costume flew up, revealing black shorts that barely covered my rear end. I glanced up at the security camera, but the red light wasn't blinking. Bad for security, good for me, as I suspected the sight had been less Marilyn Monroe over an air grate and more like intrepid reporter out in a hurricane.

I spotted a dark mound on the deck as soon as I rounded the corner. I rushed over, crouching to get a closer look.

Legendary trumpet player Alexander St. Jacques, the life of any party, appeared lifeless before me.

"Xavier! Over here!" My voice was swallowed by the wind.

I pulled out my phone and with trembling fingers texted Xavier and Jane.

FOUND HIM. MYKONOS OBSERVATION DECK. NOT GOOD.

The only movement I detected was the brisk sea air ruffling the fur he'd stuck onto his face for his werewolf costume. Blood soaked the left side of his tattered shirt, open at the collar to reveal more faux hair and a thick gold chain. Or I thought it was fake. Perhaps he really was that hairy.

As I collapsed onto the ship's deck, my foot kicked a small object. A full moon emerged from behind the clouds, and its glow reflected off the metallic item, a small silver cylinder.

It was a bullet casing.

I leaned forward to get a closer look without touching it. I held my breath so as to not contaminate what was clearly a crime scene.

ROUGAROU.

No, that couldn't be right. I'd misread it, certainly.

I blinked.

ROUGAROU.

It was like I'd fallen asleep and woken inside a B movie. Perhaps we'd set sail with not one, but two legends. Alexander was known worldwide for his musical prowess and New Orleans style. Had he fallen prey to another New Orleans legend, the Rougarou?

Chapter Five

JANE AND EMMETT arrived at the scene shortly after Xavier but before Pike and Lonnie. Word must have gotten out that Alexander had been found shot dead, because soon a crowd began to gather on the observation deck. The two officers did their best to hold the onlookers at bay.

It was an odd-looking mob: An eighty-year-old balding Dracula whose natural hairline couldn't support the iconic widow's peak and thus had crudely drawn it on with a Sharpie, an off-brand baby Yoda, Joe, the guy from *Tiger King*, and three iterations of Lucys, a.k.a. Lucille Ball.

Noticeably absent were all the members of Canailles Nous. Probably Xavier had ordered his security team to escort them to the captain's lounge to wait for further information.

This wasn't my first rodeo, so to speak. My nephew's fiancée had been murdered on their wedding cruise, and Xavier had gathered the bridal party in the same room. It was expedient for disseminating information, and also a good way to keep a close eye on potential murder suspects.

Ian Fraser and his wife, Becca, were examining Alexander's body. Ian was the ship's doctor and Becca was his nurse, however he'd become a de facto medical examiner of late. They collected evidence that would then be turned over to authorities at the next port of call. Xavier wouldn't wait to investigate, however. He had a ship full of passengers to protect, and it seemed murder was sometimes contagious.

Xavier leaned against the ship's railing and observed the horde of looky-loos. "Typically, at a crime scene, one would scan the crowd for anyone who appears unusual or out of place. I just saw a full-grown man wearing nothing but a diaper sucking on a pacifier."

Emmett absentmindedly stroked his tail. "Truly a bizarre sight."

"You'd think this would be an easy case to solve. No one onboard knew him—not personally, at least—except for the members of his band. And they all have motive. He screwed them over when he signed that solo deal." Jane flicked a strand from her orange Daphne wig over her shoulder.

"Yes, but it's also quite a complex case," I said.

"In what way?"

"That's five people who have motive. Not one or two. And the motive is basically the same."

"Except that is not entirely true," Xavier said. "It is said that the motive for murder is often based in one of three root causes." He ticked them off on his fingers. "Money. Love. Revenge."

"That's right! One of them has double motive. Actually, I'd argue all three."

Jane nodded at me. "I think you're onto something."

Emmett gave her a blank stare. "Who?"

"Ophelia."

⚓

"It wasn't me. I didn't even know Alex had left the party. I sure didn't shoot him, although Lawd knows there were times I wanted to kill him." Ophelia blinked at Xavier with bloodshot eyes rimmed with smudged black eye makeup.

Had she been crying? Hard to tell. She'd certainly been rubbing her eyes. On second thought, the makeup may have been an intentional smoky eye.

Xavier glanced at me, as if asking me to corroborate what she'd said. Almost willing me to do so. Why was he so intent on eliminating her as a suspect? Because she was beautiful? Beautiful people could be killers too.

I shrugged. Let someone else verify her whereabouts.

I'd seen her throughout the party, sure, but I hadn't kept tabs on her the whole time. Why would I? No one but the killer knew they needed an alibi, and I hadn't known I might be called upon to give one.

Come to think of it, I couldn't verify anyone's alibi, or even when Alexander had slipped out. I'd seen him milling around throughout the evening. Or had I? There was another werewolf that looked similar in the dim lighting. At one point, I thought I'd seen Alexander kissing a zombie, but then it turned out to be the other werewolf. Not the Teen Wolf, though. His yellow basketball jersey was hard to miss.

The other thing that kept bothering me was the etching on the bullet casing. ROUGAROU. Yes, Alexander was dressed as a werewolf, but who knew that was to be his costume? When would they have had time to engrave the casing once onboard? It's not like they'd have brought it with them on the ship just in case.

Unless...no.

No one actually believed he was a real werewolf.

Or did they?

"Alex had a lot of groupies and stalkers. Maybe one of them did it." Ophelia waved her hand at the other members of Canailles Nous. "Tell them, guys. He was always dealing with obsessive fans."

"Ya." Webster's singular utterance somehow conveyed the breadth of all he didn't say.

A grunt came from Percy, whose face was buried in his hands. Technically, I couldn't see his hands because of his bushy Hagrid wig, but that was his posture.

"Quite so." Victor, perched on the sofa with his white-stockinged ankles crossed delicately, pursed his lips. His powdered wig, along with ruffled blouse and gold brocade jacket, made it difficult to take him seriously.

Heath nodded in that slow way of his. "Sure. Of course, he fed that beast."

"How do you mean?" Xavier asked.

"Alex had a way of making these women believe they were the only one in the world he was interested in. Which was probably true at the exact moment he was telling them that while things were heating up. But then afterward, he could be one cold cat."

"Dog."

Everyone's attention turned to Emmett, who was spinning his tail in a circle like a cabaret dancer's boa with a faraway expression.

Heath cocked his head to the side. "Pardon?"

Emmett's tail stopped mid-rotation. "Oh, sorry, I didn't mean to say that out loud. It's just you said *cold cat*, but he was a wolf, which is in the canine family. *Canis lupus*, to be exact."

Ophelia briefly closed her eyes and guffawed. "He wasn't a wolf. He wasn't even a werewolf. He was a man in a costume. A selfish, self-centered…" She stopped herself like she'd suddenly realized she was openly confessing to despising the murder victim.

Xavier held up his hand. "Have any of you seen anyone onboard with a known history of involvement with Alexander?"

One by one they slowly shook their heads.

"This makes us suspects, don't it?" Webster asked.

"I have a ship full of passengers pretending to be someone—or some*thing*—they are not. Until I sort out who may have had prior interactions with Monsieur St. Jacques, no one is clear of suspicion. We have a few days before we will reach our next port of call, and I hope to turn our killer over to the authorities at that time, so my team and I will be conducting a full investigation."

Ophelia stood and made her way over to Jane and me. "I heard from one of the staff that you helped exonerate her the last time there was a murder on the ship." Her eyes filled with tears. "I—I think I could use your help as well."

Jane and I exchanged glances. Xavier cleared his throat in a way that sounded suspiciously like a warning not to get involved.

I gave her a sympathetic smile. "I think our days of meddling in murder investigations are over. I'm sorry. I don't think we can help you."

Ophelia's face fell. "I don't understand."

"I promised Jane no more murder investigations. No more putting ourselves in danger."

Not that I'd meant that promise. It had been made under duress.

What was it about Ophelia that left me less than inclined to help her?

Chapter Six

"WE'RE NOT REALLY going to sit by while Xavier investigates this murder all by himself, are we?" Jane hustled to keep up with me as I walked toward the elevator.

Emmett followed close behind her.

"He's not all by himself. He's got Pike and Lonnie."

"Char, come on. They never would have solved the other cases if we hadn't been there to help."

I stopped to face her. "Why are you giving me grief about this? I did what you wanted. *No more murder investigating.* Weren't those your exact words?"

"That was land Jane. Land Jane forgot what it was like to be stuck on a floating crime scene in the middle of the ocean. Plus, we're good at it."

"Did you hear Xavier practically growl a warning not to interfere?"

"Pshh. You know he likes having our help."

"I know nothing of the kind." I stepped inside the elevator and pressed the number 7 button. "Emmett, you're staying on this floor, aren't you?"

He held the door. "Oh, yeah, uh, I thought maybe we'd

keep the party going in your room." He arched a single brow at Jane.

Ew.

She yawned. "I think I'm done for the night. Can we meet for breakfast in the morning?"

"Of course, of course. I've got some writing to do tonight anyway. I'm feeling inspired," Emmett said.

What was it about murder that he found inspiring?

⚓

IF I HADN'T known better, I'd have thought it was still Halloween when Jane and I walked into the dining room for breakfast the next morning. For the most part, the decorations were still up, although in the aftermath of the party they were torn, askew, and sagging in places. Hungover partygoers may have changed out of their costumes, but as they slogged through the omelet bar, their dark circles, unkempt hair, and dazed expressions were evocative of a zombie apocalypse.

Emmett waved us over to a table by the window.

"Good morning, ladies. How did you sleep?"

Jane grunted. "Like a baby."

"Wonderful."

"Like a baby who saw a dead body," she clarified.

He grimaced. "It does make for an unsettled feeling."

"Did you accomplish your goal?" I asked.

He looked at me for a moment, like he was trying to give context to my question.

"Your writing. Did you get done what you were hoping to do?"

"Oh, yes. Thank you."

Haimi Dara, one of the regular servers onboard, brought over a carafe. "Coffee?"

I didn't know much about her, other than that she was from Northern India and she aspired to be an actress.

Judging by the pink that was spreading from his collar up his neck to his cheeks, Emmett had noticed how beautiful she was. Creepy. He was more than twice her age.

Jane didn't seem to notice, though, as she nudged her cup forward. "Looks like the party didn't stop when the entertainment showed up dead."

"Yes, they decided to drink and dance their sorrows away rather than mope around. I don't think we got everyone out of here until after 2 A.M." Haimi poured coffee into Jane's mug. "I cannot believe it has happened *again*."

I offered my own cup. "You didn't happen to see anything that might shed light on what happened to Alexander, did you?"

Haimi glanced over her shoulder. I followed her gaze to the bar where Hawk was pouring mimosas. He caught sight of her and returned her stare.

"Um, not really."

Not believable.

She scurried to the next table before I could call her out.

Was Hawk intimidating Haimi into silence about something she'd witnessed?

While I knew little about her, I knew even less about

Hawk. He'd joined the crew on our voyage to Yokohama. At the time, he'd commented that it wasn't really his scene. I hadn't yet determined what that meant.

Jane leaned forward and whispered. "You're investigating!"

"I am not."

"You are!"

"I was just curious."

Emmett shifted in his seat. "I'm with Jane. I think if the three of us put our minds together, we can figure out exactly what happened."

I expected Jane to give him a placating pat on his hand and explain this was a her and me thing, not a three of us thing, but instead she gave him a broad smile and nodded enthusiastically.

Blerg.

⚓

AFTER BREAKFAST, JANE and Emmett went looking for members of Canailles Nous to interview, while I headed for the security office. Luckily, I checked my hair and teeth in the elevator's reflection. Not a lot I could do about the cowlick I was fighting at the back of my head, but I could extract the spinach leftover from my omelet that had wedged itself between my two front teeth.

Jane was slipping. Normally, she'd have caught that. She'd been too busy mooning over Emmett to notice.

"Hey, Charlotte." Lonnie was alone in the security office.

"I half expected you to be here when I relieved Pike from duty this morning."

"It was such a late night that I wasn't sure what time anyone would get here. Xavier in yet?"

"He stepped out for coffee. He should be back anytime."

I leaned on his desk. "What can you tell me about Alexander's death?"

Lonnie chuckled and shook his head. "You trying to get me in trouble?"

"Of course not. Anything you tell me will go in the vault." I twisted my fingers in front of my mouth like I was locking it.

Lonnie glanced at the door. "I'm starting to think it was some sort of voodoo thing."

"Like the dolls you poke with pins?"

"Maybe. It was something spooky. Did you see that bullet casing?"

"I did. But I don't think Cajun werewolf legends are necessarily related to voodoo."

"Look, I'm no expert, but you've got a full moon on Halloween, we've just left New Orleans, and some dude dressed like a werewolf gets shot by a silver bullet. That's some hoodoo-voodoo kind of thing."

"I'm pretty sure voodoo is a religion."

"No disrespect intended."

Something he'd said finally registered. "Did you say silver bullet?"

"Do not answer that." Xavier stood in the doorway holding two paper coffee cups.

"Hey, boss man. Thanks for the coffee."

Xavier set one of the cups on Lonnie's desk. He gave him a pointed look. "Irving, how many times do I have to tell you not to share details of our investigations with passengers?"

Lonnie nodded somberly. "I figured since it was Charlotte—"

"Especially Madame McLaughlin." He side-eyed me. "Follow me."

As he led me back to his private office, which was much less utilitarian than the lobby, I noticed a barely perceptible shake of his head.

He was already exasperated with me, and I hadn't even asked him a single question.

"No coffee for me?"

"I did not know you were coming."

"Well, we both know that's a lie." I plopped myself in a leather chair.

A slight smile twitched at the corner of his mouth as he sat at his desk. "This is becoming a habit for you."

"Barging into your office demanding information?"

"Finding corpses."

A shiver ran down my spine. It was true, although I didn't like to think about it that way. "I always wondered how law enforcement handled seeing so many tragic sights. I think I've begun to understand it."

"What have you determined?"

"Compartmentalization."

He tented his fingers. "This is quite perceptive. Intuitive.

Of course, you have already proven yourself to be so."

"A compliment. I'll take it."

"However." He exhaled and shifted in his chair.

"Here it comes."

"You are not on my investigative team. You are a passenger on this ship. You are a customer, not an employee. You are neither trained nor are you licensed in any way to be involved."

"So you're saying I should go through P.I. training?"

"What? No, that is not what I am saying in any way."

I sat back and gave him my sternest look. "When are you going to come to terms with the fact that I'm an asset to you?"

My words must have caught him off guard, because he seemed to struggle for a response.

"How about this. A compromise. Most of the time I'm just one of the pampered passengers. I stay out of your hair. But when and if there's a major incident—such as a werewolf shot dead with a silver bullet under the light of a full Halloween moon—perhaps you can deputize me for the duration of the investigation or until we reach our next port of call."

He opened his mouth to speak but I preempted his rejection.

"That way we don't have to waste precious time doing this dance of you pretending you don't want my help and me pretending I'm not snooping around where I'm not supposed to be."

He observed me silently for a moment, wringing his

hands. "If I agree to this arrangement—"

"You'd be a fool not to." I caught his look of annoyance. "Sorry. Continue."

"If I agree to this arrangement, I have some stipulations."

"Lay 'em on me."

"First, you must communicate with me or my staff every step of the way. No more sneaking. No more letting me know after the fact."

I nodded. "Reasonable."

"Second. You are a member of *my* team. You are not chief inspector of your own team. Therefore, you are not to be conducting missions with your sister and whichever tagalongs you've recruited."

"Wait. You're saying Jane can't be part of this? We work together. Bounce ideas off each other."

"I am less concerned about Madame Cobb as I am about Monsieur Guidry. But seeing as how they seem to be involved on some level, I do not want her sharing information with him that is to be kept confidential."

"Have you discovered something about him that makes you wary?"

"Gut feeling. His rental request came through Travel the World Rental Properties, and since they vetted him, I did not do a full background check on him as I normally would have. I have decided perhaps I should run my own check after all."

"Oh, well, that makes sense. Frankly, I'm not sure what to make of Emmett either. He seems harmless enough, although I find his handsome and charming act a bit annoying."

Xavier cocked his right brow. "You find him handsome and charming?"

"No, I find him annoying. And I don't like how Jane behaves when he's around. Objectively, however, he's handsome."

"I see. Can you elaborate on how Madame Cobb is behaving in an unusual way?"

"You've known her for a year. Don't you think it's time you call her Jane?"

"Despite your efforts to the contrary, I try to keep my relationships with the passengers on this ship as professional as possible."

Was he suggesting I've gotten under his skin? "Mm-kay. Well, Jane met Emmett Guidry about thirty-five years ago while she was a student in one of his classes at UDub."

"UDub? What is this?"

"University of Washington. UDub for short."

"Ah. Continue."

"He was a newly minted professor, barely older than most of his students, and she developed a crush. Fast forward to a few days ago, and we ran into him in downtown New Orleans. Turns out he's originally from here, and he's a professor at Tulane now. Immediately, she morphed from a grown woman into a giggly schoolgirl. It's gross."

Xavier chuckled. "I have seen this phenomenon before. People tend to regress to the age they were when they first connected. Other than his, how did you put it, annoying charm, has anything stood out to you about the professor of which I should be aware?"

"Other than his obsession with werewolves and other Louisiana folklore, I can't think of anything."

He stared down his perfectly straight nose at me. "He has an obsession with werewolves?"

"Well, yeah, but that doesn't mean anything. Alexander St. Jacques wasn't actually a werewolf. It was a costume."

"Tell me how you came upon this information."

"Jane and I were in a bookstore in the French Quarter. She was actually referring to the professor when he walked through the door. It was uncanny."

He narrowed his gaze. "That's quite a coincidence."

It sure was. "Sure, I mean what are the odds? Except it's a Faulkner bookstore and Emmett is a big fan, which is what Jane was saying when he came into the shop looking for a book on the Rougarou."

"This is the word etched on the bullet casing. Do you know what it means?"

"It's Cajun for werewolf."

He nodded slowly. "Similar to *Loup-Garou*."

"Not similar. Same. The details might be different, but the creature is the same. Acadians from France eventually settled in Louisiana and their name evolved to Cajun. Same with Rougarou from *Loup-Garou*."

Xavier blinked at me several times. "So a mysterious man from your sister's past appears out of nowhere, has a fixation on this Rougarou, and joins a cruise where a man in a werewolf costume is shot by a silver bullet with a casing that has the word etched on the side. And you believe that means nothing?"

Not good. I'd gone to Xavier in hopes of getting in on the action of the investigation, not to throw my sister's crush under the bus.

Chapter Seven

"FIND OUT ANYTHING?" I asked Jane when I arrived back at our cabin.

She and Emmett had scoured the ship searching for members of Canailles Nous to interview, but he'd left her to go for a jog on the Kalispera level where the track was.

Of course he was a jogger. He had that toned frame and outdoorsy kind of tan that only came from running, cycling, or hiking. I'd pegged him as more of a cyclist, but I wouldn't have been surprised if he was a triathlete.

"We ran into Ophelia at Azure Lounge. She was three mimosas in and babbling about how unfair the whole situation was."

"Meaning what?"

Jane shrugged. "Not sure exactly. She seemed less broken up over Alexander's death as she was about how it impacted her."

"Because without Alexander there's no Canailles Nous?"

"Something like that. Then we came across Heath, hanging out on the observation deck not far from where the crime scene tape is still up."

"That's kind of creepy. What was he doing out there?"

"Smoking."

"Could he have been returning to the scene of the crime?" I asked.

"Could be. He's a tough one to read. He's the kind of guy with such a cool exterior, you can't tell if he's really as detached and unbothered as he seems, or if below the surface he's a complete mess but he's really good at hiding it."

I thought back to the night I'd met him outside Buddy Dupree's. Even when Ophelia and Alexander were fighting in the alley, he'd seemed unruffled by it. "Mom and Dad are fighting again."

Jane screwed up her face. "Pardon?"

"That's what Heath said the other night when Ophelia threatened to quit. She'd marched out the door of the club yelling about wanting to choke Alexander. He'd followed her into the alley. At first, he'd tried to calm her down, but then when she wouldn't budge, he hammered her with the consequences of breaching their contract."

"It's got to be her, right?"

Xavier had insisted on my discretion when sharing information with Jane that might make its way back to Emmett, but he didn't say I couldn't poke and prod a bit, see if I could get her to see things she might be blinded by because of her infatuation. I'd never forgive myself if I stayed quiet and she got hurt.

"It could be her, but there's something else I believe is worth considering."

"What's that?"

I steeled myself for the fact she wasn't going to be

thrilled with what I had to say.

"It's the whole werewolf thing."

Her brows pulled together. "What about it?"

"Well, you see…" I was stalling. I just needed to spit it out. "Is it possible that someone might have a bit of an obsession with werewolves and might have, you know, gotten worked up and thought Alexander was a real werewolf and—"

"Char, what are you getting at?"

"The only thing we know about Emmett is that he's consumed by legends of the Rougarou."

My words had come out in a flurry, so it took a minute for the realization to flash across Jane's face, followed by shock and then anger.

"That's ridiculous. How could you even think such a thing?"

I held up my hands in mock surrender. "I'm not saying I believe it. I'm saying it's a working theory."

"It's a stupid theory. And also, it's based on a fallacy."

"What fallacy?"

"That I know nothing about Emmett. That's simply not true. We go way back."

"But Jane, there's nearly a four-decade gap in your knowledge of who he is. What else do you know about him other than he's a fan of Faulkner and is into folklore?"

"I know he's a kind and decent man. I know that he lost his wife in a tragic way, and he's smart and kind—"

"You said that already."

"Because it's true!"

"I've just noticed that he has quite an effect on you, and your infatuation with him may cloud your judgment a bit."

Jane clucked. "Char, how many times have I trusted your judgment, despite all evidence to the contrary? Countless. And now that the shoe is on the other foot, I don't get the benefit of the doubt in return?"

Her face was flushed, and it was clear the conversation wasn't getting anywhere.

"You're right. I'm sorry. Of course you deserve the benefit of the doubt. I think we should be cautious, though, when it comes to jumping to conclusions about what we know or don't know about anyone involved."

"I hope that restraint in jumping to conclusions extends to Emmett. The only way he's involved is that he's trying to help us solve this."

I wished I were as convinced of that as Jane, but something about Professor Emmett just didn't sit right with me.

⚓

JANE AND I called a truce when it came to my suspicions of Emmett. There was no point in arguing with her regarding something she felt so adamant was a nonstarter.

And Jane had a point about Ophelia. Despite her protests to the contrary, Ophelia did have the strongest motive. Not only had she lost out financially when Canailles Nous broke up, her career had stalled, and she'd been publicly humiliated by Alexander's affair. He had betrayed her in every possible way. Throw in his threats about what might happen to her if she broke the tour contract, and it was almost unfathomable that she *wouldn't* want to murder him.

Oh, and the threat. It had seemed offhand at the time. The kind of thing people said in anger but had no intention of following through on.

I literally want to choke you with my bare hands.

Had she meant it literally? Often when people threw the word *literally* around, they meant *figuratively*. I suspected she had meant it literally, but that didn't mean she'd actually do it.

And she hadn't.

Alexander St. Jacques hadn't been strangled or choked to death. He'd been shot.

Where was the gun? How had it gotten onboard the ship? Xavier was adamant about scanning luggage, and everyone walked through metal detectors.

I thought about the cruise to Yokohama when the former head chef had been killed.

The murder weapon had been brought onto the ship via the cargo loading dock.

I invited Jane to accompany me on my quest to determine how a gun might have gotten through Xavier's security measures, but she said she needed a nap.

On my way to the security office, I passed the ice cream shop. Percy Brown was reading a book and licking a chocolate ice cream cone.

"Hey."

He looked up from his book and pushed his horn-rimmed glasses farther up the bridge of his nose. "Oh, hey.

Charlotte, right?"

"Yes." I indicated the open chair opposite him. "Mind if I sit?"

"Be my guest." He set the open book—Dickens's *A Tale of Two Cities*—facedown on the table.

Jane would have thrown a fit.

"How's the ice cream? I've lived on this ship for nearly a year, and I've never tried it."

He grunted. "It's fine. It's no Angelo Brocato's."

"How are you holding up after last night?"

Percy stroked his full beard. "It's tough. Not gonna lie. Alex was like a brother to me."

"Even after Canailles Nous broke up?"

"Of course. Alex did what he needed to do for himself and his career. He had a golden opportunity, and he took it. I don't blame him for that."

"Even though it had a negative impact on you?"

"He took care of me. Got me hooked up with the producers of *Celebrity Court*."

"Do you like your job on that show? It looks like a bit of a circus anytime I've watched it. I remember one case involved two nepo babies fighting over who was responsible for the cost of a rented fur that accidentally got left on the hood of their Uber."

"Yeah. Clementine Brooks and Farrah James." He chuckled. "I had to play bouncer along with my P.A. duties that day."

"Seems like you've played that role a lot. I saw you trying to keep the peace between Alexander and Ophelia the other night outside Buddy Dupree's."

Percy exhaled a deep sigh. "Yeah. They were always at each other's throats. That's been the case since the day they met. Fire and ice, the two of them. Oil and water."

"And yet they weren't exactly oil and water, because for a period of time they were engaged. There had to have been good moments in their relationship."

"Sure." He smoothed his hair back. "Never lasted long, though. I had the impression they got off on it, the fighting. Some people are just like that. The bigger the fight, the better the making up."

"So their relationship was always volatile?"

"Not in an abusive way if that's what you mean. Just a lot of yelling."

"What about at the club when she threatened to choke him?"

Percy rubbed his heavily tattooed arm, a full sleeve of jazz instruments, music notes, and a fleur-de-lis. "Fee was angry about the contract, no doubt, and that woman has a temper. But I can't see her doing him that way. At the end of the day, after all the ways he's done her wrong, I believe she still loves him—*loved* him—passionately."

I didn't doubt that. The question was, had Ophelia's passionate love for Alexander led her into committing a crime of passion against him?

Chapter Eight

"TWICE IN ONE day. How fortunate am I?"

I ignored Xavier's mildly acerbic tone as I sat in the chair I'd vacated just a few hours earlier. "If you don't want people hanging around, perhaps you shouldn't have put in such comfortable seating. All I need is a blanket."

"Note to self: order new chair, stiff and unyielding."

"Ha."

"To what do I owe this pleasure?"

"You know I can hear the sarcasm in your voice."

"It is not sarcasm. I am genuine."

"The twitch at the corner of your mouth says otherwise." I waved him off. "Doesn't matter. I came to discuss strategy."

"Do tell."

"After speaking with Jane regarding Emmett—"

"I asked you not to do that."

"I didn't tell her anything. I asked her to consider the werewolf obsession as a possible motive. That inevitably led to a conversation about Emmett. She rejected the idea outright and says his only interest in the case is helping us solve it."

His expression was unreadable but not expressly unhappy, so I continued.

"They are actively working the Ophelia angle. Which, unfortunately for her, looks pretty viable. Alexander's betrayal of her was multifaceted. It impacted her negatively on many different levels from her career to her financial stability, and of course her broken heart."

Xavier leaned back in his chair and crossed his arms. "This is not anything of which I was unaware."

"Right, but I spoke with Percy, the bassist, and he said Ophelia and Alexander's relationship was pretty volatile from the start. Lots of fighting, lots of making up. It was a dance for them."

He shook his head. "I cannot imagine this. I could not live that way. Why choose to be in a constant state of unrest with your partner?" He absentmindedly rubbed his left ring finger with his thumb.

I knew very little about Xavier's private life, much less his relationships. We'd first met nearly a year earlier when that finger still had a faded band that alluded to the end of a marriage. For what reason it had ended I'd yet to learn, and I hadn't wanted to push the issue with him. The line had since faded completely, which meant the demise of the relationship—or his wife—had happened not too long before that fateful cruise. As he toyed with the phantom ring, a sting of empathy mixed with jealousy about this person who'd once—and apparently still—held a significant place in his heart pricked my chest.

"I can't imagine choosing to live in conflict with your

spouse," I said. "I know some people fight because as long as the other person is engaged, they know they're still invested. Gabe and I had the opposite dynamic. We rarely fought because we were too emotionally disconnected to have anything to fight about. Or for. Maybe for them, it kept the spark alive. They were fairly young, too, when they were together. Probably immature."

A quick tap on Xavier's door was followed by Lonnie's orange head poking through the crack. "Sorry to interrupt, but there's been a major development."

Xavier leaned forward and placed his elbows on the desktop. "What development?"

Lonnie glanced at me.

"It is fine. Madame McLaughlin can hear."

A flicker of surprise flashed in Lonnie's eyes. "You sure? It's a significant development."

Xavier sighed. "*Oui*. We have an agreement. A *tentative* agreement."

Lonnie squeezed the rest of his body through the doorway and into the office. "I went to interview Ophelia Thibodeaux as you requested."

"*Bon*. And?"

Lonnie glanced at me once more. "Are you sure you don't want me to wait until you're finished in here?"

"Irving." He flicked his hand urging Lonnie to continue.

"She answered all my questions, didn't ask for an attorney or anything, which is good, since the only one on this sailing is Mr. Weintraub and he's recovering from surgery. His wife asked they not be disturbed."

"Surgery?" I asked. "Is he okay? I hadn't heard he was ill."

Lonnie chuckled. "Not ill. Facelift. Botched job is the rumor, but he was bandaged when I saw him board."

Xavier cleared his throat. "For such a significant development, you are taking quite a while to reach the point of this."

"Sorry, chief. Her interview yielded very little in terms of new information, but I asked to do a search of her cabin, and she agreed."

"She agreed? Without hesitation?"

"Yep. And guess what I found, hidden beneath some very sexy black lingerie?"

"Sex toys." The words came out before I had a chance to think about who was in the room with me.

Lonnie laughed. "Good guess, but nope."

Xavier briefly closed his eyes, probably trying to banish the thought of Ophelia's personal massager. Or maybe he wanted to envision it. She was a gorgeous woman, and he'd already shown a flicker of interest in her.

"Just tell me."

"How about I show you?"

Lonnie held up a plastic bag. Inside the bag was an engraved silver revolver with a wooden handle. "Second generation Colt Single Action Army, also known as the Peacemaker."

"Is that real?" I asked. "It looks like a novelty gun that would come with a Lone Ranger costume." Had I seen a Lone Ranger at the Halloween party? I couldn't recall.

"Without a doubt it's real." He shook the bag to indicate its weight. "This thing is heavy. And definitely holds the right caliber. She claims it's not hers."

Xavier took the bag from Lonnie, held it up to the light for closer inspection, then set it on the desk in front of him.

"I am not very familiar with this gun. What can you tell me about it?"

Lonnie sat in the chair next to me. "My dad had a pretty big collection when I was growing up, and he insisted on teaching me everything he knew about 'em. He was a big believer that educating me on firearms, the history of the weapons, how they'd been used, how they'd been misused was part of responsible gun ownership. He was also a stickler for safety protocol. Anyway, we went to a lot of gun shows, and part of my training was learning how to spot fakes, replicas, or reproductions."

"Is this a fake?" I asked. "You said second generation."

"Not a fake. The first-generation SAA—Single Action Army—was produced from the late 1800s up to World War II when Colt put all its energy into manufacture for the military. They didn't resume commercial production until about ten years later with the rise in popularity of Westerns. This is likely a Buntline Special circa early 1970s, but I can't tell for certain because the serial numbers have been filed off."

"Impressive," I said.

Xavier nodded. "Quite impressive."

"So, silver gun, silver shell casing, silver bullet, discharged beneath the light of a silvery moon," I said. "Doesn't that lean heavily toward the werewolf wacko theory?"

"Poetic, but no."

"Why not? I thought you were leaning that way?"

"Beside the fact the possible murder weapon was found in Ophelia's drawer, there's one problem with your little…ditty." Xavier's mouth twitched the way it always did when he teased me.

"Which is?"

Xavier indicated for Lonnie to answer.

"It's not a silver gun, and it wasn't a silver shell casing. It was nickel-plated brass. I use 'em all the time."

"Etched with the word *Rougarou*!" I insisted.

Xavier made a dismissive humming sound. "This is true. Perhaps Ms. Thibodeaux believed Alexander was a werewolf, but more than likely, she simply wanted revenge for his treatment of her as his fiancée and bandmate."

"It was a silver bullet to the heart, though. Wasn't it?" I asked.

"As far as I am aware, Dr. Fraser does not have the equipment to test the metal content of the bullet, and from what I have read, a pure silver bullet would be difficult to create, but the one retrieved from Alexander St. Jacques's body does have a silvery appearance."

"See!" I slapped the desk.

Xavier rocked back.

"Sorry, didn't mean to get carried away. It seems pretty convenient the gun was found hidden in the drawers of the most obvious suspect. If Emmett Guidry killed Alexander out of some misguided belief he was a werewolf, and then planted evidence in Ophelia's suite to throw you off the scent—so to speak—Jane could be in danger."

"Understood." Xavier addressed Lonnie. "Have you gone over the security recordings?"

"Not yet. I was going to have Taylor do it tonight."

"I would say that should be a priority. Dr. Fraser will determine what he can and preserve any evidence he finds, but in the meantime, I would like to have you bring Ms. Thibodeaux here for questioning."

Lonnie jolted upright. "Oh."

"What?"

He jerked his thumb toward the door. "She's handcuffed to my desk out in the lobby."

⚓

OPHELIA'S TEAR-STREAKED FACE was flushed with fury. "I can't believe you left me chained here like a junkyard dog!"

Lonnie grimaced. "Sorry, I got so caught up in the conversation I forgot you were out here."

"Uncuff me this instant," she growled through gritted teeth. "Before I sue you all for kidnapping and unlawful detainment."

Xavier indicated for Lonnie to release Ophelia from the handcuffs. "You are aware of the reason Officer Irving brought you here, are you not?"

Ophelia jutted her pretty chin. "I've never seen that gun in my life. I've never even held a gun!"

Lonnie eyed her skeptically. "I find that hard to believe."

She clucked her tongue. "Not everyone is as obsessed with guns as you law-and-order types."

"Officer Irving, would you please escort Ms. Thibodeaux to my office? I will join her there in a moment."

She glared at Lonnie. "Keep your hands off me."

He held up his hands in mock surrender. "I won't have to lay a finger on you as long as you cooperate."

She shuffled toward Xavier's office.

Xavier turned to face me. "I have an idea."

"Okay."

"I would like you to sit with her for a few minutes. Tell her I've been held up by something and will be briefly delayed so you will keep her company. Nurture her. See if she opens up to you."

"Because I'm a woman?"

"That, and because you are approachable. People seem to want to confide in you."

I glanced at his ringless left hand. Why wasn't he one of those people? "I'll do my best. I can't promise anything."

"That is all I ask. Tell Irving I need to speak with him, *s'il vous plaît.*"

After giving Lonnie the message, I sat next to a pouting Ophelia. She seemed less scared and more annoyed. In my experience, neither the guilty nor the innocent behaved in predictable ways, despite conventional wisdom to the contrary.

"Let me guess." She sniffed. "They've sent you in here to play good cop."

"I'm not a cop at all." Hopefully, she didn't notice my

evasion of the question.

"It's too bad that big redheaded dope arrested me. He's kinda cute. Not as cute as the boss, but I've got a strict policy of not dating people who believe I'm capable of murder. Besides, he's already seen my unmentionables. How humiliating is that?"

"He's a good guy. Can you blame him for thinking the person in possession of the likely murder weapon might have committed the crime?"

"I thought it was innocent until proven guilty."

"In a courtroom, sure. In an investigation, however, it's more like everyone is presumed guilty until the evidence proves them otherwise. Especially on a ship where there's a limited suspect pool and no place for the perpetrator to escape. Sometimes the killer ends up hurting more people simply because they feel cornered. Trapped." I didn't tell her I was speaking from experience. *Recent* experience.

"Then I need protection as a victim. The murderer may come after me too!"

"I have no doubt Xavier will keep his eye on you." I hoped the note of envy didn't give me away.

"Well, I didn't kill Alex." Her voice cracked. "Despite everything, he was still my person, ya know?"

"Tell me about him."

She exhaled a bitter laugh. "Where to start? You know that saying *it was the best of times, it was the worst of times?*"

"Yes, from Dickens's *A Tale of Two Cities*."

How coincidental, her bringing up the same book Percy had been reading at the ice cream shop. Or perhaps not so coincidental after all. Maybe he'd been talking to her about the book.

"That's what it was like with Alex. The best of times and the worst of times. Sometimes it felt like the good times would last forever, but he was always so spooked. Always looking over his shoulder. Jittery. Like a cat."

"Any idea what made him so anxious?"

"No clue. It definitely got worse when *Lamoreaux* charted. He hired extra security—never went anywhere without them—and got some high-tech system installed in his house. He was so paranoid that—" She stopped herself.

"So paranoid that what?"

She chewed her lower lip. "I shouldn't have said anything."

"Ophelia, Alexander is dead. Murdered. Anything you know that might help solve who did this is vital information. It could mean the difference between his killer getting the justice he deserves or walking away from this ship like nothing happened."

Her hands briefly covered her face. "This feels like a betrayal." Her guffaw was bitter with irony. "I have guilt about betraying the secrets of a dead man who had no qualms about betraying me. How messed up is that?"

Messed up—but familiar.

The placid smile I'd worn throughout Gabe's funeral to protect his reputation with anyone who didn't know about his double life. The fumbling response I'd given to his ninety-five-year-old mother about the identity of the weeping woman holding the baby who reminded her so much of

Gabe when he was young.

I'd burst into tears when I called the cable company to cancel one of our extra subscriptions and the woman asked why.

B-because my huh-husband wanted it so he could watch all the global financial news, but he's dead now. He wrapped his car around a tree with his mistress and their b-baby inside. S-so I don't n-need it any-muh-muh-more.

"Let's just say I understand more than you may know."

She gave me a wan smile but thankfully didn't press for details.

"At the height of Canaille Nous's popularity, Alexander had kind of a…mental break. He went to a facility in Beverly Hills for three weeks. Our publicist claimed he needed vocal rest, but that was a lie. He was convinced someone was after him."

"How did it get resolved?"

Her despondent shrug said more than her words. "Dunno. He signed the solo contract and that was that." She wiped a stray tear.

I gave her a moment to process her feelings of grief—about his betrayal and about his death. She was suffering, of that I had no doubt.

"Ophelia," I began tentatively. "Is there any way someone could have gotten into your room to hide the gun in your drawer?"

She knit her brows. "Hard to say. I mean, there's the staff. They come into my room several times a day for various reasons. To tidy, to make cute little animals out of my towels, to bring me food or coffee. Other than that, no one has been in my room that I am aware of other than the guys in the band."

"They've been in your room?"

"Of course. Oh, and that author guy."

"What author guy?" I scanned my brain for any authors among the other passengers but came up blank.

"You know, the silver fox."

"The who? The what?"

She groaned. "The dude that looks like Clooney and sounds like Harry Connick Jr., Professor McHottie. I've seen him with your sister. He showed up at my room. Said he's working on a book and had some questions."

Oh no. "Do you mean Emmett Guidry?"

"Maybe." She shrugged. "I'm not good with names."

"What did he want?"

She scrunched her forehead. "Well, first, he asked me if I'd sent him some email. I said I had no idea what he was talking about. Then he started asking a bunch of questions about Alex. I asked him if he was some kind of stalker, but he said he just wanted to know if I'd noticed anything unusual about Alex, any strange behavior. It was like he was trying to ask questions but didn't want to give away too much about why he was fishing. I told him it was not my job to keep tabs on that man, and frankly I found most of Alex's behavior strange and abhorrent." She tilted her head. "This Emmett guy…I think he said he's writing a book about werewolves."

He was indeed writing a book about werewolves. And Jane had fallen under his spell.

Chapter Nine

XAVIER CAME INTO the room where I sat shell-shocked next to a defiant Ophelia Thibodeaux. He took one look at me and then did a double-take.

"What is wrong?"

He'd directed the question at me, but Ophelia answered.

"What's wrong is, I'm being held in a claustrophobic room under a cloud of suspicion while the real killer is getting ready to eat their weight in king cake and bananas foster."

I felt a kinship with Ophelia. I often measured loss in terms of dessert as well. At the moment, however, my appetite had vanished.

"May I speak with you outside, pretty please?" I pointed toward the door.

"*Bien sûr.* Of course." He tented his fingers and gave a quick bow toward Ophelia. "My apologies for this taking so long. I promise I will return shortly."

Ophelia made a raspberry sound and crossed her arms.

Xavier carefully shut the door behind him. "What is it? Did she tell you something regarding her involvement in the murder?"

"On the contrary. I'm pretty sure she didn't do it."

His left eyebrow arched. "Is that so?"

"Yes, it's so. I asked her who might have stashed the gun in her drawer. She said not only did the members of Canailles Nous visit her at her cabin, but she also had another visitor."

"Who was this visitor?"

"Our good friend the professor."

⚓

XAVIER PROMISED TO take my theory about Ophelia's innocence under advisement but informed me he could not in good conscience ignore the evidence—namely, her possession of what appeared to be the murder weapon—and had no plans of releasing her following their interview. He also said he would follow up on Emmett's visit to her room.

I had no intention of waiting for him to do that.

The night's dinner theme was La Toussaint—All Saints' Day—which seemed especially morbid in light of the previous night's murder. The staff had transformed the dining room into a New Orleans-style cemetery, filled with electric candles of all shapes and sizes, with tombstones, flowers, and crosses placed for decorative and dramatic effect. The artificial trees draped in Spanish moss from the welcome reception had returned, with glowing candelabras hanging from their plastic branches.

It was all in very poor taste, and in no way struck me as honoring to the dead.

At least the music was less raucous than the first two nights. With Canailles Nous mourning their leader, a soothing jazz soundtrack had been substituted for their scheduled live performance.

I planned to set aside the topic of Jane's and my argument for the time being so we could both enjoy the evening, but it was difficult, especially after hearing what Ophelia had to say about Emmett visiting her at her room. Not to mention, he was standing three feet from me with his arm slung around my sister in a proprietary way.

In his all-white suit with white patent leather shoes, he looked like a groom figurine atop a wedding cake.

"What's with the getup?" I whispered into Jane's ear, hoping Emmett didn't overhear. "It's not a costume theme night."

"I think he looks handsome. Like a Southern gentleman."

"You mean like Colonel Sanders?" That would at least be preferable to the alternative, an antebellum plantation owner.

Jane glared at me, so I backed away from her. We weren't on the same page, and my teasing Emmett wasn't helping.

Ulfric seated us in the corner at a table for four.

"This is a good spot," Jane said.

"Why's that?" Emmett scanned the room.

"Because we're able to observe everyone coming and going. Maybe someone will show their hand."

"Oh, good plan. No varnish can hide the grain of the wood, and the more varnish you put on, the more the grain will express itself."

"Faulkner?" I asked as we sat at the table.

He shook his head. "Not this time. Dickens. *Great Expectations*."

I wagged my finger. "It's funny you should mention Dickens. I've heard two people reference *A Tale of Two Cities* just since we boarded in New Orleans."

Emmett gave an approving smirk. "A classic."

"Who was talking about that?" Jane asked.

"Well, Percy was reading it, and then Ophelia quoted it."

"Strange," Jane murmured.

"Quite," agreed Emmett. "It's not even his best novel. I'd argue it's not even in the top five."

"What? You're joking." Jane turned to fully face him.

I observed Emmett as subtly as possible as he and Jane bickered about their rankings of Dickens novels. He didn't look like a deranged werewolf hunter, but having never encountered one in real life, I had nothing to compare him to other than Van Helsing. Wait. Van Helsing *became* a werewolf in order to go after Dracula, Mr. Hyde, and Frankenstein's monster, hadn't he? Something like that. Regardless, I had no context of werewolf hunter encounters from which to draw.

Jane—having had enough of Emmett's assertion that *Bleak House* was Dickens's best book—got up to use the restroom, leaving the two of us alone at the table.

"Emmett, I was sorry to hear you lost your wife. I'm sure Jane mentioned I'm a widow."

His face clouded over. "Yes, she did. And thank you."

I waited for him to elaborate, but he didn't. One more try. "Car accident?"

He looked up at me with a bewildered expression. "Come again?"

I fiddled with my silverware. "Oh, Jane had said it was some sort of accident rather than illness. I assumed it was a car accident. That's how Gabe died. Sort of. Heart attack that caused a car accident, but nonetheless, suddenly. People often say it's better for all concerned, but it certainly hasn't felt that way."

"Not a car accident." He took his napkin from his lap and set it on the table. "Would you please excuse me for a moment?"

I mumbled something that sounded like acquiescence, but he was already halfway across the room, headed straight for the bar. He exchanged brief conversation with Hawk, who handed him a cocktail of some sort.

Also bellied up to the bar was Percy Brown. Percy was dressed in black cargo pants and a short-sleeved black button-up that showed off his tattoos. He had an empty glass in front of him and one that was nearly empty. He tapped his large index finger on the bar. Hawk glanced over at him and gave a quick nod.

Emmett turned to Percy and held up his glass. Percy raised his own glass, and after clinking them together, he downed the remainder of the amber liquid.

Jane returned to the table. "Where's Emmett?"

"He seems to be getting a drink." I indicated the bar. "I tried to get him to open up a bit about his wife. No go."

"Char, you didn't!"

"Of course I did. I figured if he'd open up to anyone about what happened to her, it would be someone who'd gone through something similar. I couldn't even get him to give a straight answer on how she died. It's bizarre."

Pink crept up her neck. "How would you like it if someone gave you the third degree about your husband's death, huh, Torquemada?"

I brushed off her unfair implication that I'd been grilling him like the Spanish Inquisition. "Don't you think it's odd that he doesn't want to talk at all about what happened to her?"

"You of all people should know everyone processes grief in their own way."

"Sure, but I'm starting to wonder if the reason he doesn't want to talk about what happened to her is because he's in some way responsible."

Jane slammed her hand on the table. "Enough!"

Diners at nearby tables stopped eating and glanced over at us.

"I do not appreciate what you are doing, and I'm starting to think you are purposely sabotaging any possibility for romance between Emmett and me."

"You think I'm jealous. Of Emmett?" I scoffed. "Not my type. Did you know he visited Ophelia at her room? Maybe you should ask him what he was doing th—"

"You know what, Char?" She rose from her chair. "I think I'm done for the night."

She marched away to join Emmett at the bar. She placed

her hand on his shoulder, and whatever she said to him caused him to glance my way. His expression was unreadable but certainly not friendly. He swigged the remainder of his drink, slapped Percy on the back, and looped his arm through Jane's.

Haimi hustled over to me. "Sorry it has taken me so long to get to you." She looked around. "Did Ms. Cobb and Mr. Guidry have a change of plans?"

"Something like that," I murmured.

⚓

FOLLOWING MY SOLITARY dinner, I made my way over to Azure Lounge. The indigo lighting and bluesy music playing overhead were apropos for my mood.

Egan was tending bar, and I found Heath Hubbard nursing a drink. I slid onto the stool next to him.

He acknowledged my arrival with a slow nod. "Evenin', Ms. Mack."

I was about to correct him about my last name when I realized he'd given me a nickname.

"Heath, how are you holding up?"

He grabbed a handful of nuts from the dish in front of him and popped them in his mouth. He chewed quietly for a moment. "I don't mean to be callous, but I've seen my share of death. Grief is not a new phenomenon for me, sad to say."

"That is sad to say. I'm sorry to hear it."

He shoved the bowl my direction. "Pecans?" He pronounced it PEE-cans rather than pee-CAWNS, which is how

I'd learned to say it growing up on the West Coast.

"Thank you." I popped one in my mouth and immediately realized my mistake. It was as if my entire mouth, throat, and esophagus were on fire. I coughed and waved at Egan. "Water," I rasped.

Heath chuckled. "Forgot to let you know they're called hellfire pecans, on account of the five kinds of pepper and paprika."

I gulped down the water, but the scorching continued.

"Prolly shoulda drank milk. They say that's better for the burn."

"Helpful to know after the fact." I stuck out my tongue, not in response to Heath but to cool it down. "How did you just eat a handful of those things without needing medical intervention?"

"*Chère*, I was raised on those spices since the day I was weaned from my mama's breast. Heck, I probably got it vicariously through her nursing me."

"My ancestors came from the UK. Not exactly known for seasoning. What's that saying? Britain conquered half the world for spices and decided it didn't like any of them."

"*Au contraire, ma chère*," Heath said. "Some of the most flavorful food I've ever eaten was in London and Dublin. Of course, all from cultures they appropriated, but still."

"Hey now." Egan wiped a glass and set it on the counter. "Don't lump us Irish in with the Brits. We weren't the ones out colonizing—we were the colonized."

Heath tipped his glass toward Egan in a conciliatory gesture. "My apologies, good man."

"Mrs. McLaughlin, can I get ye anythin' other than water?" Egan flashed his bright blue eyes and brushed his glossy black hair out of his face.

"I wouldn't mind something, but I don't think I'm up for a hurricane or anything like that. What else have you got?"

"How about a Pimm's Cup? That's a French Quarter classic."

"Never heard of it. What's in it?"

"Pimm's number one, which is a gin-based liqueur with fruit juice and spices, paired with lemonade, lemon-lime soda, and topped with a fresh cucumber slice."

"That sounds refreshing, but not quite right for my mood. Any other suggestions? Maybe something more dessert-y."

"Milk. That's it." Egan pointed at me. "I've got just the thing. If I'm wrong, I'll make you something else."

"Deal."

He pulled a gallon of milk from the fridge and poured about a cup into the shaker. He then added a shot and a half of brandy, followed by a tiny bit of powdered sugar and a whole lot of ice. He poured the concoction into a coupe glass and topped it with freshly grated nutmeg.

"Brandy milk punch a la Brennan's."

I took a sip. "Delicious. Thank you."

"My pleasure."

"Have you been to Brennan's?" Heath asked.

"I have, as a matter of fact. I had brunch there the morning before we left." I took another sip. "It's funny. While I was there, I met some kids who were talking about the Rougarou, and now here we are."

Heath side-eyed me. "What do you mean, here we are?"

"Well, the whole werewolf thing."

He spun his stool to face me. "Are you speaking of the fact Alexander was wearing a werewolf costume?"

I tried to read his expression and demeanor. Was he playing naïve, or did he really not know that the shell casing from the silver(ish) bullet used to kill Alexander was etched with the word *Rougarou*?

"There are a few factors that might—I stress *might*—indicate that the killer believed they were shooting an actual werewolf. A Rougarou."

Heath screwed up his face. "You're kidding."

"I'm not."

"Is that what that Scooby-Doo guy was talkin' about in the captain's lounge last night?"

"Emmett is writing a book about Louisiana myths and legends, so he's particularly fascinated with the myth of the Rougarou."

Heath leaned back and crossed his arms. "Well, I can tell you having grown up in the bayou, to the people who live there, it's no myth. My *granmère* would swear on her own life that a Rougarou roamed the area and was responsible for heinous things. That's why she never allowed her children or grandchildren out alone after dark."

"What do you think?"

"I think when it comes to people's beliefs, it doesn't matter whether it's real or not. As long as they think it's real, they will behave accordingly."

"Can you tell me what you know about the legend?"

He swigged his drink. "As with anything like this, there are variations on the myth. I've heard all sorts of things like that just looking in its eyes may cause you to be cursed. In order to protect your home, you should lay thirteen small objects outside your door."

"Why's that?"

Laughter rumbled in his chest. "Because supposedly when you're a werewolf, you lose your ability to count past twelve. Something to do with being obsessed with midnight. The theory is that they will be so consumed with counting and recounting the objects, they'll keep doing it until the sun comes up and they have to go hide."

"Odd. Okay. So, let's say you looked in its eyes or were bitten or whatever, and you become a Rougarou. What then?"

"I was taught that in order to be released from the curse, a Rougarou must incite someone into shedding its blood. Not kill it, mind you, just draw blood. But then the attacker falls under the curse for one hundred and one days unless they can transfer the curse to someone else."

"Vicious cycle."

"Literally. But here's the other thing you should know about the Rougarou."

"What's that?" I sipped my brandy milk.

"Many families see them as guardian angels."

"How can that be? I thought they were considered monsters."

"Yes, but more like the avenging injustice type. They protect the good-hearted from those who might harm or wrong them. They look out for orphans, widows, the poor. Anyone who's been rejected by society but remain kind and compassionate."

"Benevolent beasts."

He nodded. "Benevolent beasts."

I made my way back to the suite I shared with Jane, but it sat empty and dark.

Perhaps it was the brandy. Perhaps it was the fact I'd dined in a makeshift cemetery. Certainly, it was all the talk of full moons and werewolf curses.

The idea that someone had killed Alexander because they believed he was a werewolf was becoming more plausible to me by the hour.

Especially with that latest tidbit of information that Rougarous were known for their advocacy on behalf of the downtrodden.

A little internet sleuthing revealed that just two months ago, Alexander St. Jacques had announced the formation of a charity called *L'Aumône* Foundation. The word meant *charity* in French. Its mission was to clothe and feed families in the Lower Ninth Ward, the area of New Orleans hardest hit by Hurricane Katrina.

Had someone seen his act of charity as a confession of the curse he was under?

Chapter Ten

By 11:00 P.M. Jane still hadn't returned to our suite. I attempted to read a book, but my mind kept wandering and worrying.

Just before midnight, she walked through the door. She didn't seem to notice me at first.

"Jane, can we talk?"

She nearly jumped out of her skin. "Ack! Don't sneak up on me like that."

"Sorry. I'm not sure there was any way for me to let you know I'm here without startling you."

She set her purse on the kitchen counter and leaned against it. "I'm really not happy with you right now."

"I know."

"Do you have anything to say for yourself?"

"Just that I love you, and I hate when we fight."

Her shoulders slumped. "Me too." She joined me in the living room.

"Where did you end up going with Emmett after you left the dining room?"

"Casino. Then we discovered Victor Lutz was playing piano in the theater lounge next door."

"How was that?" I asked.

"Lost fifty bucks. But the music was good."

"Victor was performing by himself?"

"Yes. Webster Powell was in the audience, though. What did you do?"

"I ended up at Azure talking with Heath Hubbard at the bar."

"Anything come of that?"

If I brought up the Rougarou stuff, would she get defensive again? I was too exhausted to find out. "Not a whole lot. Hey, did you know that Alexander St. Jacques had recently started a charity?"

"Not surprising. Celebrities are always looking for tax write-offs."

"I'm not sure that's what this is. It's a pretty important cause for New Orleans, and I get the feeling it's one that's close to his heart." I winced, both at my inadvertent use of the present tense when referring to Alexander, but also the location of where the bullet that had taken his life had entered his body. "It's called *L'Aumône* Foundation, and it supports low-income areas of New Orleans, particularly the Lower Ninth Ward."

"*L'Aumône?*"

"I looked it up. Roughly translated it means money given to the poor."

"That's a little on the nose."

"Gets the point across, though." I picked a piece of imaginary lint off my pants. "I have a proposition for you."

She narrowed her gaze. "Why do I sense I'm not going to

love this proposition?"

I held up a hand. "Just hear me out."

She arched her left brow but said nothing.

"You know how Xavier is always saying everyone is a suspect until they're ruled out?"

"Mm-hmm."

"I think we need to keep an open mind. The motive isn't clear. It's only been twenty-four hours since Alexander's murder, and I think there are still a lot of facts to gather before we jump to any conclusions about who is guilty."

"Agreed."

"Or who is innocent."

Jane pursed her lips and exhaled through her flared nostrils. "Are you saying you don't think I can be objective? Are you saying I'm naïve? Easily manipulated?"

"I'm not saying any of those things. I'm saying I will not focus too much on one particular theory if you don't."

She shifted her jaw back and forth. "Fine. I will keep my eyes wide open."

"And?"

"And what?" she snapped. "I already agreed to keep an open mind. What more do you want from me, Char?"

"To openly discuss all aspects and all potential theories without it getting contentious."

"Of course." Her stiff posture and clenched jaw said otherwise.

"Okay."

She gave an abrupt nod. "Okay. I'm tired. I'm going to bed."

"Night, Jane."

"Good night, Charlotte."

It was never good when she called me by my full name.

⚓

JANE WAS GONE when I got up the next morning. She hadn't left a note.

No matter how much I wanted to believe she understood where I was coming from and that I was only looking out for her, I suspected there were things at play that clouded her perception. Hormones, for one. Jane hadn't been in any romantic entanglements in years. She'd kind of sworn off relationships after a particularly nasty breakup about ten years prior, announcing that she was done with the whole thing. If I remembered correctly, she'd said something to the effect of there not being any men in Turlock worthy of shaving her legs.

As I sipped my coffee, I considered the possibility that, regardless of my admonition to her to remain open-minded about the evidence, I was hesitant to do the same when it came to Emmett.

Something about him was off. He was strangely cagey about his wife's death, his charm struck me as inauthentic in some way, and my protective instincts toward my sister were ringing all the alarm bells.

Unfortunately, Jane and I were so far from being on the same page about him, we were barely in the same book.

Why couldn't she understand that everything I was doing was to protect her?

I checked my phone. No missed calls or texts.

It was after nine. There was a Mardi Gras mask-decorating class at ten I was planning to attend, and I had yet to shower.

I'd intended to stop by the security office to see if there were any updates, but it would have to wait. I wanted to make sure I got to the theater lounge in time to snag a table. The theater served as a multipurpose room for everything from performances to owner meetings to craft making events, and crafting was a big draw with the *Thalassophile* crowd.

I'd found in my previous investigations that it was a primo place to gather information.

Jane and I had planned to attend together, but when I arrived, she was already seated at a table with Emmett. A table for two.

"Morning. You guys got a good spot. Mind if I pull up a chair?"

Emmett smiled at me and opened his mouth to respond, but Jane cut him off.

"It's a small table, and we're going to need room to work."

"Ah, I see." I swallowed a grapefruit-sized lump. "Okay." I scanned the room, tamping down the tears threatening to well up in my eyes. "Oh, there's Percy and Webster. Looks like they have room at their table."

Jane gave a curt nod but no response. As I made my way across the theater lounge, I could hear Emmett whisper something to her, but I couldn't make out what he'd said or her grumbled response.

Things were rapidly devolving between us, and I couldn't shake the unease it bred within me. Not to mention, if Emmett really was a killer, how could I protect her if she was barely speaking to me?

"Hey, guys, how's it going?"

Webster grunted and pulled down the brim of his bucket hat.

Percy nudged him. "C'mon, man. Show some manners."

"Sorry. Too many hurricanes last night."

"That'll do it. Can I join you?"

Percy held out his hand. "By all means. We could use a woman's touch."

"Not sure how much help I'll be. I'm kind of surprised to see you two here."

"Not a lot else to do, now that all our gigs are canceled, our leader is dead, and our vocalist is in jail for his murder." Webster pulled at the collar of his tie-dyed shirt.

He'd worn a similar shirt nearly every time I'd seen him. He must have owned a dozen of them unless it was the same shirt. But I hadn't noticed any odors, and there were slight variations, as happened with tie-dye.

"She's not in jail, man, I keep telling you." Percy ran his hand over his shellacked hair. It didn't move even a tiny bit. "She's just temporarily detained because they found a gun in her room."

Webster slowly turned to look at him. "Man, are you smoking something? She hated him with every fiber of her being. The murder weapon was literally found hidden in her drawers."

Percy wagged his finger. "Now, that's not exactly true. They found a gun, but they don't know it's the murder weapon. Not officially." He glanced at me. "Unless you know otherwise."

I held up my hands. "I know nothing."

He narrowed his gaze at me. "Hmph. I doubt that's true."

"Ladies and gentlemen." Hawk stood on the stage holding a microphone. "For some unknown reason, I have been chosen to lead you all in this activity. I am not from Louisiana, I've never been to Mardi Gras, and I haven't used a glue gun since elementary school. However, I have watched an instructional video, and we're all going to figure this out together."

Each table had an array of plain masks in purple, green, gold, and black, along with similarly hued feather boas, bead necklaces, bottles of glitter, gold paint, and artificial jewels.

"According to the video, Mardi Gras masks were a way for people from different social classes to mingle together during the celebration without fear of repercussion. Of course, that's not an issue onboard this ship. You're all high-class folks, amirite?"

A titter of laughter moved across the room. Webster grunted.

For the next forty-five minutes, I struggled with paint, feathers, beads, glitter, and a glue gun to decorate my mask for the evening's event.

I loved the various themed events the ship's entertainment director put on, but consolidating a region's culture into one or two weeks' worth of activities often meant an odd amalgam of holidays and traditions jumbled into one.

For example, decorating a mask for a Mardi Gras masquerade ball two days after Halloween rather than in February.

"This is a mess." Webster held his mask up to his face. "Not to mention it's way too small. Did I get a child's size on accident?"

"That's not a small mask. It's normal size." Percy chuckled. "It's your head that's too big."

An ironic statement considering Percy's giant stature. His hands were the size of a Little League baseball mitt, and his wardrobe most definitely came from the big and tall shop.

I glanced at Jane, smiling and chatting with Emmett.

Her accusation that my prejudice against him was born of petty jealousy and possessiveness was harsh and unfair.

Sure, it was true that in the weeks after Gabe died, I'd never felt so alone, and when Jane and I embarked on our new life at sea, suddenly I had a full-time companion. A buddy. Partner in crime. If Jane fell in love and moved out of our suite and back into a land dwelling, that would impact me. No doubt.

But couldn't she see it wasn't about that? I wasn't being selfish. I was concerned for her well-being. Her safety, even. Why did that make me the bad guy?

⚓

"You're just in time." Lonnie Irving waved at me as I entered the security office.

"Just in time for what?"

Pike Taylor sat at the edge of Lonnie's desk. "We just learned something quite interesting about our victim."

I sat in the chair opposite them. "Intriguing."

"Mesnier had us fingerprint Alexander St. Jacques. I thought it was unnecessary, but he insisted." Pike shrugged. "Turns out his instincts were correct."

I clucked my tongue. "He had a criminal record?"

Lonnie smirked. "Yes, but that's not the most interesting aspect of the report we just got."

"Are you going to keep me in suspense?"

Xavier opened the door to the security office. "What have we got?" He caught sight of me and stopped in his tracks. "You did not tell her anything." He ignored my indignant cry. "I do not want you releasing information to Madame McLaughlin without my approval. I have explained this."

A chastised Pike slumped his shoulders and returned to his own desk.

Lonnie's neck and cheeks flushed pink. Of course, with him being a redhead, that happened with regularity. "I thought you said there was an arrangement."

"That arrangement means I will share information with her at my discretion." Xavier turned his attention from Lonnie and gave me a pointed look.

"If you have something to say, you can just say it." I crossed my arms.

"Perhaps you can wait in my office while Irving and Taylor update me on what they've found."

"And then you'll come share that information with me, right?" I chewed on the inside of my cheek.

"If I deem it appropriate to do so."

Judging by the clenching and unclenching of his jaw, this was a battle I wasn't going to win. "Fine. I'll be waiting."

In his office, I availed myself of his built-in bar. What did it matter than it was before noon? The events of the past few days justified a little tippling.

Besides, I had a lot of nervous energy I didn't quite know what to do with. I suspected the information Pike and Lonnie were sharing with Xavier was going to be a game-changer for the case. My anticipation for knowing what that was, while also trying to reconcile the possibility he wasn't going to share it with me, made me buzz with adrenaline. In addition, the unease I'd been feeling surrounding the Jane situation or, more accurately, the Jane and Emmett situation, had begun morphing into full-fledged dread.

About fifteen minutes later, Xavier entered his office. "Sorry to keep you waiting."

"Hopefully, it was for good reason."

He tilted his head at the sight of my half-full glass. "I see you've started happy hour several hours early."

"I figured you wouldn't mind."

"Not at all. That is why I have it."

His face showed none of the telltale signs of alcohol abuse, and I'd rarely seen him drink. Perhaps he really did have a minibar for guests rather than himself.

"So?"

He rubbed his chin. "Can I count on you to keep this information confidential?"

"Of course."

He arched one brow.

As I had previously with Lonnie, I pretended to lock my mouth and throw away the invisible key.

"Monsieur St. Jacques was not as he appeared to be."

"This isn't about the werewolf thing, is it?"

He gave a brief shake of his head. "It is not."

"Okay, not as he appeared in what way? I mean, he's a public figure. What could he be hiding that TMZ hasn't discovered?"

I considered mentioning what Lonnie had told me about Alexander having a record but refrained. I didn't want him getting in trouble. Then he'd really never share any information with me.

"His fingerprints matched a criminal database from an arrest more than twenty years ago."

I feigned surprise. Judging by his narrowed gaze, I may have overplayed it a bit.

"You knew this?"

"Not at all." I crossed my fingers and slipped them under my leg.

"Hmm."

"What was he arrested for?"

"Accessory to a robbery. He pled the charge and served six months in Lafourche Parish Detention Center. Apparently, this facility is no longer open. It has been replaced by a more modern correctional facility."

"Accessory to robbery. That's pretty bad. But if it was two decades ago, it must have been before the success of Canailles Nous, and he must have been fairly young."

"*Oui.* Nineteen."

"Well, good for him for remaking his life in a more positive direction."

"Oh, he remade himself all right."

I waited for him to elaborate, but he merely sat there looking smug.

"You gonna tell me or what?"

"The man who spent six months in jail in the late nineties wasn't Alexander St. Jacques."

"You just said it was."

"No, I said Alexander St. Jacques's fingerprints matched with a convicted felon in Lafourche Parish."

I waved my hands. "Isn't that what we're talking about here? You're speaking in riddles."

"The fingerprints of the man who called himself Alexander St. Jacques matched an inmate who spent time in Lafourche Parish Detention Center. That inmate's name, however, was René Defaux. Alexander St. Jacques was a fraud."

Chapter Eleven

"If Alexander St. Jacques was actually René Defaux, who was Alexander St. Jacques? And did anyone know about this false identity?"

"We are working on that."

"This information changes everything. Maybe someone from his past who knew him as René wanted revenge for something he did. Robbery's not a small crime, and likely not his first offense. Maybe he was on the run, and that's why he changed his name. Did he escape from prison?"

"No, he was released on parole. His original sentence was three to five years and a thousand-dollar fine. And it was accessory to robbery. There must have been extenuating circumstances that prevented him from being charged with first- or second-degree robbery."

My nervous energy was now causing my entire body to vibrate. "Who did he assist in committing the robbery? Was it a gang thing?"

"We are still ascertaining the facts."

I tapped my mouth with my fingertip. "I wonder if he kept in touch with his parole officer. Maybe he didn't escape prison, but if he didn't abide by the rules of his parole, they'd send him back to finish out his sentence."

"The record shows a completed program. The fine was paid."

"Do you mind if I do a little digging?"

Xavier exhaled. "In what way?"

"I'm a fantastic researcher, and I have access to newspaper archives and family tree websites. Let me see what I can find out about René. Maybe I can also find information about the real Alexander St. Jacques—if there was one."

He nodded. "I would appreciate that. I'd like my team to focus on checking all the security camera footage, conducting interviews of guests, staff, and the members of Canailles Nous."

"Speaking of Canailles Nous, we should ask Ophelia what she knows about Alexander's real identity."

He looked down his nose at me. "We?"

I jutted my chin to the left. "Yes, we. She asked for my help before, and she trusts me."

His expression was skeptical as he rose from his seat. "One moment."

A couple minutes later, he returned with Ophelia in tow. Her hand was touching his arm. I resisted the urge to jump up and slap it away.

"Hey, Charlotte." She sat in the chair next to me.

I held up my nearly empty glass. "You *really* look like you could use one." It was a petty jab, but I felt no remorse. After seeing her pawing at Xavier, I needed another shot—or two—of bourbon.

Her laugh was bitter as she smoothed her hair. "I should

be offended, but I'm sure I look a fright." On the contrary, she was still stunningly beautiful, despite the dark circles under her eyes.

"No offense intended. Even after a night on Xavier's cot, you look more put together than I do on my best days."

"It is not a cot. It is a bed with a deluxe mattress. This is a luxury cruise ship. I do not have passengers—whether I suspect them of a crime or not—sleeping on a camp bed."

Ophelia nodded. "It's actually more comfortable than a lot of the motels and tour buses I've slept in over the years. Not to mention the fact someone's dog was making racket all night next to my suite the first couple nights onboard. I kept banging on the door, but it just kept at it."

"Ophelia," I began.

Xavier cleared his throat.

"Yes?" I asked him.

"I would like to conduct my own line of questioning if I may."

Through gritted teeth I said, "I thought I was asking the questions."

"You were mistaken."

Ophelia shifted her attention back and forth between us. "Would someone like to let me in on what's happening here? Am I free to go?"

"Not yet. I have uncovered some information I would like to ask you about."

"Okay..."

He pulled a pen and paper from his desk drawer. "We are aware that you previously had a romantic relationship with Monsieur St. Jacques that did not end well, *n'est-ce pas?*"

"Is this about the texts I sent him? I swear I didn't mean them. That was a long time ago. Obviously, if I really meant I was gonna kill him, I would have done it way back then."

Halfway through her confession, I started shaking my head in hopes she'd stop incriminating herself, but she apparently hadn't noticed. By my count, she'd threatened to kill Alexander at least three times, and that was just in my presence.

Xavier blinked rapidly. "I was not aware of old text messages between you and Monsieur St. Jacques that were of a threatening nature. Do you still have them?"

"Of course not. I think they were even pre-flip phone. Probably on Blackberries."

"I am, however, aware of a threat you made against him the night before you boarded the ship."

I hadn't shared that information with him. The only other person who witnessed it was Heath Hubbard, and the only person I'd told had been Jane. Had either of them told Xavier? Or had Jane shared it with Emmett, who had then in turn used the information to deflect suspicion?

"Can you blame me?" Ophelia asked. "He was always taking advantage. He talked us all into this reunion gig, but then we found out he'd snuck some clause into the contract that paid him on both the front and the back end. He was double-dipping despite the fact we're all broke because he decided to break up the group."

"So you threatened to kill him?" Xavier's tone was calm

considering the explosive nature of his accusation.

"No, I threatened to leave. He enlightened me about the penalty clause for breaking the contract. *That's* when I threatened to kill him."

I had to give it to her, she was being transparent. Usually, the guilty tried to subvert the truth getting out, but she was bold in her honesty.

"Didn't you read the contract before you signed it? Had a lawyer look it over?" As soon as I asked the question, I remembered how many things Gabe had me sign over the years that I never really read. He was my husband, though, and I hadn't yet discovered how untrustworthy he'd been.

Ophelia had already been burned by Alexander before this latest incident. But then again, love clouded judgment, and if she was still in love with him, that would make it easier for him to manipulate her.

She fiddled with her fingers in her lap. "It was dumb. I get that now, okay? It's just…my *mère* is about to lose her home, and the contract was offering enough money to save it from foreclosure. The guys had already signed it. I thought it would be okay." She looked up at Xavier, tears spilling onto her cheeks. "Do you think the people who hired us for this gig will still honor the contract?"

His grim expression wasn't encouraging. "I do not know. Those decisions are not under my purview." His face softened, and his pen hovered above the notepad. "I would like to take you back to the beginning if I may. Tell me, when and how did you meet Alexander St. Jacques?"

Still consumed with her thoughts, she didn't immediately answer him. "Oh, uh, I was singing at a club back in my hometown, and he approached me. Asked if I wanted to join him for a performance he had coming up in Baton Rouge. Well, of course I did. I'd have done anything to get outta there."

Xavier looked up from his notes. "What is the name?"

"Thibodaux."

"No, not your name, madame, the name of the location where you met Monsieur St. Jacques."

"That is the name. Same as mine, different spelling. T-H-I-B-O-D-A-U-X. Mine is E-A-U-X. Although, I am certain that is simply because my ancestors were trying to differentiate themselves."

Xavier typed something into his computer. "That is in Lafourche Parish." He gave me a knowing glance.

The same parish where Alexander—René—had served time.

"Yes, sir, it is in Lafourche."

"And you had no knowledge of him prior to this?"

She crooked her head. "What do you mean?"

"You did not know him, nor did you know about his past?"

"What past? You mean his ex-girlfriends? There was this one chick named Meg who was a real psycho."

"I am not referring to his previous romantic relationships."

"Then I'm not sure I know what you mean. What's this all about? You think someone from his past did this? But not an ex?" She scrunched her nose. "I can't help you if I don't understand what's going on."

I gave Xavier a look I hoped conveyed my agreement; however, sometimes my face didn't always align with my intentions.

He tapped his fingertips together. "Have you ever heard of a man named René Defaux?"

"Possibly. He's an artist, isn't he? I think he does those abstract paintings of naked women."

"Oh, he's an artist, all right. A *con* artist." I smiled to myself over my clever pun. "Can't speak to naked women, though."

Xavier shook his head, but a slight smile twitched in the corner of his mouth. "Not a painter if that is what you mean."

Ophelia shrugged. "Then no, I don't believe so."

I really wanted to burst out with the news, but I restrained myself. I was slowly making progress with Xavier allowing me into his inner circle, and I didn't want to find myself on the outs.

"During the examination of Monsieur St. Jacques's body, I instructed his fingerprints be scanned and matched against the AFIS database—"

"What's AFIS?" she asked.

"Automated Fingerprint Identification System. I also sent it to Interpol."

"Interpol? Like James Bond?"

"*Oui.* Sort of."

Did Xavier not always realize when he switched from English to French or was it strategic? I couldn't tell, but I'd begun keeping a mental tally.

"Wow. Are you saying Alex was a spy?"

"No, that is not what I am saying."

Her eyes opened wide. "He's a criminal mastermind? Like Dr. Evil? I knew it! I knew I wasn't crazy. He's a bad dude."

Xavier emitted a half chuckle, half grunt. "No, as far as I can tell, not an evil mastermind. More like small-time thug."

"So he *is* a criminal?"

Xavier glanced at me. "You are fidgety over there. Am I to assume you would like to be the one to share this information with her?"

Yes! A thousand times yes. "I'm fine with whatever you decide," I answered casually.

His long, dark lashes fluttered, no doubt trying to suppress the eyeroll he wanted to give me. He could read me like a Dr. Seuss book. To me, he was *War and Peace*—in the original Russian.

"Go ahead, madame."

I turned to Ophelia, who stared expectantly back at me. "Okay, here's the deal. Alexander's records match a former inmate of the Lafourche Detention Center named René Defaux."

Her jaw went slack. "What?" She glanced briefly at Xavier and then back at me. "That can't be."

She hadn't known. That had to bode well for her. At least in terms of that being connected to her motive.

Xavier tilted his head to the left. "I find it interesting it is easier for you to believe that he was an international man of mystery rather than a felon who changed his name for a fresh start."

"Well, that's because," she sputtered, "that's because I've known him my entire adult life! We were nearly married, for gawd's sake. You're telling me that if we'd gone through with it, I would have been Mrs. René Defaux? Wife of a convicted criminal? What did he get in trouble for, anyway?"

I hadn't expected her to be the traditional *take your husband's name* type, but it didn't feel like an appropriate time to question her about it. Especially since now that he was dead, she would never be Mrs. St. Jacques or Mrs. Defaux. What did it matter at this point?

"He was involved with a robbery."

His nonchalance was disrupted when Ophelia burst into tears. He threw me a wide-eyed look and slid the tissue box toward her.

I reached out and touched her on the arm. "I'll bet you're feeling a lot of emotions about now. I can relate. I promise."

"How could anyone possibly understand?" She pulled out a tissue and dabbed the corners of her eyes.

"The day my husband died, I discovered he'd been living a double life. Pretty much the only thing that was true about our lives together was his name."

"Ouch."

"Yeah. And I had to process all that stuff at the same time. Grief over his loss, anger over his betrayal, confusion about what was real and what was a lie. I'd never understood the phrase *having the rug pulled out from underneath you* until that day."

She nodded, tears streaming down her face. "I did love him. And I hated him." She jerked her attention toward Xavier. "But I didn't kill him. I had no idea he was hiding a secret identity. We'd hardly had any contact since Canailles Nous disbanded."

Xavier observed her. "I'd appreciate your discretion regarding this matter."

She snorted, and a bubble formed at her nostril. She quickly wiped her nose with the back of her hand. "Who am I gonna tell? The cockroach I hear scurrying in the wall at night?"

"I have decided to release you at this time. I do not believe you pose a danger to anyone on the ship. We have retrieved the murder weapon. And it is not as if you can leave."

She jumped from the chair and ran around his desk to hug him. "Oh, thank you! Thank you so much!"

Xavier's expression was one of shock but not displeasure. Unsurprising considering the beauty of the woman embracing him. Even with her being unshowered, I still felt insecure next to her.

When she released him, she smoothed his shirt. "Sorry if I got my tears and snot all over you."

He held up a hand. "No apologies necessary. As I said, please do not share this information with anyone."

She nodded, but something about her gaze darting around the room told me she wasn't debating *if* she'd break her promise but to whom she'd break it first. "Absolutely.

Am I free to go?"

"You are."

She turned to me and opened her arms. "Charlotte?"

I ambled to my feet and allowed her to hug me.

"Okay, bye!" She waved and hustled out the door, which she shut behind her.

I watched him for a moment, attempting to understand what had motivated him to do what he'd just done. He stared back at me, like he was daring me to ask.

I crooked my neck. He mirrored me. I craned forward. He smiled.

"Okay, explain it to me."

"What is there to explain?"

"You released her despite her having motive, means, opportunity, and the probable murder weapon in her underwear drawer. Not to mention she threatened his life multiple times."

"*Oui.*"

"Don't *oui-oui* me, *monsieur*. Help me understand. Despite your warning to the contrary, aren't you concerned she's going to go running off and tell anyone who will listen that Alexander St. Jacques was not the man he pretended to be?"

"Am I concerned? Not at all. I'm counting on it."

Chapter Twelve

JANE WAS STILL not in our suite when I returned from the security office. It felt like I was living with a phantom. A stranger. She was acting so unlike herself; it was almost like she'd become someone I didn't know.

I climbed in bed and set up my laptop. One of my favorite pastimes was researching our ancestry, so I had subscriptions to family tree websites as well as newspaper archives. I decided to start by building two family trees: one for René Defaux and one for Alexander St. Jacques. I didn't have a lot of information on either of them, other than they'd both lived in Louisiana at one point and were both in their mid-forties, give or take a few years.

I moved on to the newspaper archive. Because of his fame, a search of Alexander's name came back with an absurd number of matches in Louisiana newspapers: 5,803 to be exact. There was no way I could scour that many articles in a timely manner. Especially without Jane's help.

I then searched René Defaux. There were a lot fewer matches. All of the mentions ceased around the time Alexander left prison and started his new life.

One article in the *Golden Bayou Daily Gazette*, dated

February 6, 1997, was from the day of his sentencing.

Nineteen-year-old René Defaux was sentenced Wednesday for his role in the robbery of Moulton's Grocery on Carmouche Avenue back in October. In January, Defaux pled guilty as an accessory to the crime orchestrated by his uncle, Marty Defaux, 43, of Lafourche Parish. The younger Defaux claimed to have been coerced into being the lookout for his uncle and another man, Lucien Broussard, 39, also of Lafourche Parish, as they robbed the night manager of $461 along with fifty books of postage stamps with a value of $370. The judge in the case, Aaron Rubin, censured Defaux—a music major at Nicholl's State University—for not standing up to his uncle and advised him to cut all ties once he is released from Lafourche Detention Center. He's expected to spend at least six months of his sentence behind bars. Marty Defaux and Lucien Broussard are scheduled to go to trial later this spring.

René/Alexander must have taken the judge's words to heart. Not only had he cut ties with his uncle, but he'd also changed his name. Of course, once he became famous, his family must have recognized him. Perhaps that was why he'd been so diligent with his security. That also probably led to his paranoia.

If it had gotten out that he was a fraud and a convicted criminal, it likely would have been career-ending.

It sounded to me like he was a generally good kid with poor role models.

I switched back to the tab with the Defaux family tree and added his uncle's name.

Since René became Alexander sometime after going to prison in 1997, I adjusted the newspaper archive search for Alexander St. Jacques to any matches before that date. I got a hit in the fall of 1978.

> *Services were held today for 11-month-old Alexander Marcel St. Jacques IV at Our Lady of Perpetual Help Catholic Church. Father Batiste presided over the mass, which was attended by friends and family of the infant. His parents are Alexander III and Lynette St. Jacques of Raceland. Following the funeral, the family held a private Rite of Committal at the adjacent cemetery.*
>
> *Born January 9th of this year, the child succumbed to cholera on the 17th of November, following a visit to extended family in Vermilion Parish.*

It was so sad. The boy I suspected was the real Alexander St. Jacques had died as a baby. I'd read that cholera was a horrible death. René must have searched local cemeteries for the graves of children who were about his age but had died before there were any paper trails for them other than birth certificates and maybe social security numbers.

Just as I was about to call down to the security office to tell Xavier what I had found, I came across yet another old article about an Alexander St. Jacques. The original ASJ.

It was a review of a book written in the 1930s called *When the Hunter Becomes the Hunted: The Monstrous Life and*

Legend of Alexander St. Jacques.

⚓

JANE FINALLY CAME back to the suite around four. At least, I assumed it was Jane. I heard the door, but she didn't come into my room. She headed straight for her own.

The ball started at seven, but at this point, I wasn't sure whether she was going, much less whether we were going together. We'd each purchased formal gowns from a specialty shop in New Orleans. That was the morning Jane had reunited with Emmett.

Everything changed after that. Nothing had been the same since.

I wiggled my toes as I contemplated my next move. I wanted to know, *needed* to know, what her plans were. I also didn't want to get my head bitten off if she was still annoyed with me.

One thing was certain: I couldn't tell her what I'd discovered about Alexander St. Jacques's connection to the werewolf legends of Louisiana.

I'd come to believe René had stepped into the identity of a renowned werewolf hunter's great-grandson and thus had made himself a target. According to the book review I'd just read; the St. Jacques patriarch had become obsessed with Rougarou legends—sounded like someone we knew—and ultimately fell victim to its curse.

I didn't believe in curses or werewolves, but I harbored no illusions about the influence of those beliefs when they took hold over someone and how that person might behave as a result.

I also harbored no illusions or delusions of how Jane being twitterpated with Emmett was influencing her.

"I won't know her plans if I don't ask." I set my laptop aside and marched across the hall.

I gave a quick rap on her door.

"Come in."

At least she was speaking to me. I pushed open the door. She was sitting on her bed, reading.

"When did you get back?" Like I didn't know. Like I hadn't been listening for her all afternoon.

"A few minutes ago. I wasn't sure if you were taking a nap."

"How's your day been?" I wasn't used to walking on eggshells with my own sister, and I didn't like it. I also didn't like the idea of withholding information from her, but she'd backed me into a corner.

"Pretty good." She placed a bookmark in her book, closed it, and set it on her nightstand. "Guess who I ran into?"

"Who?"

"Ophelia Thibodeaux."

I pretended to be surprised. "Oh yeah?"

"Yeah. I guess Xavier didn't have enough to hold her. Not sure how that's possible." She clenched her jaw.

"Is that all she said? That Xavier didn't have enough to hold her?"

She narrowed her gaze at me. "Considering she'd just

been with you in the security office, I'm guessing you already know exactly what she might have told me."

I twisted my mouth to the right. "I can guess. Although she wasn't supposed to say anything to anyone."

Jane scoffed. "Probably why she said, *don't tell anyone where you heard this* before spilling the tea about Alexander's true identity."

Xavier's ploy had worked, although to what end I had yet to know.

"What did Emmett think about that?" It was a risky move to ask her but a necessary one. How Emmett reacted to discovering Alexander wasn't really a St. Jacques could shed light on many things.

"He wasn't with me. He'd gone to the library to work on his book."

Interesting. "Is he coming to the ball with us?" I purposely phrased it to imply she and I were still attending together rather than ask if that were the case. I'd always found presumption was a powerful tool in getting my way. Most people didn't like to correct wrong ones—particularly when it came to social occasions—if it meant having to explain why they were excluding someone.

"Of course he is."

I took it as a good sign she hadn't said they were going without me.

The silence was awkward. I'd had a lot of practice being awkward, but it never got easier knowing how to handle it.

The emotional distance between us felt much further than the few feet I was standing from her. It felt like I had a kumquat lodged somewhere in my esophagus.

"Jane—"

"Char—"

We both laughed.

"You first," I said.

"I was just going to say that, even though things have been strained between us, I love you and I know you love me."

"That was exactly what I wanted to say."

She smiled. "Let's just have fun tonight. Let loose. It's Mardi Gras, after all."

"Mardi Gras in November."

"Not only that, but it's also Wednesday, not Tuesday. You took French. If it's not Fat Tuesday, what should it be?"

"*Mercredi Gras.* Doesn't have quite the same ring to it."

"Definitely not." She tilted her head. "What have you been doing all afternoon?"

"Um, just doing a little family tree work."

"I thought you already finished our family tree."

"You know how it is. They're always adding new resources and databases."

"Find any root rot?"

"I'm working on something, but it's too early to tell."

"You'll tell me if you come across anything I should know, right?"

"Of course." My fingers were crossed behind my back.

Chapter Thirteen

"WOWZA!"
Emmett shoved his mask up onto his forehead, revealing his eyes nearly bugged out of his head as he stared at Jane's ruby-colored floor-length silk gown. It was sleeveless with a sweeping neckline and sequins along the edges. Large magenta roses dyed into the shimmering fabric perfectly matched her lipstick. Her hair was swept into a sophisticated updo, and her harlequin mask accented her high cheekbones.

She'd never been one for dressing up, so I couldn't help but think this transformation was for Emmett's benefit.

"You look nice, too, Charlotte." He didn't actually look at me when he said it.

That was fine, though. I'd rather he only had eyes for Jane. If he wasn't a murderer—the verdict was still out on that one—I hoped he would make her feel special and loved.

Xavier was stationed in the corner of the dining room. Even if he had been wearing a mask—which he wasn't—I would have recognized him. His broad shoulders and dark hair were unmistakable to me at this point.

He scanned the room and stopped when his gaze landed

on me. The quick crook of his head told me he recognized me—or at least he thought he might. A slight smile played upon his lips, causing me to shiver.

"Oh look, there's Xavier." Jane's tone revealed way more than I was comfortable with. "Char, did you see Xavier?"

Emmett, who had yet to replace his mask, gave Jane a strange look. "Should I be jealous? Is there something I should know about Xavier Mesnier?"

"No," I snapped. "I'll go say hi." I threw a glare at Jane, but she had already returned her attention to Emmett.

She straightened his black-and-white herringbone necktie and smoothed his jacket lapels.

She really liked him. There was no denying that.

I sighed. Perhaps instead of trying to find evidence he was a werewolf-crazed murderous lunatic, I should have been working to exonerate him instead.

For Jane's sake.

By the time I'd made my way across the room to Xavier, I had a hurricane cocktail in my hand.

"I hear those drinks are dangerous." He nodded at the glass.

"They are, but Haimi shoved the tray in my face as I walked past. What else could I do but take it?"

"I see." The glint in his eye was playful. "Your dress is the color of an emerald."

"Is that a compliment or merely a statement of fact?"

"It is a nice dress."

"Thank you, although it holds less weight when I gotta drag it out of you."

He gave a light chuckle. "There was no dragging, I assure you."

"Thank you." I took a sip. "Sheesh, that's strong. Anyway, that's not why I came over here."

"I see. And what is the reason?"

"I was going to call you earlier."

"Is that so?"

"I did some research on the family tree websites and the newspaper archives. I came across a few interesting things."

I shared with him everything I'd learned about René and the real Alexander St. Jacques, along with his werewolf-hunting ancestor.

"Is your conclusion that Monsieur St. Jacques was merely unlucky and that someone who did not know of the false identity took revenge on him, believing he was a descendant of this other Alexander St. Jacques?"

"I wouldn't call it a conclusion so much as a working theory." I took another sip. It burned less going down than the previous one. "You think I'm silly."

"Not at all. Why would you say that?"

"Because I'm down this weird rabbit hole—"

"Rougarou hole." The corner of his mouth twitched.

"Yes. Rougarou hole. It's not grounded in reality."

"Perhaps not, but it never matters as much *what* someone believes as what they will say or do as a result of that belief."

"That's what I've been saying!"

"You have? I do not recall."

I blinked twice. "I may have been saying it to myself at

the time."

"Ah. I do have a question for you."

"What's that?"

"Is it that you believe Monsieur Guidry has a reason to want Monsieur St. Jacques—" He made a gurgling sound and pretended to slice his own throat.

"What was that sound you made?"

He repeated it, along with the accompanying gesture.

"Do it again."

He wagged his finger at me. "Ah. Ah. You are teasing me."

"A little. Besides, he was shot, not killed with a knife."

"You know what I am meaning."

"Of course. And the truth is, I have no idea. My gut is telling me something is off with Emmett. Coincidentally running into Jane and me in the French Quarter, the book he's writing about legendary creatures—it's all too convenient for my taste."

"Is that all?"

"What do you mean?" I chugged a bunch of my cocktail rather than answering directly. I knew exactly what he meant, but I had no intentions to give him the information that easily. He needed to spell it out.

"I mean, I have come to know you and your sister over these past several months. You are very close. It is a beautiful thing. This man, he threatens the new life you have been building together. That must make you feel insecure."

It didn't matter that I knew deep down he was right. I didn't like being called out. Maybe it was the exceedingly strong alcoholic beverage. Maybe it was the stress. Maybe it was the undergarments digging into my lungs.

I held the rim of my glass up to his nose. "You don't know what you're talking about." With that, I turned on my heel and marched back to where Jane and Emmett had been seated.

"Everything okay?" Jane eyed me with concern.

"Yeah."

"Charlotte, would you like me to get you another drink?" Emmett asked.

My glass was empty. When had that happened? "Maybe one more."

Jane placed her hand on Emmett's forearm as he stood. "And some water please." She glanced at me. "For all of us."

He nodded.

Jane clasped her hands and rested them on the table. "Did that conversation with Xavier not go as well as you hoped?"

"It was fine." I threw back my glass, but all I got was a face full of ice. I took a napkin and patted myself dry.

"Char, if Ophelia didn't kill Alexander—and I'm not saying I think that's true—but I have another person I've been keeping my eye on."

"Really? Who?"

The obvious choice was Emmett. Had she finally come to her senses?

"Hawk."

"Hawk!" I glanced around and whispered conspiratorially, "Why would Hawk kill Alexander?"

"I have no idea. I'm just certain that I saw him acting suspicious up on Santorini near Alexander's suite, and he denied it."

I declined to mention that Emmett's room was on the same floor. "Hmm. I don't know why he'd be up there even if it were him. There are only ten or so suites plus the captain's lounge. There's nothing else."

Jane tapped the edge of the table with her fingers. "That's what I'm saying!"

Percy, Webster, and Heath appeared next to Jane.

"What are you saying, Miss Jane?" asked Heath.

She waved him off. "Oh, nothing. Just chewing the fat."

"Do you ladies want company?" Percy asked. "Looks pretty lonely at this big table."

"We aren't alone. Professor Guidry is getting us another round, but you're welcome to join us." Jane indicated the empty seats on the opposite side of the eight-person round table.

"Great." Percy pulled out the chair next to me and sat. "You look great."

"Thanks, back atcha." I nodded at Heath. "You should have come to the mask-making class. You can't show up to a masquerade ball without a mask!"

Laughter rumbled in Heath's chest, accompanied by his smoker's cough. "Nah. I've got nothing to hide."

Webster fiddled with his mask, causing the rubber string holding it on his head to break. "Ow!"

"I told you to stop messing with it, Webb. Here." Percy held out his hand. "Lemme try to fix it for you."

As Webster handed him the mask, I was struck by the idea that once again Percy was playing fixer of the group. Literally this time.

"Where's Victor?"

Heath shrugged in that cool cat way he had.

"Last I saw him; he was headed for the cigar lounge." Webster nudged Percy. "Did he say whether he was coming tonight?"

A shiver came over me. I'd found a dead man in the cigar lounge a few months earlier.

Percy's tongue stuck out the side of his mouth as he tried to thread the string through the tiny hole on Webster's mask. "Nah, I don't think so. He said he met some hot guy earlier at the gym and they were supposed to meet up for drinks."

"Well, I'll be darned." Heath let out a slow whistle. "Look who it is."

Everyone at our table—and nearly everyone in the room—turned to look at the source of the buzz.

Ophelia stood at the entrance of the dining room in what most would consider the ultimate revenge dress. Revenge for what, I wasn't sure. Revenge for having been accused of murdering her ex? Revenge for having been framed? For having to spend a night in what Jane referred to as boat jail?

Light from the chandelier above her reflected off the gold sequins that covered the form-fitting gown in an ombre pattern. The halter tied at her bare nape, with her dark hair twisted into a chignon accented by a bejeweled tiara. Long lashes fluttered behind her delicate gold filigree and crystal mask.

She possessed the kind of breathtaking beauty that caused men to start wars.

Alexander was a dummy for cheating on her with a groupie. I immediately banished the thought. Gabe was a dummy for cheating on me, despite my ordinariness, merely because he'd made a commitment to me and then broke it. Beauty had never been, nor would it ever be, insulation against infidelity and betrayal. Infidelity was about something lacking in the relationship or in the character of the cheater.

Despite her confident posture, something about the way she looked around the room gave the impression of an underlying insecurity. Her attention lasered toward the back of the room. I followed her gaze.

Xavier.

He offered her a warm smile as she approached. Most of the time, he tended to keep a serious expression, and I found this shift in temperament unsettling. Between the dustups with Jane and now this, that uneasy feeling was becoming a frequent but unwelcome companion.

She leaned toward him and whispered something in his ear. He nodded. Her lips brushed across his cheek before she stepped back. She was still too close to him for my comfort. At some point, I needed to examine why the scene had affected me so much.

She glided across the room toward our table just as Emmett arrived with two hurricanes in hand. He lifted the glasses to indicate for her to move ahead of him.

"Well, if it isn't the belle of the ball." Percy dropped

Webster's mask on the table and jumped up to pull out an empty chair for Ophelia.

"Thanks, P." She gave him a warm smile, and his ears turned pink. She glanced around the room. "Good turnout."

Percy nodded. *"A multitude and yet solitude."* A quote from *A Tale of Two Cities*.

Heath cocked his left brow. "So, Fee, how does it feel being a free woman?"

Ophelia exhaled. "Slightly relieved, although I'm not in the clear yet."

Emmett appeared to be trying to solve something. His forehead was wrinkled, and his mouth was pursed tight. "I'm curious as to what exonerated you enough that you've been released. I heard they found the murder weapon in your room."

Emmett had visited her room prior to the discovery of the gun. Because of the tension with Jane, I hadn't had a chance to grill—ahem, ask him about it.

Had he planted it?

She straightened her already straight silverware. "Xavier is a good judge of character."

"Xavier?" Jane crooked her head. "You two all chummy now and on a first-name basis?"

Ophelia smiled. "Not a bad person to have in my corner."

Emmett shifted in his seat. "Still, I can't help but wonder what development is leading the investigation away from you."

Ophelia's laugh was like the tinkle of a windchime.

"Well, for starters, I'm not a werewolf hunter."

Emmett's face froze and Jane stiffened.

"Speaking of werewolves, did anyone hear something that sounded like howling last night?" Webster asked.

Emmett tilted his head. "What did you hear?"

Ophelia gasped. "I heard it too! Not last night, I was…otherwise occupied, but the first night."

I didn't like her implication. She probably meant that since she was detained, she hadn't slept in her room on the eighth floor, but she made it sound like Xavier had kept her company in the security office.

"What? What was it?" Emmett bounced in his seat. "What was the information that prompted Mesnier to release you?"

Ophelia shrugged. "All I know is, there's a good chance someone from Alex's—or should I say René Defaux's—past had a score to settle, and so they did. With a bullet."

The color drained from Emmett's face. "What did you say? Who's René Defaux?"

"Alex's ghost."

Emmett wrinkled his forehead. "Are you saying Alexander St. Jacques wasn't his real name?"

She glanced at me and giggled. "Oops. I wasn't supposed to let that cat out of the bag. Hope Xavier doesn't throw me back in that cell of his."

Chapter Fourteen

Jane narrowed her gaze at a shell-shocked Emmett. "Why is this so upsetting to you? So he used a stage name. Lots of performers use pseudonyms. Authors too."

Emmett's faraway look indicated he hadn't heard a word she'd said.

"Well, I can tell you why it's upsetting to me." Webster leaned back in his chair and folded his arms. "I thought of that man like a brother. Now it seems I didn't know him at all."

Heath pulled a pack of cigarettes from his inside jacket pocket. "I need some air." He stood and walked out of the dining room.

Percy slapped Webster on the back. "Don't take it too hard, man. He must have had a good reason for using a stage name and not telling us."

"It wasn't just a stage name." Ophelia's smug expression diminished her beauty.

If it weren't for the fact this was exactly what Xavier had said he wanted, I would have given her a warning to stop sharing the information. A quick glance over my shoulder confirmed my suspicion: he was watching the entire interaction. He'd likely interrogate me later about what was said.

"What do you mean?" Webster leaned forward. "Was he transgender?"

She reared back. "What? No, of course not. Don't you think I would have noticed if I wasn't dealing with original parts?"

"Then what?" Percy blinked behind the mask he was still wearing.

She lowered her voice to a conspiratorial tone. "He was a convict."

"Whaaa?" Webster twisted his mouth to the side. "That can't be right. That man wouldn't even jaywalk. He and I were alike in that way."

"Probably because if he got in trouble again, it would come out who he really was," Jane offered.

Emmett turned to her. "You knew he had an assumed identity and you didn't tell me?"

Jane's eyes widened in horror. "No! It's not like that. I just found out."

"Right now?"

"Well, no, this afternoon. I didn't have a chance to tell you yet."

That answer didn't appear to satisfy a scowling Emmett.

"So, who was this—what did you say his real name was again?" Percy removed the mask, leaving creases at his temples where the rubber band had been tight against his skin.

"René Defaux. I don't know much about him, only that he spent time in Lafourche Parish Detention Center for robbery," Ophelia said.

I cleared my throat. "Accessory to robbery, actually. I looked into it a bit, and it seems he was forced into it by an uncle. He was only nineteen at the time."

"Well, he'd have to have been. We formed Canailles Nous not too much later than that." Webster shook his head. "You think you know a guy."

Ophelia glared at him. "You act like he was a saint. He wasn't. He was a liar and a cheat." Her chin quivered. "He ruined my life."

"Careful, *cher*." Percy placed a big paw on her shoulder. "Don't be making statements that will draw suspicion back your direction."

She'd already done that with her multiple admissions that she'd threatened him.

Jane's attention was squarely on Emmett, who had the look of a kid who'd just been informed the truth about the tooth fairy or Santa Claus. Lost. Bewildered.

It was at that moment Haimi arrived with a tray of hush puppies and a cup of rémoulade sauce. "I will be back shortly with a crock of chicken and sausage gumbo, another of jambalaya, and a shrimp étouffée."

Ophelia frowned. "We don't get to order whatever we want?"

"Tonight, the meal will be served family-style."

Percy grunted. "Some family this turned out to be."

⚓

EMMETT REMAINED SUBDUED throughout the rest of the evening. Jane fussed over him, to no avail. Ophelia picked at the food. Whether because of lack of appetite, not liking the selection, or if that was how she maintained her svelte figure, I didn't know.

Webster was somber, but that didn't keep him from taking seconds or even thirds of the dishes.

Percy maintained his usual affable disposition.

When the king cake arrived, our table barely mustered an *ooh* or an *ahh*. Haimi gave me a perplexed look, and I grimaced in return.

She attempted her spiel despite the mood. "For those who do not know, the colors of the king cake each have a special meaning."

"Of course we know," muttered Emmett. "Nearly everyone here is from Louisiana."

"Well, I'm not." I forced a smile. "I'd love to hear about it, Haimi." My gritted teeth and clenched jaw were intended to serve as a warning to anyone who might give Haimi a bad attitude.

"Okay, then," she continued. "The cake is made of an enriched sweet dough filled with praline and then twisted into a ring. It's topped with white cream cheese icing and sprinkled with colored sugar. Purple for justice, green for faith, and gold for power. As per tradition, there is a porcelain infant figurine hidden within the cake." She gave a quick bow and scurried off as soon as she finished.

I didn't blame her.

"It's a fairly macabre tradition, don't you think?" Jane asked.

Everyone turned toward her.

"I beg your pardon?" Offense rolled off Emmett in waves.

"I—I only mean that it's weird to think about accidentally chewing on baby Jesus."

He blinked at her. "First, it's not necessarily baby Jesus. Many people celebrate the tradition without including the religious aspects. Second, you're supposed to pay attention to what you're putting in your mouth."

Ophelia choked on her laugh. Jane glared at her in return.

Percy, doing what Percy always did, gave Jane a conciliatory smile. "I get where you're coming from. If I hadn't grown up eating king cake, I might think it strange as well."

I jumped into the fray to divert the conversation and save Jane from further contention. "I love the meaning behind the colors. I'd never heard that before."

Webster cut himself a large slice and shoveled it onto his plate. "There are a lot of similar traditions and celebrations of the season throughout the world, but none have the history behind them that N'awlins has. We were a confederate city. Those colors and their meanings were chosen over a hundred and twenty-five years ago to honor the beauty of the true melting pot the city is." He took a bite and chewed for a moment. "You know, many of my ancestors living in the region at the time had been emancipated just thirty years or so earlier."

"I think you're reading too much into it." Percy grabbed his own slice of cake. "I recall that they were chosen to honor a visiting Russian Grand Duke, and purple and gold were chosen because those are the colors of royalty. The meaning was attached later."

"Alexis Romanov, son of Czar Alexander the second," Emmett mumbled.

Ophelia ignored Emmett but narrowed her gaze at Percy. "Can't we just have this?"

He jerked his head back. "I didn't mean—"

She waved him off. "Forget it. Y'all will never understand."

He set his fork on his plate. "It's my home too."

"Mm-hmm."

He cocked his head to the side. "Fee, please don't be this way. All I'm saying is, the history belongs to all of us. Everyone who loves that city."

"My mama's family was brought to that city against their will. We've made a place for ourselves there, against all odds. The culture of that place is because of what we've brought. The food, the music, the energy. People look at you and Alexander and think the Cajuns are responsible for all of this." She made a sweeping gesture. "But don't you forget that much of what most people consider quintessential New Orleans comes from our ancestors, not yours."

Jane jumped up from her chair and leaned over the cake. "This looks delicious. I've never tried king cake." She cut one slice and handed it to Emmett, took one slice for herself, and handed me a third slice.

"Thank you, *cher*." Emmett smiled at her.

Jane's ears turned red. "You're welcome."

"Yes, thanks, Jane."

She gave me a quick nod.

I jammed my fork into it, but instead of it slicing through soft pillowy dough, I hit something hard. I picked up my knife and used the two utensils to spread the cake apart.

A tiny little baby tumbled onto my plate.

"Well, lookie there," rumbled Percy. "Mizz Charlotte's got the baby."

"Congratulations, Char." Jane's tone sounded less than congratulatory. Resentful would be the word I'd have used.

"That makes you the king," Emmett said. "Or in your case, queen. That position comes with its own set of responsibilities. You're in charge of next year's Mardi Gras celebration. And since we are celebrating in November, you've only got about three months to prepare."

"I'm happy to let someone else have the baby." I shoved my plate toward the center of the table. "Webster, you take it."

Webster pushed it back to me. "Not how that works. This is your *fais-do-do* to plan, not mine. Besides, don't you know that it also comes with a horde of blessings and good fortune? Eat up, now, Queen Charlotte. Enjoy your reign and the luck that comes with it."

Later, I thought about that moment and a deep sense of regret washed over me.

If I hadn't given in and kept the good luck for myself, would Webster have still died?

Chapter Fifteen

WEBSTER'S COLD BODY was found by the cleaning crew in the captain's lounge just after 6:30 A.M.

Jane and I got the news when Windsor brought our morning coffee service just after eight thirty.

A native of Brighton, England, Windsor Hadwin had the quintessential look and sound of a butler with his accent, his white fluffy hair—what was left of it anyway—that encircled the crown of his head, and his matching eyebrows darting in all directions.

"They say he was wearing only his robe and a bucket cap," he whispered conspiratorially, despite the fact the walls were well insulated for sound. "And the room smelled of tobacco and sandalwood."

"So basically; every old library." Jane clucked. "He was so nice. Who would want to kill him? He always wore tie-dye. Tie-dye is the universal symbol for peace."

"I thought that was a dove," I murmured. "Or an olive branch. Or a dove holding an olive branch."

"Whatever." She waved me off. "His face was so cute and round. It reminded me of one of those—" She snapped her fingers several times trying to jog her memory. "Ah! Those

Campbell's Soup kids."

Windsor furrowed his bushy brows together. "Pardon?"

"Maybe you didn't get those ads in the UK. Campbell's Soup kids were these chubby little characters they used as mascots on soup cans, advertisements. I think they even had a Saturday morning cartoon at one point."

"I don't think it was a whole show," I said. "I'm pretty sure they were just elaborate commercials."

She shrugged. "Could be. Windsor, did you hear anything else? Like, *how* was he murdered?"

He scrunched his already wrinkled face. "Murder is an assumption I cannot make. I was only told he is deceased, but I did not get any details."

Jane and I exchanged glances.

"I mean, it has to be murder, right?" she asked me.

"Not necessarily. I suppose he could have had a heart attack or something."

"He was too young for a heart attack."

"He was our age."

"Exactly."

"Jane, you know that people our age can have heart attacks, right?" Did I have to remind her my husband had died of a heart attack?

"I know no such thing. I am young and vibrant, and I refuse to accept someone so young died of natural causes. What could he possibly have been doing in the captain's lounge at midnight in his bathrobe?"

"His room wasn't too far down the hall from there." I left out the part about Emmett's room being on the same floor. No need to start the day with contention.

She tutted. "You should go talk to Xavier. He'll tell you what happened."

"I suspect he's not going to be in the greatest of moods. Another death on this ship that may or may not be murder."

"It was totally murder. And of course; Ophelia has to be the prime suspect."

"Why does Ophelia have to be the prime suspect?"

"Because no one got murdered while she was in custody." The *duh* was implied by her tone.

Windsor had the look of a man desperate to escape. "I would love to stay while you two hash this out, but alas, I have others to attend."

"Thanks for letting us know about Webster," I called after him as he hustled out the door.

"That's the fastest I've ever seen him move."

"Probably because he sensed an argument coming," I said dryly.

"What's there to argue about? Ophelia hated Alexander and then he was murdered. No one was murdered while Xavier had her locked in the security office, and as soon as she was released, Webster's dead."

"Like Windsor said, we don't know for sure he was murdered."

Jane scoffed. "Sure, we do."

"We don't. Maybe the stress of everything got to him. Gabe wasn't that much older, and we didn't see it coming. He had no symptoms leading up to that day."

Jane's face softened. "That's true. I just feel like it would be too much of a coincidence."

"Probably. But the thing I can't quite figure out is, why would anyone want to kill Webster, especially Ophelia? I get why she'd have motive against Alexander. But Webster?"

Jane sipped her coffee. "One thing is certain."

"What's that?"

"Xavier always likes to gather the friends and family of the victims slash possible suspects."

"Yeah, and?"

"He's gonna have to find a new spot. He can't use the captain's lounge to question them about a murder that took place in the captain's lounge."

⚓

JANE WAS RIGHT. It was definitely not a heart attack. Dr. Ian Fraser estimated Webster had been killed sometime around midnight. This time there was no silver bullet, just your garden variety bonk on the head by a blunt object. In this case, the suspected object was a crystal lotus flower paperweight that had been on the side table. The ship's designer must have bought them on bulk, because there were dozens of them throughout the ship. We had three in our unit alone.

Jane was also right about the captain's lounge. Due to it being a crime scene, it was off limits. The security office wasn't large enough to fit everyone, so Xavier had us all congregate in the theater lounge.

By all of us, that also meant Emmett, who believed he'd

been included as part of the crime-solving team. I knew better. Xavier hadn't tipped his hand yet, but I felt certain he and I were on the same page when it came to Emmett.

Ophelia looked quite a bit more haggard than the last time I'd seen her, which meant she was still gorgeous like those women who say things like, *Don't look at me—I'm hideous*, because their flawless skin is without makeup and their hair is mussed in that *just woke up from a sexy dream* sort of way.

Jane whispered in my ear that she probably had terrible morning breath, but I held little hope of that.

Percy kept shaking his head and muttering, "This can't be happening."

Victor Lutz fiddled with his gold medallion necklace as tears streamed down his face. Next to him was some guy I'd never seen before who was gently rubbing his back and cooing words of comfort.

Even cool, calm, and collected Heath seemed anxious, his leg bouncing up and down in frantic agitation.

Xavier stood on the stage. "Can everyone hear me?"

"It might be better if you used the microphone," Hawk called from the back of the theater.

Xavier looked at the mic stand like it was a venomous snake. "Is that necessary?"

"My ears are a bit plugged from all the crying." Victor blew his nose into a silk handkerchief.

Resigned, Xavier pulled the mic from the stand and put it up to his mouth. "Better?"

Heath gave a thumbs-up.

"Yeah, man," Percy said.

Xavier held the mic in his left hand and the cord in his right like he was getting ready to belt out a Broadway showtune. "I appreciate you all for coming down here this morning. As I am sure you are all aware by now, we have had a second death connected to Canailles Nous. Early this morning, the body of Webster Powell was found in the captain's lounge."

This wasn't news to anyone in the room, but still Percy let out a yelp of sorrow that nearly cracked my heart. Ophelia whimpered, and Victor sniffled. Heath just kept tapping his foot.

"I can imagine this is quite a shock, especially considering it comes on the heels of what happened to Monsieur St. Jacques."

"Which you still haven't solved!" Percy jerked back and covered his mouth. "I'm sorry. I know you're trying. I let my emotions get the best of me."

"Your feelings of grief and frustration are understandable. My team and I have been working around the clock to gather evidence and interview witnesses. I have an entire ship full of passengers and crew, it is my solemn duty to protect. In the aftermath of Monsieur St. Jacques's death, we were working with a variety of theories as to motive. It was possibly a random attack, or one committed by a fan, or even one related to myth and legend. It is now my feeling that these are targeted attacks against members of Canailles Nous. To what purpose, we have yet to determine. If you have any information that might shed light on these events, please come forward now."

The room was silent other than Ophelia's whimpering, Victor's sniffling, and Heath's tapping.

Ophelia's lip trembled like Marilyn Monroe's. "Thank you so much for all you're doing."

"Does this mean you've exonerated Ophelia?" Emmett's tone held bitter accusation.

Jane turned her head to look at him. He arched his brows in return.

Xavier held the mic too close to his mouth and it squawked. "Pardon. The answer to your question is that no one other than the deceased has been ruled out in this investigation."

"What about the threatening note someone slid under Alexander's door? Have you figured out who wrote that?" Victor asked.

"We have not. Another piece of evidence being examined and analyzed. Did any of the rest of you receive threatening notes?"

They all shook their heads.

Percy sat upright. "Wait. Did Webb get a note too?"

"Not that we have found thus far. We are still processing his suite."

I scanned the room. From our booth at the side of the theater, I had the ability to view everyone other than Emmett, who was on the other side of Jane. I had to crane my neck in an obvious fashion to look at him, and with Jane between us, I didn't dare.

"We're all in danger," Victor said. "I don't feel safe, and

we still have how many more days left on this ghost ship?"

The man next to him squeezed his shoulder. "I'll protect you. I won't let you out of my sight. Don't you worry." Medium-sized gold hoop earrings swung side to side as they hung from both his ears.

At least ten years younger than Victor, the man had the muscular frame of a body builder. His hair was trimmed short—nearly a buzz cut—and his ethnicity was unapparent beneath what was most certainly a spray tan.

"Thank you, *cher*." Victor patted the man's leg.

"I definitely don't want to be alone." Ophelia's gaze drifted between Pike, Xavier, and Lonnie like a lion determining its prey.

Xavier cleared his throat, which showed signs of pink, even in the dim lighting. "It is important to stay vigilant at this time. When you are in your suite, do not answer the door to anyone without first alerting security. Do not get in an elevator with only one other person, and avoid using the stairwells. Stay together or remain secure in your suite."

Heath spoke for the first time. "You say we're safe together, but that's making a pretty big assumption, don't you think?"

"What assumption is that?" Xavier spread his legs shoulder-width apart and crossed his arms, tucking the microphone into his body.

"That one of us isn't the killer."

Chapter Sixteen

"HEATH HAS A point, you know." Jane chased her salad around the plate with her fork. "There's not safety in numbers when one of them is probably a killer." She stabbed at a piece of romaine, to no avail.

"Of course he has a point. And I think Xavier knows that. But he's only one man, and eventually, he's got to sleep. Same with Lonnie and Pike. There's only so much they can do. There are hundreds of people on the ship."

Emmett sliced one of his beets with the precision of a surgeon. "The murder ratio is quite startling when you think about it. A person has about the same chance of being murdered on the *Thalassophile* as they have of being audited by the IRS." He popped a tiny red cube in his mouth with his fork tines facing down and chewed thoughtfully. "Not sure which is worse, frankly."

I blinked at him. "Pretty sure being murdered is worse than an IRS audit."

"All I'm saying is one should be prepared for either."

"Char, what did you make of Heath's behavior?" Jane caught the shred of lettuce on the end of her fork. "He seemed rattled, when normally he's cool as a cucumber."

"My thoughts exactly. He's usually unflappable."

"He's probably the murderer," Emmett declared. "The walls are closing in on him, the trail is red hot, and he knows it's only a matter of time before he's discovered."

"Maybe," I allowed, feeling generous now that I wasn't hangry. "He just doesn't strike me as the murdering type. None of them do."

"Speak of the devil." Jane nodded at the entrance to the dining room.

Heath ambled in and sidled up to the bar where Hawk, who'd attended the meeting in the theater lounge, was now making cocktails for the lunch crowd. They exchanged a few words, but I couldn't read either of their lips.

"It's tricky," I mused, as much to myself as anyone.

"How do you mean?" Jane asked.

"Each member of Canailles Nous is equally a suspect and a potential victim."

Emmett dabbed the corners of his mouth with his napkin. "My money's still on Ophelia. Woman scorned and all that."

As if summoned like Beetlejuice, Ophelia sauntered into the dining room. She spotted us and beelined for our table. We were at a four-top, with one open spot. She pulled out the empty chair and sat.

A whoosh of air came out of her. "Hoo boy, can you believe this?" She picked up a piece of bread and took a bite. "Y'all don't mind if I join you, do you?"

As if we had a say. "Of course not."

She craned her neck and spotted Heath at the bar. "Well,

that's a relief. At least I know he's safe. Victor should be fine with Conan the Barbarian, but I am a bit worried about Percy. He's a gentle giant, and I know he's taking all of this so hard. He can take care of himself—physically, I mean—but emotionally I'm not sure."

"Aren't you?" Jane asked. "Taking the deaths of two of your bandmates hard, I mean."

Ophelia absentmindedly ripped her bread into smaller pieces. "Of course. I'm all torn up. Webby was my friend. Alex was…well, you know my thoughts on Alex. But Webb did nothing to nobody his whole life. Who would want to hurt him?"

Emmett narrowed his gaze and looked down his nose at her like she smelled of rotting cabbage. "I can think of someone."

She fluttered her lashes at him. "Who? Me?" She scoffed. "Not only did I adore Webby, take a look at me."

She flung her arms open wide. Not a jiggle. If I were to make the same motion, the swaying of my loose underarms could hypnotize the entire restaurant.

"I can't kill anyone. I'm a hundred-pound weakling. I don't even go to the gym."

I could have sworn I heard Jane mutter something derogatory under her breath, but when Ophelia said, "Hmm?" Jane waved her off, holding her arms close at her side.

And Jane was svelte. She hadn't inherited the strong Eastern European genes I had. Gabe used to tease me that he felt safe walking in dark alleys as long as he was with me. One of the many reasons it stung that he'd fallen in love with Kyrie Dawn, who was pocket-sized.

Emmett wasn't dissuaded, however. "It's not like they were strangled with their bare hands. One was shot and the other was likely bludgeoned by a glass paperweight. That doesn't take much strength."

Jane leaned back in her chair and fanned her face with her napkin.

Emmett put his hand on her shoulder. "Are you all right? You look like split pea soup with a dash of tabasco."

He was right. Her entire face was a sallow green except for her brightly flushed cheeks.

"Picturing him being bludgeoned made me queasy, and that triggered a hot flash." She increased the intensity of her fanning.

"What's your plan to stay safe?" I asked.

Ophelia pasted a crazed smile on her face. "I was hoping to hang with you guys."

Jane stopped waving her napkin. "Like…all the time?"

"Well, only if it's okay with you. I'm okay to stay in my room alone. It's got a pretty hefty lock. But I thought maybe we could all go to my room to get my costume for tonight and then get ready together." She clapped her hands. "It will be so fun!"

"So fun," Jane repeated wanly.

"So, *so* fun," I agreed without mustering any more enthusiasm than Jane had.

⚓

THE FOUR OF us had shuffled up to Ophelia's room to gather her costume and a suitcase full of hair and makeup products. Jane and Emmett escorted us back to our suite before heading off to the spa for a couple's massage. I used every ounce of mental restraint to keep from picturing that scenario.

I handed Ophelia the TV remote and headed for the bedroom to decompress.

Ophelia settled herself on the living room couch with a blanket and began scouring all the streaming services for a rom-com.

"Can you believe they're already showing Christmas movies?" she called to me. "It's only November third, for goodness' sake."

"Seems like it's getting earlier and earlier every year. Christmas in July used to be a novelty because it was so far away from the holiday. Now it's practically the start of the season."

I climbed onto the bed, picked up my laptop from the nightstand, and opened it. Whenever the world didn't make sense, research always made me feel like I was making progress in figuring it out.

It was an illusion. Or a delusion. Could be either or both.

The newspaper archive website was still up from my last search that had revealed Alexander's—or should I say René's—origin story. Now that Webster was also dead, the idea that Alexander had been killed because he'd taken on the identity of someone associated with a Rougarou legend had become less plausible.

More likely than not, whoever had shot him had used the legend to throw investigators off the scent, so to speak.

It was possible that some obsessed fan was taking out the members of Canailles Nous one by one, but so far there hadn't been any evidence to indicate that was the case.

I kept going back to the idea that murder almost always had at least one of three motives: money, love, and/or revenge. It was almost always someone known to the victim.

Alexander was easy to figure out. He'd broken Ophelia's heart, he'd abandoned his group, and he'd shafted them financially, both by going solo and by this latest contract where he was set to get paid on the front and the back end. Any number of those factors could have been a motive for his murder.

But why Webster? Webster had been the victim of Alexander's selfishness, not a co-conspirator. He'd lost as much money and as many opportunities as the rest of Canailles Nous. He'd gone along with the reunion, but as far as I could tell, he hadn't facilitated it. I didn't think he'd been romantically involved with any of the members, so that pretty much ruled out the love theory.

It made no sense.

"Ophelia?"

"Yeah?"

"Who planned the reunion tour?"

"Alex."

"Right, I know it was his idea, but who helped him get the rest of you on board?"

She was quiet for a moment, presumably thinking. "You know, I'm not positive, but I think it was Heath. Yeah, I'm pretty sure it was Heath who reached out to me. Why?"

"Just curious. It might be nothing."

She appeared in my open doorway. "Not buying it. You've got a thought brewing in that clever brain of yours."

"Flattery will get you nowhere." That was a lie. "I'm trying to understand how a single motive could apply to both Alexander and Webster."

She pursed her mouth into a pout and nodded. "I've wondered the same thing. Not just to solve it—and don't get me wrong, I want to solve it—but I must admit a bit of self-preservation is kicking in."

"That's nothing to feel bad about. Can't help anyone else if you're dead."

She gave a solemn nod. "Very true."

"And you've never had any crazed obsessed fans?"

She laughed. "Don't be absurd. Of course we have. Who said we didn't?"

"I don't know. I guess it's because that idea seemed to get dismissed right off the bat."

"Probably because there were a thousand and one reasons someone who actually knew Alex would want to murder him. Now that Webster has—" her voice caught. "Now it feels like that's the most likely scenario. Some psychopath taking us out because they lost touch with reality. Maybe they tried to get an autograph and one of us spurned them. I've had a ton of guys approach me in bars, and I must admit I haven't always been the nicest when I've rejected them."

A spark flickered in my mind. "Wait. What if that's what this is all about?"

"What do you mean?"

"What if this is a fan obsessed with you? What if they didn't like the idea of you being surrounded by these guys who are your bandmates and decided to get rid of them? Alexander would be an easy first choice, for all the obvious reasons. But maybe they're worried you might have something going on with one of the other guys."

She wrestled with my statement. "I don't know. Those are some pretty extreme lengths to go to in order to try to be with me."

I nodded. "It is extreme. But somebody murdered two men close to you, and an obsession with you is as good a reason as any."

⚓

JANE RETURNED JUST after two in the afternoon. The sound of the door had awoken me, and I reached for my phone to check the time. I had no idea how long I'd been out, having fallen asleep with my laptop open to an article about the upcoming reunion tour. I'd been scanning the comment section—an activity I typically avoided at all costs—searching for any obsessive fans. No luck, at least no luck before I lost consciousness. Most responses to the tour announcement were tepid, which was understandable for a twenty-year-old one-hit wonder band. Some were excited, although those were sprinkled few and far between political arguments that had broken out—how that occurred on an apolitical post I had no idea other than that seemed to be the way these days—and discussions about other groups who should reunite.

Jane was standing in my doorway when she knocked on the frame. Her face was aglow.

"Hey, how was your massage?"

"Amazing."

"You look happy."

"I am, Char. I really am."

"I'm glad."

"Ophelia's asleep on the couch. How did that go?"

"Fine." I set my laptop on the bed next to me. "Mostly she just watched TV, but at one point we tried fleshing out some theories."

"What did you come up with?"

"Not a lot. I keep coming back to this obsessive fan theory, but I can't quite make it stick."

"Better than your werewolf theory."

I bit my tongue rather than retort. I'd done my best to let go of the idea Emmett was a murderer. It seemed farfetched when Alexander was killed, but with the body count at two, I couldn't see Emmett as a serial killer. Of course, that's what everyone said about serial killers, right? Never saw it coming. He seemed like a nice guy. Kept to himself.

It seemed to me the werewolf theory had only made sense when it came to Alexander, not Webster.

"I was thinking we should arrive at pirate night around

five thirty."

"About that." She picked at an imaginary piece of something on the doorframe.

"What?"

"I'm only back here for a few minutes. Emmett was sweet enough to book me an appointment with Teresa Corazon at the salon to do my hair and makeup. Then we're going to meet for pre-pirate party drinks at four thirty."

"Oh, I guess I assumed we were going together."

"Yeah, that was the plan, but you're okay going with Ophelia, right?"

"Sure. Sure! Of course. How fun getting pampered at the salon."

"I'm excited. I have an idea for how I want her to do my hairstyle and my makeup. I think I'm going to use extensions!" She pulled at her shoulder-length wavy brown hair.

"Extensions! Wow." What else was there to say but wow?

She clapped her hands. "I'm going to grab my costume and toiletry bag, and then I'm out of here!"

It was fine. It was totally fine. Jane and I weren't joined at the hip. We didn't need to do everything together. And it wasn't like I'd be showing up to the party alone. On the contrary, I was arriving with the most beautiful woman on the ship. No one would even notice I was standing next to her.

After a few minutes of me rummaging and running around, the front door opened.

"What in the world?" Jane's voice carried into my bedroom.

"What's wrong?" I called to her.

"Come look."

I scrambled off the bed and into the living room.

Ophelia was still on the sofa, stretching her arms above her head. "What's with all the racket?"

Jane stood in the doorway holding a piece of white paper. She handed it to me.

"Oh, this isn't good," I said.

Ophelia rose from the sofa to join us. "What isn't good?"

I handed her the paper, and her gaze widened.

"Oh, my gawd," she whispered.

It was Ophelia's photo with a target superimposed onto her face.

Chapter Seventeen

I SLAPPED THE paper with the target photo of Ophelia onto Xavier's desk. "Special delivery."

He pulled the picture toward him with the eraser end of his pencil and scanned it. "Where did you get this?"

"Just arrived on my doorstep."

"Thank you for letting me know."

"That's all you've got to say?"

"For now. May I keep this?" He tapped on the paper.

"I guess."

He opened his desk drawer and removed a gallon-sized clear plastic food storage bag and a single blue latex glove. He pulled on the glove, picked up the paper, and slid it into the bag. "It would have been more useful if you hadn't gotten your fingerprints on it. Who else has touched it?"

Oops. "Uh, Jane and Ophelia."

"Walk me through this discovery."

"It had to have been dropped off between two o'clock when Jane got back from the spa and two thirty when she went to leave, because she swears it wasn't there when she got home."

"It was outside the door, not slid underneath it?"

"She's not sure. She said she didn't notice it until she was walking out the door, but it could have drifted into the entryway from the hall."

"Where were you?"

"I was in my bedroom all afternoon. I'd been doing some research and then fell asleep. I woke up when Jane got home, but I never left my room."

"And Ophelia? Where was she?"

"Asleep on the sofa. She says she binge-watched TV until she passed out."

He sucked his teeth, sighed, and narrowed his gaze.

"What?"

"It occurs to me that the best way to deflect from yourself as a perpetrator is to make it appear you are a victim."

"You don't think she did this."

"I cannot rule out that possibility. It is convenient that she handled the paper, so her fingerprints will be on it."

"When would she have had time to print this photo?"

"I do not know. I merely find it to be an intriguing theory."

I observed him for a moment. "I thought you liked her."

"Who says I do not like her?"

"You keep accusing her of murder."

"I do not know the woman enough to like or dislike her. Which is my point. I do not know whether or not she is capable of this level of malfeasance."

"That's a fifty-cent word."

He smiled. "My wife once gave me a daily word calendar to help improve my English."

I froze. He'd never directly mentioned that he'd been married, nor had he ever spoken of his wife. Current wife? Ex-wife? Dead wife? I'd spent months wondering and it seemed the revelation was at hand. A million thoughts raced through my mind as I attempted to keep my composure and not make a thing about it. All my synapses were firing as I formulated what I hoped was a casual response.

"Oh?"

His head tilted slightly to the right. "You do know I was married."

Was married. "You never wear a ring." Sure, when we first met, I'd noticed the mark where it had been, but this was technically an accurate statement.

He examined his bare left hand like he hadn't been aware.

A heaviness fell across his office.

"My wife died five years ago. She was in labor, and something went wrong."

Labor? As in baby?

He continued, "It was three weeks before she was due to give birth. Her water broke, and she called the midwife. She labored at home for quite some time, not knowing that the baby was in distress. I was traveling for work at that time. I hopped aboard a plane, but by the time I arrived, the child was gone and Louise was in a coma. She did not recover."

It was as if a dagger had been thrust underneath my ribcage. A whimper of heartache escaped me, and I immediately covered my mouth. I didn't want to burden him with my emotions about his loss.

A melancholy smile touched the corner of his mouth. His chai latte eyes held a compassionate sadness that resonated to the core of me.

We were members of the same horrible club. He'd known about my loss but had kept his to himself.

"Thank you for sharing that with me." A single tear escaped my eye, but I brushed it away as deftly as I could.

I had so many questions. Mostly I wanted to understand why he'd chosen this moment to reveal such a painful personal tragedy to me.

My terrible poker face must have given my thoughts away, because he said, "For a while now I have wanted to tell you my story, to let you know that you are not alone in this experience. I did not know how you might react to the fact I was not there for her when she needed me most. It has been my greatest shame, and I did not want you to think poorly of me. I waited for a moment to arise in our conversation, and now seemed as good a time as any." He smiled again, this time with less sadness. "There are times it is nice to know there are other people in this world who understand, *n'est-ce pas?*"

My chest squeezed like it was going to burst. His willingness to use his vulnerability to connect with my experiences made me feel significant in a way I hadn't for quite some time, if ever. He trusted me. He wanted to share his grief, his regret, and his heartbreak with me. It was an invitation to deepen our relationship, something I'd longed for in my own marriage but hadn't ever found.

And it was absolutely terrifying.

I rubbed my sweaty palms on my thighs. I felt heat creep up my neck, along with a rising panic. I might not be up for the task of an authentic connection with a man I cared about.

"Are you all right?"

His question broke me out of my stupor. "Yes. Yes, I'm sorry. Uh, hot flash." For once, something helpful about being in menopause. I fanned my face.

"Do not apologize."

"Can I ask—" I stopped short of forming my question, regretting I'd allowed that much to slip out of my mouth.

"Of course you may."

I stopped fanning. "The child. Did you name them?"

He winced slightly. *Dammit, Char, you should have left it alone!*

"I did. It was a little girl. I named her what Louise had chosen. Céline. It means heavenly. That is where she resides with her mother."

A lump formed in my throat. No crying. I had to keep it together. "Beautiful," I whispered.

He cleared his throat and began idly straightening and rearranging items on his desk. "Back to the issue at hand."

I had no intention on fighting him. Changing the subject brought huge relief. "I left Ophelia with strict instructions to keep the door locked and not answer it for anyone. I'm heading back to my room to get ready for tonight's event, and I won't let her out of my sight."

"*Merci.*"

"Do you have a pirate costume?"

"I do not."

"Why?"

"I have to draw the line somewhere."

There was no arguing with that. I awkwardly stood and said my goodbyes, still reeling from his revelation. As I left the security office and headed toward the elevator, I was as jittery as a hummingbird.

I waited for what felt like forever for the elevator to arrive, but it seemed to be stuck down on three. That tended to happen when the crew was preparing for a big event.

After a while I gave up and headed for the stairwell. Xavier had cautioned the members of Canailles Nous to avoid the stairs, but that warning hadn't applied to me.

I was dragging myself up the stairs and had just made it to the seventh-floor landing when a large figure burst through the doorway, knocking me to the side and causing me to thwack my head against the wall. I slumped to the ground.

Chapter Eighteen

"Oh man, Charlotte, I'm so sorry. Are you okay?"

Percy Brown's round face hovered over me. Make that Percy Brown's round, concerned, flushed, and sweaty face. And he was winded.

"Percy, what the heck? You made me crack my head against the wall." I rubbed the point of impact. "Am I bleeding?"

He leaned in to look closer. "Not that I can see. I'm really sorry. Does anything else hurt? Do I need to take you to the medical center?"

I checked in with my various limbs and found nothing throbbing in pain other than my head. Oof, and my shoulder. I was really going to be feeling that later, no doubt. Percy looked so upset about hurting me I didn't have the heart to make a fuss.

"I'll be okay."

He reached out his hand to help me to my feet. "I didn't think anyone would be in here. Every other time I've come this way it's been empty."

I brushed my backside of any possible debris. "*You're* not supposed to be in here. Xavier was quite clear about that.

You're supposed to stay where you're in view and can't be cornered or caught unawares by persons with nefarious intent."

Percy chuckled. "Look at me. You think I can't take care of myself?"

"Webster wasn't exactly a small man."

Percy's expression darkened. "True dat."

"Why are you in such a hurry?"

"I was headed to the security office."

"Funny, I just left there."

"Oh yeah?"

The area where we were congregated wasn't a large space, and with his size, Percy took up most of it. His scent was musky, like an old library.

I took a half step backward, and ran into the wall, bonking my head.

He reached out to cradle the spot where I'd hit, invading my space further. "Geez, Charlotte, you gotta be more careful."

There was no more space to retreat so I shifted to my left. "I'm clumsy that way. So, why were you headed to the security office?"

He must have sensed my discomfort with our proximity, because he took two large steps away from me. "Sorry, didn't mean to loom over you. Sometimes I forget how intimidating that can be."

I waved it off. "No worries."

He pulled a wrinkled paper from one of the many pockets of his black leather jacket. "Someone shoved this under my door."

It was a photo of Percy with a target over his face, just like the one Ophelia had received.

"When did that happen?"

"Not sure. Maybe an hour or two ago? I was out having lunch, and then I was reading in the library. It was in my room when I got back."

"*Tale of Two Cities*?"

He squinted at me.

"The book you're reading. Still *Tale of Two Cities* by Dickens?"

"Oh, yeah. So, why were you at the security office?"

"Ophelia got the same note."

"What? You're serious? Oh, man. You know, I went by her room after I got this to show it to her, but she didn't answer."

"That's because she's in my cabin."

"Well, that explains it."

"What about Heath and Victor?" I asked.

"What about 'em?"

"Did they get notes?"

"Not sure."

"Maybe I'll go ask them. What are their suites?"

"Oh, uh, I think Vic is in 810 and Heath is in 807. Anyway, after Ophelia wasn't at her place—which is 809—I decided it was best to give it to security, let them handle it. I got impatient waiting for the elevator."

"Me too. I think the crew is using it to transport stuff for the event tonight. That always slows things."

He held up the paper. "I'm going to take this down to Mesnier, see what he's gonna do about it. Makes me feel like I've got a target on my back."

More like on his face, but I didn't say it. "Good plan. I'm just warning you. He's going to lecture you about taking the stairwell."

He arched his left brow. "Maybe we keep that a secret between us." He winked and headed down the stairs.

All I had to do was open the door and I'd be in my cabin in minutes.

That would have been the sensible thing to do.

Instead, I trudged up one more flight and exited on the eighth level, Santorini.

I came upon Victor's suite first and knocked. No answer. I rang the doorbell. No answer.

I moved down the hall to Heath's room. I put my ear to the door. A vacuum was running inside.

I wanted to know whether Heath had received a similar note as the others—a targeted threat, so to speak—but if I were being completely honest with myself, my growing suspicion of him had become too great to ignore. I couldn't quite put my finger on what was feeding those thoughts. Perhaps it was the absurdly calm way he'd processed Alexander's death, including taking smoke breaks adjacent to the scene of the crime. Maybe it was his nervous and jittery demeanor at the gathering to discuss Webster's death. If he were the only one of Canailles Nous who hadn't received a note, that would put him at the top of the suspect list.

Of course, I had no motive for why he might have killed

Webster, but then again, I had no idea why anyone would have killed Webster.

I knocked and, predictably, got no answer. I rang the doorbell. The vacuum kept going. I was about to give up when the door opened.

Olalla Tercero, one of the housekeeping staff, peeked her head into the hallway. "Oh, Mrs. McLaughlin. I thought I heard the bell." Her brow furrowed. "You know you are on Santorini, not Odyssey."

Claiming to accidentally be on the wrong floor wasn't a terrible idea, but it wouldn't get me inside the room. "Actually, I was coming to look for an item I may have left here the other night."

"Oh?" I could practically see the wheels turning in her head as she contemplated why I might have been in Heath Hubbard's suite at night. This worked to my advantage. If she believed we were romantically involved, she might be more willing to let me inside the room.

"What was it? Perhaps I've seen it."

What was it? What was it? "Oh, um, it was an earring." Perfect. Exactly what one would leave behind following an interlude. "It's one of my grandmother's ruby earrings. They mean the world to me."

I mustered all my eighth-grade drama club experience and attempted to squeeze a tear from my eye. Judging by the alarm on her face, I'd likely only managed to look constipated.

She blinked a couple times in that way people did when they were trying to determine whether you were a big fat liar.

Maybe she didn't think I was Heath's type.

"I haven't seen anything like that. I'm nearly done in here, but you're welcome to take a peek. I may have missed it."

She opened the door wider for me to enter and I stepped inside.

The units on Santorini were larger on average than those on Odyssey, except for the two end suites, which included my two-bedroom and the three-bedroom penthouse next door. Odyssey had forty-two units—mostly studios and one-bedroom—to Santorini's ten. Nine of those were two-bedrooms suites, while Alexander had been staying in the sole three-bedroom penthouse. The bulk of the remaining space on the eighth level was taken up by the captain's quarters and the captain's lounge.

Heath's suite was approximately 1,300 square feet. As with all the units, the first thing to draw my gaze was the glass sliders leading to the balcony. All that stood between the outdoor dining set and the ocean was a wrought iron railing. On the table was an ashtray, which was overflowing with cigarette butts.

Olalla must not have gotten to that yet. Or perhaps that wasn't part of her duty. I didn't smoke, so I didn't know what the protocol was.

Each owner had the opportunity to choose the style of décor and furnishings, and some brought in their own interior designers. That seemed to be the case with this cabin, as it had a distinctive style. The walls were covered in a linen fabric wallpaper with golden strands woven through.

On one hung a large abstract portrait of what appeared to be Frida Kahlo surrounded by various shades of yellow, while the opposite held a polyptych of Marilyn Monroe, Steve McQueen, Robert Redford, and Ray Charles. Interesting quartet. Recessed lighting within the recessed ceiling glowed lemon yellow. The sofa was gray leather with gold accent pillows, and the accent chairs were gold silk with silver accent pillows. A yellow wool throw blanket had been meticulously folded and laid across the back of the sofa.

"Lots of yellow," I mused.

Olalla wrapped the vacuum cord around the handle. "To each his own. Where did you say you thought you dropped it?"

"Hmm? Oh, the earring. Right." Couldn't bring myself to say the bedroom, despite really wanting to search in there. As it was, the rumors among staff and crew were going to be brutal. "Somewhere in here, I'm sure." I dropped to my knees and began feeling around the plush pile carpet for my nonexistent family heirloom.

Olalla's walkie-talkie squawked. "Olalla, Mrs. Weintraub is requesting you return to their suite immediately. Apparently, Mr. Weintraub's surgical bandages came loose, and there's a bit of a mess."

Olalla sighed and squared her shoulders. She pressed the button on her radio. "On my way." To me she said, "Find it?" Her voice was weary and slightly annoyed.

"Not yet. Do you mind if I keep looking? It's really important I find it."

She sighed. "I guess it's okay. Just don't make a mess.

The last thing I need right now is a complaint in my file."

"He won't know I've been here," I said, before quickly adding, "I mean, I'll tell him I was here, he just wouldn't know by looking." Didn't need her thinking I was acting shady. Which I was. But I didn't need her knowing that.

"I'll leave the door ajar. Make sure it's closed tightly when you leave."

"Will do." I gave an awkward and unnecessary salute, but she was already on her way out and didn't see it.

As she left, she mumbled something about passengers and their bloody towels.

Since I was already down on my hands and knees, I scanned underneath the sofa and the chairs. Not a crumb or dust bunny. She was great at her job.

I climbed to my feet and scanned the living room. Not a thing was out of place. There was no garbage, no used drinking glasses, no personal items of any kind. It made sense. The owners of the unit likely locked away any of their belongings other than what guests needed to use the unit. Heath had been onboard only five days and, other than his smoking habit, he had struck me as a clean and tidy person.

I moved into the bedroom, where the gold and silver theme continued.

I finally hit paydirt in terms of things belonging to Heath: a moleskin notebook on the bedside table, toiletries in the bathroom, a backpack on the floor tucked under the bench at the foot of the bed. In the closet was a large empty suitcase. This wasn't a surprise considering Windsor was his assigned butler, and Windsor always insisted on unpacking luggage the moment I arrived on the ship.

I checked every pocket of the suitcase, just in case something small had been left inside, but there was nothing. I checked the pockets of every clothing item hanging in the closet. I found three cigarette packs, one lighter, two books of matches—one from Maple Leaf and the other from Dos Jefes Cigar Bar—and about nine toothpicks.

I felt around in his drawers, except for his underwear drawer, as I possessed a modicum of respect for personal space and boundaries—present activities not included. The dresser yielded nothing of interest.

I eyed the notebook on the nightstand. Would reading it make me a terrible person or a good detective? Were those two things mutually exclusive?

As I debated that invasion of privacy, I didn't hesitate to riffle through the nightstand drawer. It was a larger collection of the items I'd found in his closet: smoking paraphernalia and toothpicks. He either really hated getting food stuck in his teeth or it was part of the jazz musician persona.

I got down on my hands and knees again, this time to look under the bed. It was bare and only slightly dusty. While in that vulnerable position, a strange noise came from somewhere outside of the bedroom. I froze in place, with my rear in the air. Fluff from the rug tickled my nose as I strained to listen for more noises or an indication someone was in the suite.

I tried to process what I thought I'd heard. It had sounded like a howl, but of course, that couldn't be.

After a few moments of silence—including no sound of my breathing as I was holding all the air in my lungs—I righted myself. All the blood that had rushed to my head when I was upside down left just as quickly, causing dizziness. As soon as I felt confident that I could get up without fainting, I grabbed the bedspread and used it to pull myself to standing.

I tiptoed to the bedroom door, as light on my feet as I was capable, and peeked around the corner. The front door was still ajar, and I saw no evidence that anyone had come in. I listened a bit longer until satisfied I was alone in the suite.

I exhaled and felt some of the tingling adrenaline coursing through my veins begin to dissipate. I shook out my hands. I shimmied my shoulders. I shook my head to release the jitters so I could return to the task at hand.

A quick foray in the bathroom revealed nothing more than what one might expect in a bathroom: shaving kit, skin care, hair products, and a first aid kit.

The notebook on the nightstand beckoned me like a siren luring a sailor to his untimely demise. I inched my way toward it. Just a peek. What would a tiny little peek hurt? No one would ever know.

Unless, of course, what was written on those pages revealed the identity of the murderer, then people would know because I'd have to report it. But otherwise, no one would know.

With my left hand I picked up the pen sitting next to the notebook and used the tip of it to slowly lift the cover. I didn't want to get my fingerprints all over it in case it became evidence. I held the pen precariously from the end between my thumb and forefinger, which made it difficult to get leverage. Also, I wasn't left-handed. The pen bobbled in my pinched fingers and started to slip. The cover thumped closed, and I grunted my frustration. I tried again, this time raising my right hand in the air as if somehow that would help me balance the pen in my left.

I'd almost gotten the cover flipped open all the way when from behind me came a low and slow whistle.

Chapter Nineteen

I YELPED AND flung the pen in the air, spinning around in the process. Heath Hubbard stood leaning against the doorjamb with a toothpick in his mouth and his arms folded across his chest. He spotted the pen flying his direction and ducked just enough for it to whiz over his head.

He spit the toothpick on the ground. "Holy mother of—"

"Sorry, you startled me!"

"I startled"—he gave me an incredulous look—"I startled you? You're in my suite. In my bedroom. What are you doing in here?"

I looked around like I hadn't realized where I was. Yep. Still in his bedroom. I bared my lower teeth in contrition. "Well, I, uh, you see—"

He shook his head and held up his hand. "Let's back up. How did you get in here?"

The last thing I wanted was for Olalla to get in trouble. "I told housekeeping I'd accidentally lost an important piece of family jewelry in your room."

"That's how rumors get started. Not saying I mind, but I can't imagine that would do much for your reputation or your chances of snagging the head of security."

I didn't have to look in a mirror to know my cheeks were aflame. Did everyone know I had a crush on Xavier?

"Now, back to the more important question. *What* are you doing in my suite?"

"I ran into Percy in the—" I didn't want Percy to get in trouble either. "I ran into him downstairs. He was worked up because he received a threatening note like Alexander. So did Ophelia. I wanted to see if you did too."

Heath's expression reminded me of my mother whenever she knew I wasn't telling the whole story. "Okay, but if you knock and I'm not here, then come back later. Just because you want to know something doesn't give you the right to invade my private space." His gaze cut to the nightstand. "Did you read my journal?"

"No." This was a technically true statement.

"Would you have read my journal had I not interrupted your scavenger hunt?"

He had me there. "Prossibly."

"Did you just say *prossibly*?"

"I believe I may have."

"The answer is probably, and your mouth just ratted you out."

I exhaled. "Okay, I admit it. I was curious. I am curious."

"Curious about?"

"Look, everyone in Canailles Nous had motive to kill Alexander, but I can't wrap my brain around why anyone would want to harm Webster."

"And you thought the answer might be in there?" He

jutted his chin toward the notebook. "You think I did it and that is my confession book. *Dear Diary: today I killed a man.*"

"I didn't know."

He waved his hand in a gesture indicating for me to go ahead. "You want to know what's in there? Be my guest."

"Oh, that's okay." I eyed the doorway.

Heath wasn't a large man by any definition of the word. He was also in his late sixties, and I was pretty sure I could take him if I needed to do so.

I was also *prossibly* fooling myself.

"Go on. You know you want to see what's inside." Heath sucked in his cheeks, exacerbating his already angular features. "Go on, now, *cher*." I sensed little endearment in that term.

I picked up the pen—this time with a tight grip—and flopped open the notebook.

"Read it. Aloud."

"*'Behind these bars of steel I lay, remembering that sunny day when you and I basked in the ray. Laissez les bon temps rouler.'* What is this?" I set down the pen. "Is it a poem?"

"It's lyrics to a song Alex and I were writing. Together. He was going to put it on his next solo album. He believed it was going to be a big hit."

"Oh, wow. I didn't know you were working together on new music."

"No one did. And now no one will."

"Why do you say that?"

"Because 'Laissez les Bon Temps Rouler' is never going

to get made. Alex had the connections, not me. The record company wanted Alex to perform it. I play the vibraphone. Ain't no one gonna make an entire album featuring a vibraphone."

I couldn't think of a single example to disprove his theory.

"Now do you understand why I would never have murdered Alex? He was giving me another shot. Perhaps my last shot. I don't suppose I've got too many left. I'm a cat who's already spent eight of his nine lives."

It was a compelling argument. "Why didn't you say anything about this before?"

"What's the point? I have no proof that we were doing this together. Alex was slippery. It was hard to pin him down with things like written contracts—except, of course, when they benefited him. Then he was quick to sign."

I looked again at the notebook. His theory about the song exonerating him would have been plausible, except for one thing. "There are two sets of handwriting in here. I'll bet it wouldn't be too hard to compare it to one of Alexander's known writing samples. You could take this to the record company, and they could still release the song postmortem."

"We never recorded a demo."

"Okay, but they could have someone else perform it in tribute. The last song Alexander St. Jacques ever wrote. The song he wanted to release, but then he was murdered. It will sell like hotcakes. And you'll make a fortune from the royalties."

"I guess so, but that's a lot of ifs. Having Alex record the song was a much better and more direct way to fame and fortune. To me, that should be reason enough to know I didn't kill him."

"But Heath, if he broke his promise to you about including the song, or if he planned to cut you out of the deal by not crediting you so that you'd get paid, that might be considered an even stronger motive for murder than his original abandonment of Canailles Nous or even his latest double dipping on this gig's payout."

"But he didn't break his promise. Or at least, he hadn't yet."

"He could have told you something that might make you believe he was about to. No one would know if he had."

Heath's gaze hardened. "Yeah, I suppose you're right about that."

Something about the way he looked at me was unsettling. I didn't feel like I was in imminent danger—especially since he was across the room—but I needed to get out of here so I could get my thoughts straight. On the one hand, he'd always been kind to me, and nothing about him had ever felt threatening, but on the other, desperation sometimes led to desperate acts. I'd already been in more of those perilous predicaments than I cared to think about, and I really didn't want to find myself in one again.

I pulled my phone out of my pocket and looked at the blank screen. "Oops, I'm getting a call." I pretended to swipe and held it to my ear. Thankfully, he was far enough away he shouldn't have been able to see it was a ruse. "Oh, hey, Jane." Pause. "Oh, yeah, sorry, I lost track of time. I'm in

Heath Hubbard's room, but I was just about to leave to come meet you." Pause. "Yeah, I'll be there in about five minutes. See you then." I pretended to hang up and slid the phone back into my pocket. "I totally spaced that I was supposed to meet Jane at the, um, hair salon. To get ready for the party tonight."

Heath eyed me skeptically, once again leaning against the doorjamb with his arms crossed, still blocking the doorway. "Anyone ever tell you that you're a terrible liar?"

"Once or twice."

He stepped into the bedroom.

Uh-oh.

He gestured for me to leave. "Don't want to keep *Jane* waiting." There was no mistaking the derision in his voice. He knew I was just trying to leave.

I took him up on it. "See ya later!" I said as I shuffled past him and hustled through the living room. I didn't look back to see his expression.

As I burst into the hallway, I caught a glimpse of Hawk heading into the stairwell. He'd told Jane she couldn't possibly have seen him on Santorini because he never had need to go to the eighth floor, yet here he was, skulking there just as she'd claimed.

⚓

"WHERE'VE YOU BEEN?" Ophelia was still on the sofa where I'd left her. "You went to take the note to Xavier like two hours ago. I was starting to get worried."

Her placid expression and multiple discarded snack wrappers didn't exactly scream worried, but everyone handled stress differently.

How much did I want to share with her, and how much did I want to hold back? "I went to see Xavier just like I said. Showed him the picture of you with the target on your face—" She winced. "Sorry. Anyway, after I talked to him for a bit, I meant to come back here, but I ran into Percy, and he was on his way to the security office to bring his own threatening note." I purposely left out where I'd run into him and hoped she didn't ask. Terrible liar and all that.

Her hand flew to her mouth. "Oh no."

"Yeah. So I decided to go talk to Victor and Heath, see if they'd gotten notes as well."

"Had they?"

In the stress of the moment in his suite, I'd forgotten to ask Heath. "I'm still not sure. I tried Victor at his room but got no answer. Heath was also gone when I arrived, but housekeeping was there, and they let me in."

"They let you into someone else's room? Why?"

"Because I asked."

Unsatisfied with that answer, Ophelia pressed me again. "No, I mean what reason did you give them for going into someone else's room?"

"I said I lost an earring. Family heirloom."

"Tsk, tsk. I'm going to start calling you Shady Charlotte."

"It got me into his room, didn't it?"

"Sure, but why couldn't you just come back later and ask

him instead of poking around in his stuff?"

Good point. Should I reveal my true reason for entering his room? I wasn't quite ready to trust Ophelia with my suspicions of Heath. "I guess I was just feeling anxious and didn't want to wait. I figured if I found the note with his face and a target, I'd get my answer and no one would be the wiser."

"But you didn't find one." She had a pensive expression.

"No."

"Does that mean he's the one sending us the notes?"

I hadn't given her enough credit. "Maybe? I don't know. If I hadn't run into Percy and had gone to his room instead, I wouldn't have found the note because it was in his pocket. Maybe Heath has his in his pocket. I didn't ask him."

Her gaze widened. "Wait. Heath caught you searching his room?"

"Yeah, he came in while I was nosing around his bedroom."

"How did that go over?"

"As you might expect."

"Not good, I assume. Heath has always been a pretty private guy."

I checked my phone. "We still have a couple hours before we need to leave for the party. I'm going to do a bit more online research."

She yawned and stretched her arms above her head. "I'm going to finish this *Real Housewives* episode, and then I'll take a shower."

"Sounds good." I headed toward my room.

"Oh, by the way, that Emmett guy came by while you were gone."

I turned and came back to the living room. "Without Jane?"

"Yeah, he said she was at the salon."

"What did he want?"

"He wanted to ask me what I knew about Alex's past. He's pretty sideways about the fact that Alex wasn't who he'd claimed. Kept mumbling something about his wife. I didn't know he was married. I thought he was pursuing Jane."

"He is. And he was. Married, I mean. His wife died two years ago."

Ophelia shrugged. "Well, like I said, he seemed pretty worked up."

I ambled to my room, climbed onto my bed, and opened my laptop. In the search bar of the newspaper archive website, I entered: *Emmett Guidry wife*.

The first article that popped up was headlined WOMAN BRUTALLY ATTACKED AND KILLED IN BARATARIA PRESERVE. HUSBAND CLAIMS IT WAS ROUGAROU.

Chapter Twenty

ARTICLE AFTER ARTICLE said the same thing. Emmett's wife had been killed in some sort of animal attack, and Emmett was convinced it was perpetrated by a Rougarou. A werewolf. No wonder he was so obsessed with the legends.

Or had the legends created this obsession?

Grief did strange things to people. I'd experienced this firsthand. Terrible, unexpected things happened sometimes, and it was a normal instinct to try to find an explanation that made the unthinkable make more sense.

Even if that meant forming an irrational and extraordinary narrative around a tragedy that had a simple explanation.

When Gabe's will had been read and all his assets listed, my first thought—after the initial shock of his net worth—was that maybe he'd been involved in some sort of criminal activity and someone had run him off the road to silence him. Or maybe it wasn't a heart attack—he'd been poisoned. Kyrie Dawn was an operative who'd seduced him and then blackmailed him into some Seattle crime syndicate.

Anything was better than facing the truth that my husband had lied to me, cheated on me, and kept secrets from me.

Emmett's grief had rejected the logical for the absurd, despite all evidence.

Wildlife officials were certain the attack was from a bobcat, probably one that was ill or affected by rabies. They'd also found the tattered wrapper of a SPAM breakfast sandwich that Marie had apparently picked up with her morning coffee at a local café. Sardines, hotdogs, and spiced meats were listed as foods bobcats might find irresistible. While they tried to avoid outright victim blaming, officials made note of the fact there were signs posted all over the park stating that food was prohibited in certain areas, including the trails where Marie had been attacked. Since it was part of her routine to walk the area, she really should have known better.

Emmett, on the other hand, had claimed a coverup and insisted it had to have been the work of the Rougarou. He'd gone to the press, he'd harangued local law enforcement, he'd made many trips to the New Orleans City Hall building, and he'd sent letters to his state representatives that were not threatening, per se, but had enough of an agitated undercurrent to warrant a visit from the Louisiana State Police Bureau of Investigation.

While it wasn't stated outright, it seemed Emmett wasn't exactly on a voluntary sabbatical from his teaching duties at Tulane—it had been strongly recommended he take one in lieu of a hearing that might cost him his tenured position.

The more I read about Emmett's emotional instability and his fractured state of mind, the more I worried about Jane's safety and well-being.

While I still couldn't find an explanation for Webster's death, the articles I'd read had brought me full circle back to Emmett as my prime suspect with the werewolf obsession theory back in play.

My heart thumped wildly as I considered how to tell Jane what I'd discovered. She wasn't going to be grateful, that was a given. She'd most likely accuse me of hyper focusing on Emmett for the sole purpose of intervening in her love life out of some sort of petty jealousy and/or control.

Of course, there was a part of me that was concerned about what a change of Jane's relationship status might mean for me. Standing at the base of the Great Pyramid…alone. Climbing to the top of the Eiffel Tower…alone. Waking up in a different port of call every few days in an empty suite. Or, possibly worse, waking up to the two of them canoodling over their morning coffee as they planned their day together.

But the majority of my concerns when it came to Emmett were grounded in facts mixed with a healthy dose of intuition.

Something wasn't right with him, and now I had a pretty good idea what that was. Whether his grief had propelled him over the edge or he'd been teetering there for some time, I had no idea. In many ways, he presented himself quite rational and composed. And if it were just a fascination with werewolves, it could be chalked up to a quirky hobby. What I was reading took things to a different level.

The most jarring article came from the *Nola Gazette*.

Tulane Professor Adamant Wife Murdered by Rougarou

Jean Lafitte National Historic Park and Preserve
Jefferson Parish

It's been sixteen months since the brutal fatal attack on his wife in the middle of Barataria Preserve, but for Emmett Guidry the grief is as fresh as if her death had occurred sixteen days ago. Thirty-nine-year-old Marie Guidry was walking the trails alone just after 6 A.M. last April. Her husband claimed she'd left their home in Kenner around 5:30 that morning, something she did at least twice a week in the spring and summer months.

Her body was discovered shortly before 8 by a local hiking club. "I've never seen anything like it," Harahan Hikers Association President Remy Broussard said at the time. "We've spotted a few bobcats on the trails, but they always seemed to be more frightened of us than we were of them."

Officials say bobcat attacks are quite rare and out of character, but this animal must have been suffering the effects of rabies. Emmett Guidry, however, believes this attack wasn't the act of a rabid bobcat, but the famed werewolf of Louisiana: the Rougarou. A tenured professor of literature at Tulane University, mythology has always been a topic of interest for Guidry, 61, but since his wife's death he's delved into local lore in hopes of finding an explanation for the terrible tragedy.

"It's a conspiracy that reaches to the highest levels of government," Guidry said in a phone interview last

week. "They're all in on it. The mayor, the medical examiner, the legislature, the police. They know Rougarou attacks are happening in this area, and they're doing nothing about it. Worse than that, they're sweeping it under the rug." When reached for comment, the mayor's office said only, "We have great compassion for Mr. Guidry's terrible loss. However, his constant barrage of attacks in the media against this office will not bring her back. We wish him the best."

The New Orleans Police Department issued a statement that said only, "The death of Marie Guidry was ruled a rabid animal attack by the Jefferson Parish coroner's office. Our subsequent investigation matches those findings and those of the Jefferson Parish Sheriff's Department. Our condolences to the family of Mrs. Guidry, but this case has been closed. Until or unless new information comes to light that supports Mr. Guidry's claims, there will be no further action by this department."

"Liars, all of them," Mr. Guidry asserted when asked about these statements. "I've got proof—they just don't want to hear it, or they don't want people to know the truth. The truth always has a way of coming out, though. I'm currently tracing the family lineages of known Rougarou like the St. Jacques family. When I find out who did this to them, I'm going to shoot a silver bullet through their black heart."

A chill spread across my arms and the back of my neck. Emmett's own words in black-and-white were a confession to what he wanted to do to Alexander St. Jacques, and what ultimately happened to him.

No wonder he was so upset when he found out that the real Alexander St. Jacques died as an infant and the man, he'd (allegedly) murdered to avenge his wife's death, was an ex-con with an assumed identity.

Oops.

⚓

"I LOOK LIKE the Dustin Hoffman version of Captain Hook," I muttered to Ophelia as we took the elevator two floors up to Mykonos.

A piece of the giant white feather poking out from my oversized purple hat floated into my nostrils. I sputtered and swiped at my nose in an unsuccessful bid to stop the itching.

"I think you look hot." She watched her reflection in the door as she hoisted her ample breasts, which were already overflowing from her lowcut neckline.

"Give me phrases no one's ever uttered to me for a thousand, Alex," I said.

"What?" She was still focusing on tucking and lifting her assets.

"Nothing."

The elevator doors opened, and Ophelia strutted into the hallway outside the dining room.

To say she made her presence known would have been an understatement. An entire room of pirates and pirate wenches turned their attention to the woman standing next to me. Totally expected, of course, and who could blame them?

She wasn't even showing the most skin, either. That award went to Kyrie Dawn, whose off-the-shoulder cream ruffled minidress cinched with black leather corset and paired with black thigh-high fishnet stockings would normally have made her the center of attention.

But there was no competing with Ophelia with her black form-fitting curve-hugging full-length bodysuit, black leather pointed waistcoat, red sash tied at the hip, black leather high heeled boots cuffed at the thigh, and wine-colored tricorn hat that somehow didn't in any way look ridiculous.

It was kind of a relief, actually. Her exceptional beauty was so out of the stratosphere, I felt no need to compete. She certainly wasn't competing. Some of the women in the dining room—including Kyrie Dawn—may have been, but Ophelia appeared oblivious to them. She was at least ten years older than Kyrie Dawn, but that only showed in her high confidence level. It was an interesting phenomenon that occurred after a woman turned middle aged, where the judgment of others no longer mattered to the same extent.

Jane liked to call it the DGAF syndrome, a.k.a. don't give a f%$#.

"Stop fidgeting," Ophelia chastised. "Why are you so nervous? It's just a party full of geezers. Rich geezers, I'll give you that, but geezers nonetheless."

"See that woman?" I asked her, tipping my chin toward Kyrie Dawn.

"The blonde in the serving wench costume?"

"Yeah."

"What about her?"

"That's my dead husband's mistress. He used to bring her on this ship for romantic trysts."

Ophelia clucked her tongue. "So cliché."

"Anyway, even though she and I have come to an…understanding, I always feel shlumpy around her. She's young and cute and petite, and I feel like a giant ogre in comparison."

"Don't be silly. You're statuesque. Elegant. Hold your chin up and follow me."

She began to strut across the room. I hesitated a moment before raising my chin as instructed and following her.

Hawk gave me a smile and a brief head nod from behind the bar. He and Egan were making cocktails faster than Tom Cruise and Bryan Brown in a 1980s rom-com. As if on cue, a merengue band began to play "Kokomo." Were they always supposed to play the event, or had they been cobbled together from staff and guests following the murders of one-third of Canailles Nous? The steel drums were a nice touch, regardless.

The dining room had gone full *Pirates of the Caribbean*. Someone had created a mural of a beached wooden lifeboat on the sand under a palm tree. Several potted palms were stationed around the room. In the center of the dining room was a large chest that, like Ophelia's, was also overflowing. Strands of faux pearls, diamonds, rubies, emeralds, and sapphires had been draped across the back of every chair. Each table had its own treasure chest of desserts, a tray of cocktail accoutrements like blue cheese stuffed olives and sliced citrus fruits, and an accompanying parrot.

We headed for the table where Percy, Heath, Victor, and Victor's now-constant companion were seated. The good thing about Victor's burgeoning romance was that he was never alone, which meant he was neither in danger nor was he the perpetrator. Unless of course they were in on it together, which seemed highly unlikely.

"Ahoy, mateys!" Percy tipped his own tricorn hat, made of brown felt.

"Shiver me timbers, ladies, you look fantastic." Victor gave a broad smile and shimmied his shoulders.

"If it weren't for the fact I know you haven't got an ounce of sexual attraction to either one of us, I might feel a little harassed," Ophelia teased.

"The night's still young. I'm on my second Captain Morgan and pineapple, and by the third, who knows." He winked at his companion. "Right, Davy?"

"Can't wait."

"Davy, are you a guest on the ship or crew?" I asked him.

Both Victor and Davy burst out laughing.

"I don't get it. What did I say that's so funny?"

Victor wiped a stray tear. "Oh, geez. You wanna tell her?"

"Well, first, my name isn't Davy," the man said with an Australian accent. "It's Luke. He's been calling me Davy all night because of Davy Jones's locker."

"That seems a tad morose, considering that phrase is a euphemism for a watery grave," I said.

Luke arched his brow. "Oh, it's twisted, all right."

Victor nudged Luke. "Tell her the other part."

Luke gave a wry smile. "I'm not staff or crew. My family owns this ship."

I covered my eyes with my hand. "Oh my gosh, how embarrassing."

"Don't be embarrassed. I try to keep a low profile when I'm onboard."

"Looks like you landed yourself a whale, Vic," Percy said. "Should I call you Ahab?"

"Luke, maybe you can point me in the direction of my own whale," Ophelia purred.

"I'll see what I can do," he chuckled.

"I'm tired of busking and jiving. I want to relax on St. Bart's with a pina colada in one hand and a good book in the other."

"Fee, you haven't read a book in the time I've known you." Percy nudged her. "Not for lack of trying."

"Well, maybe I want to start, did ya think of that?" She lifted her chin in mock offense.

Emmett and Jane appeared at the entrance to the party. She'd done as she said and had added extensions to her hair, which was braided. She wore a white peasant blouse, a purple velvet lock lace bodice, and a coordinated purple velvet and black lace ruffled skirt. Around her waist a leather gun holster held what I presumed to be a toy flintlock pistol. At least, I hoped it was. I had been with her when she bought the costume, and it hadn't included a gun. Had Emmett given it to her? He wouldn't have her wear the actual weapon he'd used to shoot Alexander St. Jacques, would he? After what I'd learned about him that afternoon, anything was possible.

"You look amazing." I stood to give Jane a stiff hug.

She gave me a strange look. "Everything all right?"

"Sure, sure. Come, sit. Join us." I waved her toward the table. "We were just talking about Ophelia's retirement plan."

Emmett paused halfway into his chair. "Which is?"

"Marry rich." She stabbed a maraschino cherry with a pink plastic garnish sword.

"Sounds like you've got it all figured out." Jane laughed.

She looked happy. I had an anvil on my chest every time I thought about breaking her heart with the revelation that the man she'd admired most of her life and had developed real feelings for was most likely a deranged killer who believed people actually turned into werewolves.

Would she believe me? Would I if I were in her shoes?

I spotted Xavier prowling the perimeter, as he did at most events. He looked often at our table; whether it was because it was filled with murder suspects or his boss, it was hard to say.

I hadn't seen Lonnie or Pike yet, which made me wonder if they were in costume and blending into the crowd. Xavier didn't blend in with the crowd. In a sea of pirates, he was simply Xavier.

Ophelia nudged me. "You should go talk to him. You obviously want to."

"What? Who?"

"Xavier. He likes you."

"No."

"He does. Trust me. I'm an expert at these kinds of things. If you don't want him, though, I'll be happy to take him off your hands." She mewled like a kitten.

I looked back at Xavier, who was staring in our direction. A slight smile played at his lips, and a surge of excitement ran through me. But then his gaze shifted—just a hair—and I knew he'd spotted Ophelia.

He might as well have stabbed me in the throat with one of those plastic swords. Even from a distance I could see his pupils dilate until his light brown irises were eclipsed. His lids grew heavy, and his slight smile broadened.

I popped out of my seat like a jack-in-the-box and threw my napkin onto the table. "I need to use the ladies' room!"

As I rushed across the dining room the sound of Jane's question, "Want me to come with you?" disappeared into the din of the party.

I bypassed the restrooms and headed for the observation deck. Because most people were at the pirate night party, Azure Lounge was closed, and the observation deck was empty of passengers.

I felt alone in a way I hadn't for quite some time. Isolated. Not just literally but figuratively as well.

Being at the front of the ship, the observation deck had windows to protect from the headwinds, but nonetheless it was still pretty windy. My pirate smock was no match for the open air of the Gulf of Mexico at twenty knots.

Come on, Charlotte, get yourself together. I shook my head like I could shake loose whatever had me feeling so unsettled.

A waft of smoke drifted into my nostrils. I scanned the area but couldn't find the source. Perhaps it came from the deck above me.

How annoying. I'd come outside for fresh air and now I was ingesting pollutants. I hated the smell, and it made me nauseous.

My stomach churned like it was filled with sour milk.

I guess I had more thoughts and emotions about Jane and Emmett than I'd been willing to admit. And the murders, of course. I could never shake that nagging feeling of something undone while a murder remained unsolved.

Xavier was a category unto himself, one I hadn't allowed myself to delve too deeply.

And then there was Xavier and Ophelia, whatever that meant. So he noticed she was pretty. Who hadn't? That didn't mean he was going to fall in love with her.

And even if he did, what business was it of mine? We were friends…sort of. Come to think of it, I couldn't be sure he even saw me as a friend. He was friendly, most of the time, but the truth was, he had a job to do, and I was merely a passenger. Half the time he seemed irritated that I was interfering with his job.

I was only trying to help.

"I know."

I whipped around. "What did you say?"

Xavier gave me an odd look. "I said I know you are only trying to help."

Crap. How much of that had I said out loud? How

much had he heard? "How long have you been standing there?"

"Not long. I came to check on you. You seem to be waging some sort of battle within yourself."

"You could say that."

A gust of wind ruffled his hair. "Perhaps we could finish this conversation inside?"

I nodded and followed him into the dim Azure Lounge. "I suppose you know Luke."

He leaned against a booth. "I do."

"That has to stress you out, having one of the ship's owners onboard while two murders have occurred and the killer has yet to be caught."

"It is indeed a concern."

"I've never met him before. Has he been on other sailings?"

Xavier rubbed his chin. "Not many. After the sailing to Yokohama and all that transpired, he informed me he would be making random checks. This is the second, I believe, since then. He was on the sailing to Sri Lanka. You skipped that one. You and Jane were back in Seattle visiting your nephew. Speaking of Jane, I cannot help but notice some tension between you."

"Is it that obvious?"

"It has been to me."

"We just haven't been on the same page this whole trip."

"I do hope my admonition that you not share information pertaining to the investigation with her has not exacerbated the rift."

If I shared with Xavier the information I'd learned about Emmett's wife and his unhinged crusade against Alexander and other people he suspected of being Rougarou, would it make a difference? More than likely Emmett was still high on Xavier's suspect list, and if Jane discovered I'd gone to him about my growing suspicions, she might never speak to me again. A cautious approach to the conversation was best.

"I think part of it is, I don't particularly care for Emmett, and she's been his biggest fan since college, feels he can do no wrong. Other than his love of Faulkner, of course. Which is, ironically, how she ended up reconnecting with him. And then he decided at the last minute to come on this cruise and—"

"That is incorrect."

"What is incorrect?"

"That his decision to come aboard was at the last minute."

"What do you mean? He booked it twenty-four hours before departure."

"This is not true. His berth was reserved more than four weeks ago."

"That can't be."

"But it is."

"Four weeks?" My chest tightened. "That was around the time it was announced Canailles Nous would be performing!"

"That sounds right."

"Oh my gosh." I buried my face in my hands. "She doesn't know that."

"Doesn't know what?" Jane stood in the doorway to the lounge.

"Oh, uh." I gave Xavier a look that I hoped said *help me!*

"Did I interrupt something?"

"*Bonsoir*, Madame Cobb. No, you did not interrupt. I was informing Madame McLaughlin that initial forensic testing on Ophelia Thibodeaux's hands for gunpowder residue came up negative."

Good save. "And I was saying she isn't aware of that yet."

Despite her skeptical look, she didn't challenge the narrative we'd concocted. "So, what does that mean? Couldn't she have washed it off before you tested her?"

"Yes, this is true. Also, the time that had elapsed can be a factor."

Jane waved her hand. "Then it's inconclusive."

"She did get a threatening note," I said.

"Could have been a red herring. Maybe you should tell her, though. About the negative gunpowder test. If she's the killer, she might think she's gotten away with it and make a mistake."

"Good point." I didn't believe Ophelia was the killer, but it was imperative Jane didn't suspect Emmett was *numero uno* on my list.

On the other hand, how could I protect her—and how could she protect herself—if she didn't know? My silence opened the door for the fox to get into the henhouse. What could I say or do that might cause Jane to doubt him on her own? If she believed it was her idea, she wouldn't get angry at me for interfering.

"Let's go back to the party. I don't want to miss the sword fight."

Xavier scrutinized my face. "Are you certain there isn't more you would like to discuss?"

Did he mean about the case or his obvious attraction to Ophelia? Either way, the answer was *no*. "I need another rum punch." I closed my right eye and swung my fist sideways. "Arrrr. Get it? I'm a pirate."

He blinked at me.

"Let's all pretend that didn't just happen," Jane said. "Come on, Char. Or should I call you Charrrr?" She patted me on the shoulder as I passed her.

"Your pity isn't helpful or necessary," I mumbled in defense of my buccaneer impression.

The dining room was in full revelry when we returned. Tropical rum cocktails featuring pineapple and coconut were being consumed at an alarming rate, made more so by the fact within minutes actors would be prancing around the room brandishing swords. Granted, they were likely to be props from some third-rate dinner theater production, but still, one could get injured if they were three sheets to the wind and accidentally wandered into a skirmish.

Xavier and I parted ways so that he could resume his watchman duties.

Victor and Luke were huddled over a tall blue beverage with two straws for sharing. Three empty glasses in front of them indicated I'd either been gone longer than I realized or they were drinking faster. It must have been delicious, regardless.

I needed to get me one of those. I glanced over at the bar in hopes of catching Hawk's eye, but he was nowhere to be found. Tricorn hats collided as impatient patrons jostled for position to place an order with Egan, who worked the crowd with flair.

Emmett stirred his drink and stared at Ophelia like he was contemplating ordering her to walk the plank.

She, of course, was oblivious to any negative attention and was, at that moment, propping up a slurring Percy as he declared her the most beautiful woman in the world.

She condescendingly patted his back. "I know, darlin'. I know."

"Where's Heath?"

Percy raised his head to look at me. He waited for his eyes to focus before answering. "I thought he was with you."

"Me? Why would he be with me?"

"Becaaaause..." He huffed. "He followed you out of here. I thought maybe you two were meetin' for a rendez-vous. I hear you've been hanging out in his suite."

I glared at Ophelia for leaking that information, but she couldn't see my expression over Percy's giant head.

She pushed his face away with her hand. "Perce, you're invading my personal space, and you smell like a Bourbon Street alley on Ash Wednesday."

"I wasn't following you." The denial whispered into my ear caused a shiver to run down my neck and arms.

I flung around to find myself staring into the unreadable eyes of Heath Hubbard. "Good to know."

Maybe he hadn't been following me, but his cigarette smoke that blew onto the observation deck said otherwise.

Chapter Twenty-One

"LADIES AND GENTLEMEN!" Egan yelled into the microphone. "Are you ready for a swashbucklin' good time?"

The crowd cheered.

"Put yer hands together for—"

Hawk rushed up to him, waving his hands. They exchanged a few words, and Egan gave Hawk a few pointed looks before handing over the mic.

"Sorry about that, everyone! I got caught up in a project, but I'm here now. Thank you to Egan for stepping in."

Egan made a dismissive gesture and stomped back to the bar where a dozen people began calling orders at him.

"Let's kick this party into high gear. Are you all ready to have a *plun*derful night?"

As many people groaned as laughed.

"Oh, look. There's our beloved yoga instructor, Kyrie Dawn, or as her friends call her, K.D. If you haven't taken one of her classes yet, you're missing out. K.D. wave so everyone knows who you are!"

Kyrie Dawn pretended to play coy, fluttering her hands in front of her face in faux humility, before waving both hands like a beauty pageant contestant.

"K.D., do you know why retired pirates looove yoga?"

She laughed. "No, but I'll bet you're about to tell us, Hawk!"

"It's because of all the ex-sailing!"

A smattering of light chuckles indicated his joke hadn't landed.

"You know, ex-*haling*, ex-*sailing*?"

One person slow clapped.

"Try again!" yelled someone from the back.

Pink crept up Hawk's neck. "Oh, you didn't like that one? Okay, well, I'll find one you like...*schooner* or later." He gave a dramatic wink.

Someone pelted him with a paper umbrella.

"Ow! Now, that's not nice."

"These jokes aren't nice! They're tarrrrrible!" someone else called.

"He's about to have a mutiny on his hands," I whispered to Jane.

"He deserves it. These are some of the worst puns I've ever heard—and I taught a summer creative writing class for nine-year-olds.

"All right, without further ado, mateys, put your hands together for the Pirates of the *Thalassophile*!"

In through the doors of the dining room came a ragtag bunch of pirates, making a racket and waving guns and swords in the air.

"Where'd they get these guys—hanging around the dock at the Port of New Orleans looking for tourists to pickpocket?" Jane murmured.

"I suppose they've managed realistic costumes if they look like actual thieves," I said.

"I need another drink."

As Jane got to her feet, Emmett jumped up with her.

"I've got it, but thank you." She gently pressed him back into his seat.

She'd made her way across the floor when suddenly one of the pirates grabbed her and put a sword against her chest.

Emmett jumped to his feet once more.

"Where do ye think ye be going?" The man's pirate dialect was surprisingly convincing.

Jane gurgled. "Let me go. I have no interest in being part of the show."

"Did you all hear that? We got a rhymer here!"

Someone in the crowd at the bar whooped.

I glanced at Xavier, who was on high alert but hadn't yet intervened.

What was he waiting for? This felt sinister.

"Let. Me. Go." Jane elbowed the man in the stomach, causing him to double over and release her in the process. "Never put your hands on a woman." She marched over to the bar.

The crowd erupted into cheers, and, after a brief hesitation, the pirate bowed as if it had all been planned.

I knew better. Even from a distance Jane's shaking hands were visible. She leaned in to whisper something to Hawk, and he nodded.

As he moved away, she sneezed three times.

The pirates moved around the crowd, making theatrical threats to partygoers. Most seemed to be enjoying it a lot more than Jane had. Of course, no one else had a sword put to their throat either.

She returned and set her drink down.

"Are you okay?" Emmett's worry seemed genuine.

"I'm fine." She clenched her jaw and then sneezed once more.

"What's with all the sneezing?" I asked.

She wriggled her nose. "Must have been a gin and tonic up at the bar."

I still didn't buy the idea that smelling gin would cause her to sneeze, but it didn't seem the appropriate time to argue the point.

As the pirates marauded around the room, harassing people along the way, I observed Emmett doting over Jane.

How to reconcile this picture with the unhinged grieving husband? He was caretaking for Jane, so that fit with the devoted husband vibe, someone who, upon losing their spouse, might become overprotective in their next relationship.

But at the same time, it didn't make sense that the kind of person who obsessed about hunting down their spouse's killer to the point of murdering two people in revenge could also be so gentle and loving. He'd lied about when he'd booked the cruise, so perhaps he was a better actor than I'd given him credit for.

Still, I needed to protect Jane without her realizing what I was doing. She had to think any suspicions she developed about Emmett were her idea or she'd be resistant to them. Maybe even defiant. Where to start?

"Emmett," I began. "Do you have kids?"

Jane cut her gaze to mine, and I attempted a wide-eyed innocent expression in response.

"Unfortunately, I did not. My wife—rest her soul—and I were hoping to enlarge our family, but we waited and then…and then she was gone."

Jane glared at me, and I shrugged like Urkel asking *did I do that?*

She patted his hand. "You don't need to talk about it."

Ophelia leaned forward, causing her cleavage to spill out of her bustier even more than it already was. "I've found it's good to talk about feelings and grief. Otherwise, they get stuck. Right here." She wedged her fingers into the narrow gap between her breasts.

Every male at the table—including Victor and Luke—were mesmerized by the sight.

Jane clucked her tongue. "Emmett."

He dragged his attention away from Ophelia's bosom and back to Jane's face. "Hmm?"

"I mean it. You don't owe anyone any explanations." She threw a scowl my direction.

He took a deep inhale. "You know, maybe it's time I did talk about it. Lawd knows it hasn't done me much good keeping it all inside."

"Let it all out," purred Ophelia.

Emmett nodded at her with that wistful smile of a cartoon animal being lured by their favorite food.

Jane kicked me under the table, but I knew better than to react. I reached down to rub my shin but swallowed my yelp.

Victor and Luke leaned in to hear Emmett's story. Heath remained in his cool, reclined position. Percy was slumped facedown on the table.

Emmett tore tiny pieces from his paper cocktail napkin. "My wife—Marie—was a breath of fresh air infused into my very stale life. I'd been alone for some time, focused solely on my career. The path to a tenured professorship isn't an easy one. I wasn't looking for her; she just blew into my world and turned it upside down. In the very best possible way. She was quite a bit younger than me and a grad student at Tulane when we met."

Victor scrunched his nose like he smelled something unpleasant. "You were her professor?"

Emmett vigorously shook his head. "No, she was getting her masters in river-coastal science. She was an environmentalist who felt most like herself outdoors. I'm the complete opposite. An ideal day for me would be sitting in the library doing research or reading a great book."

"Me too." Jane gave him an encouraging smile.

While Jane had been a librarian, I wouldn't have ever called her a recluse or someone who preferred the indoors. She'd always lived an active life, which was one of the reasons she made a good companion for me.

"We were married for twelve years. We didn't start discussing children until she turned thirty-five. It was like one day she woke up and realized the opportunity was slipping away. Turns out she was right. Two miscarriages, several rounds of IVF, and no baby. We made the decision to try once more. She was thirty-nine. It would either work or it wouldn't."

Jane placed her hand over Emmett's. "And it didn't, I'm assuming."

His breath was ragged. "It did. She was thirteen weeks along when she...when she died."

I gasped. Emmett's newspaper article quote had been, *When I find out who did this to them, I'm going to shoot a silver bullet through their black heart.* I'd noticed he'd said *them* instead of *her* but didn't give it much thought. His threat had been my focus, not the word *them*. It wasn't a typo. It was an even greater tragedy than I'd known.

It also made his motive for revenge even stronger.

Jane whimpered, "Oh, Em, I'm so sorry."

She rubbed his back, and he flinched at her touch. She pulled her hand away.

Ophelia shook her head. "Mr. Guidry, I cannot even imagine how difficult that must have been for you. May I ask, how did Marie pass away? She was so young."

He clenched and unclenched his jaw several times. "She was attacked on her morning walk."

"Oh my. Robbery?" Ophelia knit her eyebrows together.

He gave a mirthless laugh. "Ha. No, that I could make sense of. It was an...animal attack."

Jane shifted in her seat. Then she shifted back again.

My plan was working. She was uncomfortable with the direction the conversation was going. So why did I feel so terrible about instigating it?

Percy popped his head up from the table. "Animal attack? Near your home? What kind of animal? How did it happen?"

Ophelia patted Percy's shoulder. "Hey, now. Let's not bombard him with questions about such a sensitive topic."

"Sorry." Percy rested his chin on his forearm. "I've just never heard of such a thing happening in real life."

Emmett swallowed. "Marie liked to walk in the Barataria Preserve."

"Isn't that inside Jean Lafitte Park?" asked Victor.

Emmett nodded. "Our house is in Kenner. She liked to start her walks along Bayou Coquille just as the sun was rising."

Victor leaned toward Luke. "It's a swamp."

"So, was it a croc attack?" Luke asked. "Or, I guess you all have gators here, not crocs."

"We have crocs around here," I said. "Usually shuffling around the pool right before water aerobics." I giggled at my own joke. I was the only one.

Luke, confused, turned to Victor, who shook his head—presumably in secondhand embarrassment for me. "She's referring to the waterproof shoes with the holes in them."

Luke's eyes lit up. "Ah! The rubber clogs. Clever."

Finally, a chuckle. I'd take it.

Jane was stiff beside me.

"You, okay?"

Silence.

Great, now she wasn't speaking to me. I thought I had

deftly maneuvered us into the territory where Emmett would reveal his motive without overplaying my hand, but she'd seen right through the ploy.

"No," Emmett said. "Not alligator." He scanned the table like he was judging how we all might receive what he was about to say. "Rougarou."

Once again Percy's head popped up. "Rougarou! As in werewolf? You believe your wife and child were killed by a werewolf?"

"I do." He didn't even hesitate. He didn't appear in any way reticent about making the declaration. He tipped his chin in the air in defiance of anyone's forthcoming argument.

Jane exhaled and her shoulders slumped. It almost seemed like she'd been holding her breath in anticipation of this announcement, perhaps hoping it might never come, but when it did, she was resigned to it.

Instead of a sense of triumph, guilt washed over me.

What was I doing?

If Emmett had killed Alexander to avenge the death of his wife and child, he'd be found out sooner or later. And if he hadn't, what difference did it make if he believed they'd been killed by a legendary creature? All I'd managed to do with my meddling was rip the scab off his wound and put a wedge between Jane and me.

I didn't blame her when she turned on me with a fiery gaze.

"Jane," I whispered. "I didn't mean to—"

She pushed out her chair and jumped to her feet, startling the pirate who was sneaking up behind her.

The withering glare she cast my way before storming out of the dining room said it all.

She was beyond angry with me.

I'd damaged our relationship.

Possibly beyond repair.

Chapter Twenty-Two

I FOUND JANE in her room packing. Her pirate braid extensions swung wildly around her head as she grabbed items from the drawer and stuffed them into a suitcase. Her smoky eye makeup had smeared so much she reminded me of a rabid raccoon.

"What are you doing?"

"What does it look like?" She threw a blouse into her bag. "I'm leaving."

"Where are you going?"

"I'm going to stay with Emmett."

"Jane—"

She waved her underwear at me. "You don't get a say in this."

"You heard him. He believes a Rougarou killed his wife and child. He's obsessed with finding what he believes is the real killer. He thought Alexander St. Jacques was descended from a family of purported Rougarou. I found articles this afternoon talking about how he wanted to shoot them through the heart with a silver bullet and—"

"Stop it!" Her arms sagged at her side. "Just stop it."

"I'm trying to protect you."

"I'm older than you. I'm in my sixtieth decade of life, much of which I've lived two states away from you, and I've done just fine without your protection, thank you very much."

"You have to admit it's concerning. This fixation he has. The inability to move past his wife's death and live in the real world. At best, it's not healthy. At worst..."

Her pointed stare cut through me. "So now you're the expert on mitigating grief? You, who would still be sulking in her giant lonely mansion if it weren't for me dragging you out of that pathetic existence and into a new life of global adventure on the high seas? Give me a break, Charlotte. You may have convinced yourself you've dealt with all your baggage from your dysfunctional marriage to Gabe and the embarrassing circumstances of his death, but I know better."

Ouch. "I understand that you're unhappy with me right now, but that's below the belt."

"You mean like repeatedly pestering a widower about the circumstances surrounding his wife's death?"

"I didn't pester him. I had one conversation about it, and he wouldn't talk about it. He was all weird and cagey and enigmatic."

"It wasn't one conversation. It was tonight too. And before you go trying to convince me that's not what you were doing, save it. I'm not buying what you're selling." She closed her eyes briefly. "You keep pushing him into talking when clearly, he doesn't want to talk about it. Did it occur to you that it's simply too painful?"

"Of course. That's why I backed off. But Jane, there are

things I haven't told you. Things you should know about him. Xavier wouldn't let me tell you—"

Her sharp eyes cut to mine. "So you've been keeping secrets from me too?" Her bitter laugh echoed off the wall. "I'm your *sister*. How could you keep things from me like this?"

"I understand why you're upset—"

"Upset? I'm not upset. I'm done."

"Jane, look, I really believe he's bad news. You should know that I found out tonight that Emmett—"

She held up her hand. "Enough! What part of *stop* do you not understand? I don't want to hear any more about it. I get it, Char. You're jealous that I have someone who wants to be with me and all you've got is an unrequited crush on Xavier."

"I don't—"

"Seriously, I can't take any more from you." She closed the suitcase and zipped it. "Please, just leave me alone. And Emmett too." There was a coldness to her voice, a finality that chilled me to my core.

I'd known her my entire life, and I knew what that meant. It didn't bode well for our relationship. When Jane hit the wall with someone, when she felt they'd crossed her boundaries one time too many, they might as well be dead to her. She took grudge-holding to the next level.

"I'm only trying to get to the bottom of these murders." My voice shook. Desperation to get her to see my point of view overtook me. "You have to know that's my reason for all of this. I'm not doing it to hurt you. If I can prove who did this, it will be better for everyone."

"You know what, Charlotte? You do that. You go do your investigation"—she used air quotes—"and Emmett and I will conduct our own. This arrangement"—she waved her hand in the air—"It's no longer working for me."

With that, Jane stormed out of the home we shared together.

I sat on her bed and cried until I fell asleep.

⚓

I WOKE TO the sound of the doorbell and a pounding on the cabin door. I checked my phone, which had fallen onto the floor next to Jane's bed. Several missed calls and texts. I'd been asleep for forty-five minutes.

I ambled down the hall and peeked through the peephole before opening the door.

"Pike? What are you doing here?"

"Xavier sent me to check on you. He's still at the event, but he said he saw you and your sister leave in a hurry, and then you weren't answering your phone. He was worried."

I held up my phone and looked again at the missed calls and texts. Most of them were from Xavier.

"Wow. You aren't kidding. Three missed calls and ten texts."

Pike shifted from foot to foot. "You, uh, look like you're having a rough night."

I whirled to face my reflection in the mirror. Worse than I expected. My hair was going in several directions, my outfit was askew, and my makeup had morphed from what Ophelia had dubbed sensual pirate as she'd applied it on my eyes to post-frat party walk of shame or deeply depressed clown.

I attempted to rub the mascara and eyeliner from under my eyes but only managed to make it worse.

I turned back to face Pike. "Thanks for checking on me. As you can see, I'm alive. Jane isn't here. I don't—" My voice hitched. "I don't know where she is. Probably at Emmett's cabin."

"I saw her return without you. She went up to Mr. Guidry, grabbed him by the arm, and dragged him out of the party."

"Well, then. There you have it."

He observed me for a moment. "Are you sure you're okay?"

"I never claimed to be okay. I said I'm alive. You can report that back to Xavier."

"I'll text him. I'm off shift. The party's winding down, but he's planning to stay until it's all cleared out."

"Okay. I appreciate it, Pike."

"For sure, Charlotte. Hope…hope you feel better soon. G'nite."

"Night." I shut the door and clicked the lock.

Even though there were many times I was home while Jane was out somewhere on the ship, the suite had never felt so empty as it did in that moment.

I felt empty too. Depleted. And yet there was an incongruous heaviness weighing me down.

What was I supposed to do now? My nap had taken the

off, and I was wide awake. The fight with Jane had left me agitated. I felt like pacing, but what good would that do?

I needed to talk to Xavier.

But certainly not in my current condition.

I washed my face, brushed my hair and teeth, and changed into a pair of leggings and a T-shirt with a picture of Frog and Toad, the children's book characters I'd loved since I was a child. It seemed appropriate for the circumstances.

Jane, as a new reader, had often practiced by reading the picture books to me at bedtime. She joked that I was Frog and she was Toad, because Frog always looked on the bright side of things like I did, and Toad was a little grumpy. Jane said being the big sister meant having more responsibilities, and it was easier to get grumpy.

The truth was, she was more the optimist of the two of us. She was the one who wouldn't let me wallow after I'd been jilted at the prom, dragging me out of bed and down to the ferry docks to catch a boat to the Olympic peninsula for a grueling hike on Hurricane Ridge. I'd whined the whole way, but the truth was it turned out to be exactly what I needed to clear my head and realize no dumb boy was worth throwing my life away.

Ironic.

I swiped some gloss across my lips and examined the result of my efforts.

Not bad.

I felt more like myself with the minimal effort rather than the elaborate and dramatic makeup I'd been wearing earlier.

I took the elevator up two floors. No one was waiting when I exited. Odd. Normally, even at this time of night, people were coming and going at Azure Lounge, but it had remained closed for the night.

The party had wound down. No more merengue band playing. No more roving pirates. No more cocktail tricks. What remained were streamers, plastic swords, a partially deflated plastic palm tree, and balloons scattered across the dance floor. The lights were still dim as staff swept and wiped tables.

"Hey," I said to Haimi. "Why are you cleaning in the dark?"

She looked up at the ceiling and laughed. "I have no idea. I started picking up trash when people were still dancing and just kept going."

"I'll turn them on. Where's the switch?"

"Over there." She pointed at a panel near the entrance.

I flipped the switch. "Let there be light!" I swirled around in dramatic fashion with my arms over my head.

There were scenes I'd watched in movies where someone turned on the lights and cockroaches scattered. This moment felt like that. Only the creatures scattering were Ophelia Thibodeaux and Xavier Mesnier, who'd been huddled in a dark corner of the room. In an instant, they pulled away from each other like they'd been zapped.

Kind of like my heart.

Chapter Twenty-Three

I'D HAD A few surreal moments in my life. The kind of moments where my eyes saw something or my ears heard something that my mind couldn't compute.

A moment like two police officers standing on my doorstep telling me my husband was dead, but his girlfriend and their child had survived the accident, for example.

They were the moments where you wondered if you were asleep and having a nightmare. A nightmare, of course, from which you couldn't ever awaken.

Where reality was hazy and uncertain.

It was that brief moment between ignorance and the aching truth seeping into every part of your being. That moment before you couldn't escape the pain, no matter what you did, when it hadn't yet penetrated your protective walls but instead sat buzzing on the surface of your heart like it was coated in Teflon.

It wasn't, of course. Coated in Teflon. I often wished it was.

This was one of those moments.

Not that spotting Xavier canoodling with Ophelia was to the level of the death of a spouse or the subsequent revelation of his betrayal, but nonetheless it felt surprisingly familiar.

Typically, I was a freezer in the fight-flight-freeze response, like an ostrich. This time, though, after a brief panic I turned on my heel and hoofed it out of the dining room.

The ostrich was flying.

Xavier called after me, but I was on the move. I couldn't face him. I couldn't look in his eyes and see pity. I needed to escape. I needed to hide.

The observation deck was out. It would be the first place he'd look. I flung open the door to the stairwell. Up or down? Footsteps climbing a few floors below me cemented my decision. Up it was.

Using the handrail to take two steps at a time, I was winded by the time I exited on the top floor, Kalispera, and out onto the sundeck. Technically, at that exact moment, it was a moon deck under the waning gibbous.

Jane had been begging me to join her on the treadmills in the gym for months, but I'd been avoiding it. I regretted that as I tried to catch my breath.

It was only after my breathing returned to normal that I contemplated my predicament.

Not the Xavier/Ophelia predicament. The predicament of being alone at night on the top deck of a giant cruise ship with a murderer roaming around. I'd previously run into one in this exact spot, not to mention a corpse. Or was it two?

Regardless, probably not the wisest choice.

Too late now. I needed to wait to return downstairs if I were to avoid Xavier and his consolatory gaze.

Poor Charlotte McLaughlin. Always runner-up, even in

her own marriage. Even when she was the only one competing.

Then there was Ophelia. She'd expected to spend the night in my suite. She didn't have a key. Xavier had insisted she shouldn't stay in her own suite after the threatening note.

He wouldn't offer for her to stay with him, would he?

An involuntary shiver racked my body. It wasn't just from the gulf breeze.

The elevator dinged. Someone was coming.

I ducked behind the snack bar and crouched beneath the counter.

What was I doing? This was ridiculous. I was a grown woman hiding from embarrassment. That was way more embarrassing than having a crush reject me for one of the most beautiful women in the world.

As I contemplated the series of events and poor life choices that had led me to this undignified moment, a waft of smoke drifted into my nostrils.

Two voices began speaking.

It wasn't Xavier and Ophelia as I'd expected.

It was Victor and Heath.

"You really should quit, you know?" Victor's tone held more kindness than disapproval. "Our friends have been dropping like flies. I need you to stay healthy."

"What, first I gotta give up all the babes, now I gotta give up cigs? Naw, man. If I have to give up all my vices, I might as well be dead."

"One typically gives up dating other people when married. Kind of part of the deal. And by the way, I know you too well to believe you've given 'em all up."

Heath chuckled. "Yeah, yeah. So, what did you want to talk to me about?"

"This." A paper rustled in the breeze.

"Yeah, I got one too. What of it?"

"You're not at all concerned that someone is targeting members of Canailles Nous?"

"Vic, if I worried about every psychopath fan, I'd never sleep at night."

"This isn't just a threat. They've already shown they're willing to act on it."

Heath blew out a long breath of smoke, which filled my hiding space. I held my breath in hopes I wouldn't start coughing and give away my presence.

"Look, man. I get it. You're freaked out."

"The real question is, why aren't you freaked out?"

"Because I am nearly seventy years old. I've lived a long, good life, even longer than I should have. Do you know what the life expectancy is for cats who grew up in my neighborhood?"

"Now, how would I know that?"

"You wouldn't. You grew up in Lakewood, the most affluent part of N'awlins. I grew up in Hollygrove. It's 66.7, by the way."

"What?" Victor asked.

"Life expectancy. I shoulda been dead two years ago. I'm not going to run around like a cat on hot bricks. If it's my time, then it's my time."

Victor clucked his tongue. "I don't get you, man. For

...o's got so many years walking this earth, you ... to have learned a damn thing."

...h gave another long exhale, followed by smoke up my nostrils. "I've learned a whole lot. I've learned the only one who's gonna look out for me is me. I've learned people are selfish, and the one thing you can always rely on is for them to be unreliable."

"That's not fair. I've always been here for you, man." The hurt in Victor's voice was palpable.

"I'm not talking about you." Heath's words hung heavy in the air.

"We were all disappointed by Alex." Victor's voice was barely audible above the sound of the ship moving through the water. "And Webb, you know how he was. He just wanted everyone to do the right thing."

"Damn Boy Scout. He never understood that loyalty and doing the quote unquote right thing were sometimes mutually exclusive."

I covered my mouth. This was the first indication of any bad blood between Webster Powell and, well, anyone. Had Webster betrayed Heath to stay in Alexander's good graces? Heath's motive was rapidly solidifying into something substantial and viable—not just for Alexander's murder but for Webster's as well.

Another waft of smoke invaded my hiding spot and caught the back of my throat. The tickle caused me to emit a high-pitched wheeze.

"What was that?" Heath said.

I held my breath and said a prayer.

"It's nothing. Just the engines. Look, there's just four of us left. We still have a lot to accomplish. Together."

Heath responded with a raspy guffaw. "Together. I will say this, though."

"Yeah?"

"Sympathy is a strong catalyst for support."

"What are you getting at?"

Another long blow of smoke. "We've lost two members of our group in tragic circumstances. Seems like we've been presented a rare opportunity to translate that sympathy into our next recording contract."

"That's cold, man."

"No, Vic, that's business."

⚓

I RETURNED TO my dark and empty suite exhausted and weighed down by the day's events. The whole week had been a disaster.

Two men were dead, Xavier may have gotten romantically involved with one of the murder suspects, and Jane wasn't speaking to me.

The situation with Jane was beyond a disaster. It was an existential crisis.

I flopped onto my bed and stared at the ceiling.

Maybe I'd been wrong about Emmett. Maybe he was just a grieving husband with a penchant for mythology. Maybe Heath was the killer and I'd wrecked my relationship with Jane for no reason.

But it wasn't for no reason. Emmett was dangerous for her. Even if he weren't the murderer, his obsession with the Rougarou legend proved he was still mired in grief for his wife. Even though things weren't great between Gabe and me when he died, I still wasn't sure I was ready to start dating again.

Not that it mattered. Jane was going to do what she was going to do. I had two options: make amends and bite my tongue when it came to my thoughts and feelings about Emmett, allowing him to reveal his true character or stand my ground even if it meant losing my relationship with my sister. Permanently.

It was a no-brainer. If Emmett were the killer, that information would reveal itself. What good would it do Jane for me to push the issue if it meant I weren't there for her in case that happened?

If something happened to my sister with all this ickiness between us, how would I ever get over that? The answer: I wouldn't. I needed to suck it up and reconcile before it was too late. Gabe's sudden death should have been enough warning to never take a single breath for granted—mine or the people I care about.

My insistence on being right and bullying my way through our relationship had left me exactly where I deserved to be, which was alone. I hadn't considered Jane's feelings, not really. I'd wanted her to see things the way I did, and when she didn't, I forced the issue. I'd undermined her autonomy to make her own determinations about Emmett and to make her own decisions of what she wanted to do about it.

If the roles had been reversed, I'd have felt as frustrated as Jane. If it had been Xavier rather than Emmett and Jane had interfered, I'd have been furious.

Not that there was really any comparison. Clearly, Xavier saw me only as a friend at best. At worst, I was the Gladys Kravitz of the cruising world. The *Thalassophile*'s resident busybody, poking my nose where it didn't belong. A thorn in his side. The fly in his ointment. The sticky wicket in every case he investigated.

I flashed on the memory of Xavier huddled in the corner with Ophelia. Not only had I been horrified by the sight, flustered and confused, it had been uncomfortable witnessing a quiet moment of intimacy between them. But of course, he'd been entranced by her beauty, swept away by her charms. I wouldn't have expected otherwise. Hoped maybe, but never expected.

I needed to set my feelings about the Xavier and Ophelia situation aside and focus on the most important challenge I faced. A relationship with him beyond friendship was likely a lost cause. My relationship with Jane, however—and even more so her safety and well-being—needed to be my top priority.

The question was, how to go about it? A sudden about-face would bring nothing but suspicion and cynicism. Jane was way too smart for that. Groveling wouldn't work either.

Would she even give me the opportunity?

"Jane, we need to talk," I practiced out loud. No, that sounded like I was chastising her. "Janie, sweetie, I'm sorry I accused your new boyfriend of murdering two people. In my defense…" No, that wouldn't do.

I rolled myself in my comforter like a sushi roll. It made sense why mothers swaddled their newborns. Something about not being able to move my arms was surprisingly calming. For a moment it was bliss and I felt safe. Then the hot flash—followed by panic and claustrophobia—kicked in. I wrestled myself out of the cocoon and threw the bedding on the floor.

I pulled out my phone. It was well after midnight. It would have to wait until morning.

Morning. It seemed a lifetime away. How was I supposed to sleep while my soul was in turmoil? Nothing felt right in my world, and it would continue that way until I fixed this mess.

Chapter Twenty-Four

I HAD NO idea what time I finally fell asleep, but it was well after one in the morning. I'd tossed and turned, my brain shuffling through all possible ways to approach my conversation with Jane.

Ultimately, rehearsing a speech was the wrong way to go. Jane knew me too well. My approach needed to be authentic, my words genuine. We needed to connect on a heart-to-heart basis or it would make things worse between us.

I checked my phone. It was after nine. Zero missed calls or texts. No social media notifications. Twenty-three emails—all junk.

Even my sister-in-law Ronda—my brother Bernard's widow—had yet to tag me in her daily Facebook rant.

What kind of pariah woke up to no notifications from any human beings that weren't trying to sell them something? This kind of abandonment required some pretty serious self-evaluation and introspection.

Briefly, I wondered where Ophelia had spent the night, but I immediately brushed that thought away. No point in ruminating on things that would only give me indigestion.

I needed coffee.

Windsor Hadwin, in true butler style, brought a single serve French press. *Sure, pile on the fact I am alone, why don'tcha, Win?*

"*Et tu*, Windsor?"

"Madam?"

I gave a dismissive wave. "Never mind. I'm just having a bit of a pity party this morning."

"Does it have anything to do with the fact I just delivered coffee service to Madam Cobb and Mr. Guidry up on Santorini?"

I tapped the tip of my nose with my finger. "Bingo. Can't put anything past you."

"Part of the reason I am skilled at my job is that I am a keen observer. 'Tis the only way to anticipate the needs of the guests I am serving." He paused and gave a wry smile. "My therapist tells me I developed this skill as a young child. Narcissistic mother and all that."

"I'm sorry. That sounds difficult."

He poured coffee into a cup. "Life's greatest opportunities come from channeling our pain into motivation."

"Using your powers of observation for good instead of evil?"

"Perhaps. It has served me well."

I took a sip of coffee. "Speaking of powers of observation, can you tell me what kind of mood Jane was in this morning?"

He cocked his left brow in that way that said he was disappointed in me for even broaching the subject.

"I only ask because I have some making up to do, and I'd

like to know what I'm up against."

"I can only say that when I mentioned I was attending to you next, her demeanor shifted into, shall we say, less than warm and fuzzy."

A good night's sleep apparently hadn't helped my cause. I thanked Windsor for the information, despite it being the last thing I wanted to hear.

I texted Jane, asking if we could meet for breakfast to talk. I waited for twenty minutes without a response. I texted again, this time practically begging for an opportunity to make it up to her. Still, nothing.

I refused to accept this was the end of things. We'd had our tiffs in the past. We always got through them. She'd come around eventually. Wouldn't she?

One thing was certain, I wasn't going to solve these murders sitting in my robe in my room.

After my shower, I slapped on a minimal amount of makeup and left the suite with my hair still wet.

I took the elevator up two floors and marched into the dining room on a mission. Heath, Percy, and Ophelia were sitting at a table near the window.

I indicated the empty chair next to Heath. "May I?"

"Please, *cher*." He pulled out the chair and gestured for me to sit.

"How is everyone this morning?" I resisted looking at Ophelia for fear I might see something I didn't want to see. A romantic afterglow, for example. Or worse, a love bite.

Heath leaned back in his chair. "Awright. You?"

"To be honest, I've been better." I lifted my chin toward

Percy. "How about you? How's your head this morning? You had quite a lot to drink last night."

"I'm just fine. Slept like a baae-baee," Percy's deep voice rumbled.

Ophelia clicked her tongue. "Well, that makes one of us. Your snoring kept me up half the night."

I jerked my head in her direction. She hadn't spent the night with Xavier?

What were the chances the relief that washed over me wasn't visible on my face?

She pursed her lips. "Don't look so smug, Charlotte."

"I...I don't know what you mean."

She rolled her big brown eyes. "Right. As if you didn't throw a pout fit and run away so Xavier would chase you."

"Chase me?"

She huffed. "He hustled out of here so fast he practically left skid marks. Are you saying he didn't find you?"

How much did I want to reveal? "I didn't see him last night after I left the party."

"Hmph," she grunted.

Percy elbowed her. "Don't be rude, Fee. Charlotte has been doing her best to figure out what happened to Alex and Webb. You don't need to shade her just because you came across one man on this planet impervious to your charms."

Ophelia grabbed his face with her right hand and squeezed his cheeks. "Ohh, is little Percy-wercy jealous of Mr. security guard?"

Her disrespect of Xavier caused my hackles to rise. The man was French special forces, for goodness' sake.

Percy pulled his face out of her grasp. "Knock it off, Fee."

Ophelia's full mouth dropped into a pout. "Look, I think we need to focus on who sent these notes. It has to be the killer."

I was willing to set aside my annoyance with her to work together if that meant keeping Jane safe. "Probably. Do any of you have them with you?"

They all shook their heads.

Ophelia crossed her arms. "It's got to be that nutty professor, anyway. He's clearly got only one oar in the water."

"Perhaps, but I want to keep an open mind. We could really make a mess of things if we narrow in on the wrong man...or woman." I cocked a brow and gave her a look that I hoped conveyed I hadn't completely ruled her off the suspect list.

She must have received the message loud and clear, because her mouth fell open and she gave an indignant gasp. "You can't possibly still believe I had anything to do with this."

"Like I said. Open mind."

Ophelia's beautiful face transformed before my eyes. Her eyes narrowed, her brow furrowed, her nostrils flared, her mouth pursed, and her jaw hardened. She leaned forward and whispered in a tone typically reserved for parents threatening their children about what was going to happen once they were back at home and away from judging eyes.

"Who do you think you are? Just because you're some rich widow doesn't mean you're better than me." She gave a look of disgust mixed with pity. "I know you're jealous of me. You've been chasing Xavier for a year, and you've gotten nowhere. I come aboard and he's smitten right away. He only went after you last night because he felt sorry for you."

"Ophelia!" Percy pounded his fist on the table. "Stop it."

She sneered and sat back in her chair. "Come on, Percy, I'm just speaking the truth. Her husband cheated on her with that yoga instructor, she's making a fool of herself over a man who would have made a move on her by now if he were remotely interested, and her dumb spinster sister's fawning all over her old professor who, at the very least, is a creep who probably sexually harassed his female students, and at worst murdered Alex and Webb. Neither of them has what it takes to get and keep a man."

"You can say all you want about me, but leave Jane out of this. My husband may have been unfaithful, but my sister has always been there for me, since the day I was born. Maybe you don't know what it's like to have a ride-or-die, but I do, and her name is Jane Cobb."

"I—"

I leaned toward her. "I'm not finished. You may have external beauty that's fading by the minute, but my sister is a freaking goddess, and it starts within her golden soul. Her kindness and compassion are as deep as the ocean. Not to mention she's one of the smartest people I know." I leaned even farther, ignoring her squeal of protest. "I'll have you know; she skipped the second grade because she was so advanced she got bored. She had a four-point grade average and a perfect attendance record. She got full ride scholarship offers to the University of Washington, USC, and Berkely, all the while she was editor of the school paper and working at an animal shelter. She had to quit because she's allergic to dogs, but that's beside the point."

Ophelia opened her mouth to speak, but I jutted my finger in her face.

"And another thing. She never wanted to get married. She's turned down several marriage proposals over the years from *very* eligible bachelors. She likes her independence because she doesn't need a man to tell her what she's worth. If she believes Emmett is innocent, then she's got to have a darn good reason, and I'll take her side any day, any place, any time."

"Charlotte."

I jumped to my feet and loomed over Ophelia. "You'd be lucky to have Jane Cobb in your corner, whether it be for your one phone call on a trivia game show or because you've been arrested after a party in your dorm room got out of hand—"

"Charlotte."

"—or your husband has dropped dead of a heart attack and your whole world has been shredded to pieces. Jane is the kind of person to jump in the car or hop on a plane to be there for you. And she always has the right answer so she must be right about Em—"

"Charlotte!"

I whirled to face the person calling my name. "Jane!"

Her face was flushed, and tears were streaming down her face. She stood awkwardly, shifting from foot to foot. I had the sense she was battling between shaking me and hugging me.

Her posture was unsure, but her eyes said it all. I rushed toward her and flung my arms around her like we'd been estranged for years, not twelve hours.

It had felt much longer.

"I'm so sorry. I should have given you the benefit of the doubt. I just—"

"Shh. It's okay, Char." Her strangled words were punctuated by a hiccup. She gripped me tight.

"You didn't respond to my texts. I thought you didn't want to make up."

She released me and wiped her tears. "Hey, we're sisters. At the end of the day, we're all we've got, and we're all we need."

"What about Emmett?"

She smiled through watery eyes. "I like him, Char. And I don't think he's a killer."

I nodded. "Okay. That's enough for me."

"Oh, for the love of—" Ophelia stood and threw her napkin on the table. "I'd trust either of your judgments about as far as I could throw you." She eyed me up and down, presumably judging my weight. "Which wouldn't be far."

Jane started to lunge for her. Percy jumped up and blocked Ophelia from the attack. I put out my arm to stop Jane before she got ahold of Ophelia's throat.

"It's not worth it," I said. "Come on. We've got two murders to solve." I grabbed her arm and dragged her away from the potential melee.

Xavier blocked the exit, his legs spread shoulder-width apart and arms crossing his chest. "Morning, ladies. Perhaps you'd be so kind as to follow me down to the security office."

Chapter Twenty-Five

"ARE WE IN trouble?"

Xavier only indicated for Jane and me to sit in the chairs across from him as he sat at his desk.

"If it helps, Ophelia started it."

He blinked at me. "Started what?"

I glanced at Jane, who pulled her mouth to the left.

"I thought this was about the scuffle with Ophelia."

"Char was defending me."

He observed the two of us for a moment. "Perhaps we should discuss that at a later time. This is about Monsieur Guidry."

Jane blanched. "Did something happen to him? I've only been gone a little while."

"I am not aware of anything happening to him. However, I have received some information I find concerning in his background check."

Jane leaned forward. "Background check. What background check? I thought you didn't do a background check because he booked his trip right before we were supposed to leave."

"As I told Charlotte, he actually booked four weeks prior

to departure, but because he was vetted by the rental agency, I did not do the background check I normally would."

Jane's gaze was wide as she shook her head. "That can't be." She turned to me. "How long have you known this?"

"Not long. I tried to tell you last night, but you didn't want to hear it."

She swallowed. "Are you saying you found something nefarious in his past?"

He gave her a compassionate smile. I knew this smile well. It was the same one he gave me whenever the subject of Gabe came up.

"I would not call it nefarious. Necessarily. Something of note."

Her shoulders slumped with a sigh. "Just tell me. I can take it."

"Alexander St. Jacques filed a police report two weeks before our departure stating that he was being harassed by a man claiming he was a Rougarou."

Blerg.

"Let me guess." Jane toyed with her hands in her lap.

His grim expression said it all, but still he dropped the bomb. "The named defendant was Emmett Guidry. He also applied for a Louisiana abuse prevention order, but the case had yet to go to trial."

"Abuse? They didn't even know each other."

"I think that's just what they called the restraining order," I said. "Alexander must have feared Emmett might escalate the harassment. Even harm him."

Xavier shook his head. "Not Alexander. Monsieur

Guidry."

"Wait. What? Emmett was the one who filed the restraining order?"

Jane looked as shocked as I felt. "Why would he do that?"

Xavier picked up a paper from his desk. "The petition of Emmett Claude Guidry, a resident of full maturity of the parish of Jefferson, state of Louisiana, represents that one: the defendant is Alexander Marcel St. Jacques, a resident of full maturity of the parish of Orleans, state of Louisiana. Two: The defendant herein stalked, assaulted, and caused the death of the petitioner's wife, Marie Estelle Guidry, née Barrilleaux. Three: Petitioner further asserts the defendant is unable to control his violent impulses, putting not only petitioner at risk, but numerous others as well. Four: As a result of the defendant's irrational and dangerous behavior, petitioner is compelled to file this abuse protection order in Jefferson Parish. Petitioner seeks and is entitled to this temporary restraining order, restraining, enjoining, and prohibiting stated defendant from contacting the complainant except through the courts."

"This makes no sense." Jane rubbed her temples. "Why would Emmett seek a restraining order while knowing full well he'd booked a suite on the same cruise ship as Alexander and Canailles Nous two weeks prior?"

"She has a point."

He laid down the paper. "I am not certain that applying logic to this situation is useful."

"We should just ask him."

Jane jerked her head to look at me. "Have you lost your mind? We can't ask him that."

"Why not?"

"Be-because," she sputtered. "You just can't. It will devastate him to know I don't trust him."

Devastate seemed like a strong word considering they'd only reunited a week earlier. "Xavier can ask him. That's a reasonable question for the head of security to ask."

"I will consider it." He stared at me for a moment before turning his attention to Jane. "Madame Cobb, would you mind if I spoke with Madame McLaughlin alone?"

She narrowed her gaze. "I already know you've been sharing details with her about the case and not with me."

"This is not about the case." His mouth was set in a firm line.

I felt my heart drop through my stomach to my ankles.

"Oh." Jane glanced at me. "I guess I'll see you back at the suite?"

"Mm-hmm."

When the door shut behind her, I snuck a peek at him. His Mediterranean skin was sallow, and his eyes had dark circles and bags underneath them.

"What did you want to talk to me about?" My attempt at sounding casual failed.

"I could have sworn I saw you last night after the event was over, but when I went to look for you, you were nowhere to be found."

"Oh?" Dang it. My lower lip was trembling. I rubbed it, hoping either it would stop or at least keep him from noticing.

Instead, he stared directly at my mouth. I should have known nothing would get past him.

"*Oui.*" His stare lasered right through me.

"Oh, uh, I did come by briefly, but the party was over, so I took off."

His left brow arched. "Took off to where?"

I certainly wasn't going to tell him I'd been cowering under the snack bar up on the Kalispera deck because I'd seen him in an embrace with Ophelia. But then, if I didn't, how could I share what I'd overheard between Heath and Victor?

"Uh, well, I needed some fresh air."

"I checked the observation deck. All I found was my subordinate in an embrace with his date."

His subordinate? Date? "Oh! You mean Pike and Kyrie Dawn." I grimaced. "Glad I didn't run into them."

He tilted his head just slightly, still waiting for me to give him an answer. There was only so long I could play obtuse before he'd call me on it.

"I ended up on Kalispera, actually. I'm surprised you didn't see me on the security cameras."

A slight shift in his mouth revealed the horrible truth. He *had* known. He'd seen me crouch behind the counter. It was humiliating.

I clicked my tongue. "It's not nice to spy on people, you know. Doesn't exactly breed trust and intimacy."

His expression softened, as did his tone. "Is that what you are hoping for? To develop trust and…intimacy with me?"

I glanced at the door. It was too late to run. The conversation was happening whether I liked it or not.

I did have an ace up my sleeve, however. "When you were watching me, did you happen to notice I was not alone?"

He observed me, probably trying to decide whether he was going to let me off the hook or not. "I did," he said finally.

My stay was probably temporary, but I gladly took it. "Would you like to know what Heath and Victor were talking about?"

He said nothing. Maybe he hadn't let me off the hook. I certainly felt like a squirming worm or a flailing fish out of water.

"I think you're going to want to know. It pertains to the case."

He leaned back and crossed his arms, still silent.

"I'm not sure who initiated the conversation, but Heath's attitude was odd, to say the least."

"How so?"

"He was nonchalant."

"Regarding?" He shifted in his chair, antsy with my prolonged delivery.

The more irritated he was with me, the less likely we'd end up back at the part of the conversation I was avoiding.

"Regarding everything. The murders, the threatening notes, the risk to his life…actually, his life in general."

"Elaborate, *s'il vous plaît*."

"He talked about how he's lived a long and full life and outlived his life expectancy for someone who grew up in his neighborhood."

Xavier furrowed his brow. "Perhaps I do not understand what it is about this conversation you felt was suspicious or out of the ordinary. It is normal to contemplate one's mortality when loved ones die."

"I know that. Of course I know that. Me of all people," I snapped. "Sorry. That was uncalled for. I just mean it was almost as if he didn't fear death because he knows it isn't coming for him."

"Because he is the killer?"

"Exactly."

He rubbed his chin. "Perhaps. That is one interpretation."

"There's more."

"I am listening."

"They talked about Webster. Victor made a comment about Webster always wanting to do the right thing, and then Heath called Webster a Boy Scout but in a derogatory way. Like he resented that Webster was a rule follower. He said Webster didn't understand that loyalty and doing the supposed right thing were sometimes mutually exclusive concepts."

"And what did you take from this conversation?"

"It's motive for Webster's murder, don't you see?"

"I do not."

"Because first of all, I got the impression Webster may have aligned himself with Alexander. That may have brought some resentment from one or more of the members of Canailles Nous."

"That's plausible."

"Yes, but not only that, if Webster got wind of someone in the group doing something illegal—perhaps even Alexander's murder itself—it makes sense that the killer would have to take care of Webster as well."

He pondered my assertions for several minutes. I resisted the urge to continue making my case. Someone once told me the more a person overexplained, the less credibility their words held.

"You have given me quite a bit to consider."

"That's it?"

"Was there something else?"

"I'm becoming less convinced Emmett is the killer and more so that it's Heath."

"Based on what?"

"Based on what I just told you!"

It was infuriating. Why couldn't he see what I did?

"I am willing to concede the possibility. However, after receiving the information regarding the claims of harassment against Monsieur Guidry, I am afraid pursuing that will be my priority."

"Fine. Whatever. Can I at least go with you to question him?"

"Are you concerned I cannot be impartial or fair?"

"No, I just want to be there." I purposely didn't mention that I'd be reporting the entire conversation back to Jane.

He gave an exasperated sigh. "*D'accord.* Now is as good a

time as any."

Inside I did a triumphant dance. Hopefully, it didn't show on my face.

Xavier gave Lonnie instructions to call him on the radio if he was needed, and I followed him to the elevator.

As the bell dinged and the doors opened onto Santorini, a wild-eyed Hawk rushed toward the elevator and ran smack into me.

Chapter Twenty-Six

"Sorry, Charlotte!" Hawk backed away from the elevator.

I rubbed my tender nose. "You ran right into me. What's that all about? Where's the fire?"

Xavier held the elevator door open, causing it to buzz. "*Oui*, and what are you doing up here? I was under the impression you were preparing for tonight's festivities."

Hawk's eyes darted around, and his breathing was labored. "I was just checking on…someone. A passenger who told me they weren't feeling well. I'm headed back to the dining room now."

I didn't buy it, and judging by his expression, neither did Xavier, but instead of calling Hawk on his deception, he merely nodded. "Better get downstairs. I am told there is a lot of work to be done to prepare for the event." We exited the elevator as Hawk entered it.

He wagged his head. "Yes, sir."

As the doors closed, I caught a glimpse of Hawk exhaling in relief.

"That seemed suspicious." I hustled to keep up with Xavier's long stride.

"It's about seventeenth on my list of things that seem suspicious."

I elbowed him in the side. "Look who's got jokes."

He allowed himself a fleeting smile. We arrived at suite 812, and Xavier knocked on the door.

A disheveled Emmett answered. "Oh. Hello." He gave me a curious glance. "Charlotte? Is Jane okay?"

Xavier stepped forward. "Madame Cobb is perfectly fine. She is resting in her room. I would like to speak to you about something."

"That sounds ominous," Emmett said as he ushered us into the room. "Would either of you like some tea?"

"No thanks," I said.

Xavier sat on the sofa. "This won't take long."

"Good, because I'm supposed to hit the hot tub with Jane before dinner."

A tiny gurgle escaped my throat as I sat next to Xavier on the sofa.

Emmett stared at me. "You sure you don't want anything? Glass of water perhaps?"

"No, I'm good," I choked out.

Emmett returned his attention to Xavier. "Want to tell me what this is all about?"

Xavier rested his forearms on his thighs. His standard navy-blue sweater stretched across his broad back, and I resisted the urge to touch it to see what it felt like.

"It has come to my attention that you had a connection with Alexander St. Jacques prior to boarding the ship."

Emmett scanned Xavier's face, probably trying to determine how much he actually knew or whether he was bluffing.

Looking back, Gabe had done that with me often. It was only after his death that I realized how close I'd been to the truth.

"The Big Easy is a surprisingly small town."

Xavier crooked his head. "Monsieur, do not play games with me. You will not win. I promise you."

Emmett reared back. "No need to get testy. All right, all right. I suppose it was bound to come out sooner or later."

"It was all a ruse, wasn't it?"

Xavier grunted his disapproval at my outburst, but I was unfazed by it. I gripped the arm of the sofa.

Emmett cut his gaze to me. "What was a ruse?"

"Running into Jane and me. You were already booked on the cruise." Ruse Cruise. A laugh escaped me. Emmett and Xavier didn't seem to share my amusement.

Focus, Char.

"I mean, it wouldn't have been so difficult to find out who else would be onboard besides Alexander St. Jacques and Canailles Nous."

Emmett scoffed. "That's absolutely not true. They've got the owner and passenger lists locked up tighter than a gnat's a—"

"Answer my question," Xavier interrupted. "*S'il vous plaît.*"

"And mine!" I added.

Emmett sighed and held up his hands in mock surrender. "Okay. Okay. I did a search on the internet looking for any mention of Alexander or Canailles Nous. I came across the announcement about them playing the cruise, and when I looked up the ship, I discovered the company that runs this thing does an amazing job of protecting its clients."

"Then how did you—"

He gave me a look of exasperation. "I'm getting to that. The company protects the privacy of its clients, but the clients themselves do a pretty poor job of it. Do you know how many social media posts I came across with the hashtag *Thalassophile of the Seas*? Hundreds. Not only that, but they were also tagging themselves and their friends at every port of call. Including you, Charlotte. Jane too."

I sank into the cushions and glanced at Xavier. There was no doubt in my mind he was plotting to institute new safety protocols as it related to social media posts.

"Anyway," Emmett continued, "I saw Jane's name and I remembered her from UDub. She was one of the brightest students I had back then, and beautiful, too, although I kept my distance. Nothing could come of it while I was her professor. I wasn't tenured, and a scandal like that would have derailed my career before it even started." He stared intently at me. "I do care about her, Charlotte. I always have."

Not reassuring. Had he been tenured, would he have pursued her? I was pretty sure the answer was yes, and the whole idea nauseated me.

"She detests Faulkner!" I regretted my outburst as soon as I'd said it. Jane was going to kill me.

But Emmett only chuckled. "I know. She pretends she

doesn't, but any true Faulknerite can spot a fellow devotee and one who is not. And in an unexpected twist of fate, that's where I found her—in the Faulkner bookstore. It was serendipity. I'd just assumed we'd run into each other once we were on the ship. I really never expected to see her there."

Did that make it better or worse? I wasn't sure. And I wasn't sure how Jane would handle this news.

"I would like to return to the question of your previous encounters with Monsieur St. Jacques. I will save you the trouble of lying or evading. I am aware of the police report filed against you for harassment, as well as your petition for a restraining order."

"Yeah, what's up with that?"

Once again, Xavier cast an annoyed glance my way, but I was so close to finally getting answers, I couldn't help myself.

"As I told the table last night, Charlotte, my wife was killed in a vicious attack. It was such a senseless thing to happen. That morning, I woke up a happily married man with a baby on the way, and within hours I was a widower. I wasn't going to be a father. I was so much older than Marie, I believed I would be the one to go first. It never occurred to me she could be ripped from my life in such a drastic, horrific way. No warning. No chance to say goodbye. No chance to say I love you one last time."

"I understand that. Trust me. I understand it more than most. But this idea that a Rougarou was responsible—Emmett, you have to know that's crazy talk."

He jutted his chin. "You didn't see her. It was like nothing I'd ever witnessed. I had to identify her, but she was barely recognizable. Her clothes had been slashed, her face—" He choked on his next words. He swallowed and began again. "Did you have to identify your husband? It's a moment no one can prepare you to experience. In her case, it was particularly horrifying. Perhaps it was because I was already studying local myths and legends, but I'd read similar accounts of what the Rougarou could do to people."

Xavier cleared his throat. "Can you explain to me why it is you narrowed your list of suspects to Monsieur St. Jacques?"

"I had already been studying a book called *When the Hunter Becomes the Hunted: The Monstrous Life and Legend of Alexander St. Jacques*. It was about his ancestor's journey from Rougarou hunter to cursed man."

"Or so you thought," I said. "But it wasn't his ancestor."

He nodded. "Or so I thought. How was I to know he'd assumed an identity and wasn't even related?"

"However, you did not discover this fact until after his death. This makes you a primary suspect, as you believed at the time of the murder it was possible your wife's death was at his hands."

"But I didn't kill him. Even in my grief and anger I don't believe I have it in me to take the life of another. And then there's Jane."

"What about Jane?" I wanted him to keep my sister's name out of his mouth.

"Spending time with Jane has been quite healing for me. The simmering rage has dissipated with each moment I've spent with her."

I almost believed him. "What about Webster?"

"What about him?"

Xavier gave me a curious glance.

"Why would Webster be killed?"

Emmett furrowed his brow. "You want me to conjure my own motive for the murder of a man I didn't kill? You hear how absurd that sounds, don't you?"

I didn't when I said it, but I certainly did now. "You've been stalking Alexander—and tangentially Canailles Nous—for months. I'm sure you have a theory of why someone might want to kill him."

"I wish I did. Especially now that I know I'm on the top of the suspect list. Truthfully, I can't imagine why anyone in their right mind would kill Webster. He was a good man. In fact, he was about as straight an arrow as you can find."

This was consistent with what I'd already heard about Webster. Someone had called him a Boy Scout. A rule follower. I was more convinced than ever that his propensity for doing the right thing was what had gotten him killed.

Chapter Twenty-Seven

"You're awfully quiet," I said to Xavier as we rode the elevator down to Capri.

"I am processing that conversation."

"Wanna let me in on your thinking?"

He stared at me for a moment. "Not here. In my office."

I followed him out of the elevator and down the hall. We passed the yoga studio, where Kyrie Dawn was teaching a class. She gave me an enthusiastic wave, and I held up my hand in response.

Pike and Irving were both seated at their respective desks as we walked into the security office.

"Gentlemen." Xavier nodded at them.

"Sir," they each responded.

"Anything I need to know before I take Madame McLaughlin into my office to discuss next steps?"

The men exchanged glances.

"What is it?"

"Well, sir." Irving shifted in his chair. "A couple minutes ago, we received a call from Emmett Guidry."

"We were just with him."

"Right. He was calling because he said he'd just remembered something he thought might be important."

"Which is?"

"He received an email a few months back. It wasn't from anyone in his contact list. Anonymous, with a cloaked address."

Xavier crossed his arms. "What did it say?"

Irving picked up his notepad. "It said, *I hear you're looking into the connection between Alexander St. Jacques and the Rougarou. You're on the right scent. He will be reuniting with Canailles Nous for a Halloween week cruise from New Orleans to Haiti. If you are looking for vengeance and retribution, I suggest you be onboard.* It was unsigned."

"An anonymous invitation to a murder mystery cruise? That's straight out of *And Then There Were None*."

Xavier grimaced. "It wasn't supposed to be a murder mystery cruise."

"That was it?" I asked.

Irving glanced back at the paper. "Pretty much."

Xavier studied my face. "What is it? You have that look."

"What look?" I glanced at Pike and the Lonnie. "Do I have a look?"

Pike smirked. "Yes, ma'am."

Lonnie nodded. "You have that look you get when something's bugging you, but you're not sure what it is."

I exhaled. What was I feeling? Unsettled, yes. Perturbed. Anxious. But why? "If I am, I don't know what it's about."

Xavier narrowed his gaze. "Follow me. Perhaps if we talk through this, it will rise to the surface in your mind."

Once seated in the chair across from him, I couldn't get

comfortable.

"Do you know what you remind me of at this moment?" he asked.

"What?"

"The fairy tale by Hans Christian Anderson. *The Princess and the Pea*."

He was as startled by my gasp as I was by his statement.

"Did I say something offensive?" His concern was endearing.

"No. Not at all. It's just that...I've connected to the woman in that story for quite some time. Before I discovered my husband had a whole other life, I experienced a restlessness in my spirit that I often equated to that story. I sensed the presence of a disturbance, but it was hidden beneath so many layers, I couldn't quite identify it."

"Something in that message Emmett received has had this same effect on you. What could it be?"

I shook my head. "Hopefully, it will come to me, but right now I don't know what it is."

There was a quick tap on his office door, and Pike peeked his head through the crack. "Sir, Ms. Thibodeaux is on the phone for you."

"Did she say what she wanted?"

"Just that she wanted to speak with you."

I jumped up from the chair. "That's my cue to leave!"

"Wait!" Xavier also rose from his chair. "Where are you going? We were in the middle of a conversation."

"I think we covered all the important stuff. I need to check on Jane anyway."

I pushed past Pike with a muttered "excuse me," and rushed out of the office before anyone could stop me.

⚓

"JANE?" I CALLED into the suite. "Are you here?"

"I'm in my bathroom."

I wandered down the hall. "How are you?"

I found her staring in the mirror, applying makeup. "I'm okay. A better question is, how are you? You were down there forever. That must have been quite a heart-to-heart conversation."

"Oh, not really. We went to go see Emmett."

She stopped with her eyeshadow brush hovering just above her lid. "And?"

"I'm starting to think he didn't do it."

She exhaled. "Why?"

"Well, first, I trust your judgment."

She scoffed. "Not sure that's a good idea. I mean, he really thinks a Rougarou killed his wife."

"Yes, but when presented with logical facts, he absorbed them and is reconsidering his position."

"Really?"

The hint of hope in her question pricked my heart.

"Yes, and after we left, he called Lonnie and told him something that points in a completely different direction."

"What's that?"

"He got an email suggesting he come on the cruise because Alexander would be here."

Her gaze widened. "Whoa. That's something."

"It is. And something in the email sparked a fleeting thought, and now I can't figure out what it was."

"What did it say?"

"I don't remember exactly. We should ask Emmett."

Jane pulled her mouth.

"What?"

"Eh, I'm not sure I want to do that."

"Why?"

"Well, if he is a killer, I need to start, you know, breaking things off with him. At least create some space. And if he's not, I've probably already blown it with him by thinking he might be capable."

"Based on my conversation with him, he is pretty enamored with you. I don't think even a slight wavering about whether or not he's capable of shooting a man through the heart with a silver bullet under a full moon in revenge for his wife's death will impact his feelings for you."

"Well, when you put it that way..." She laughed. "I'll ask him tonight at dinner."

"I'm not sure I want to go."

"How come?"

"Who thought it was a good idea to have a Voodoo Night for dinner? That's creepy."

"You've never been one for prejudice."

"How is thinking voodoo is creepy, prejudice?"

"Well, for one thing, it's a religion."

"I know that. But eating jerk chicken surrounded by snakes and potions and spells and people sticking pins in dolls with ill intent?" I shivered for dramatic effect.

"It has its origins in Africa. The people who brought it with them to America were stripped of their own beliefs and religious practices and had those of their oppressors forced upon them."

"You're right." I nodded. "I still don't like snakes though."

"According to Emmett, ordinances were passed in Louisiana to prevent dancing on days other than Sunday and anywhere other than designated places because they were afraid it would foment a slave rebellion. The only place it was allowed was in New Orleans's Congo Square. The impact of voodoo on New Orleans culture and history is significant."

"Wow, I had no idea."

She gave me a sage nod. "The more you know…"

"Okay, fine. But if there are live snakes in that dining room, I'm leaving."

⚓

"Well?" My left hand covered my eyes.

"Not a snake in sight." Jane patted my right hand which gripped her arm like a boa constrictor.

I slowly opened my left eye.

"See? Nothing."

No visible snakes, but the room was not exactly what I would call a light and cheery vibe. The lighting was dim and eerie, made more so by the green and purple glowing lanterns positioned throughout. The floor was invisible, covered in a layer of fog emitted from a machine in each corner. Frogs croaked from the speakers between jazzy scat songs with heavy brass and drums and upbeat swing.

That was one thing about the entertainment staff of the *Thalassophile*. They knew how to go all out for a themed event.

The walls were draped in black satin, the tables were covered in purple velvet, and strands of blood red chrysanthemums hung from the ceiling. Diners wore top hats accented with bones and dark feathers or crowns of flowers on their heads. Three makeup artists were stationed around the dining room, each with a long line of guests waiting to have their faces painted with skeletal designs.

A table held stuffed dolls and a bowl full of pearl-head straight pins with a sign cautioning to use only if necessary.

Heath skulked near the bar, back in his voodoo priest costume from Halloween. An unlit cigarette hung from his bottom lip like it was attached.

Hawk caught sight of me and gave a quick nod, his standard greeting. There was nothing standard about the way he looked at me, though. I'd have called it suspicion, but it was more like he was wondering if I'd figured out his secret. I hadn't. I just knew he had one. He had been seen multiple times up on Santorini where members of Canailles Nous were staying, including the two murder victims. He had no reason to be there, and he'd been cagey about it.

I appraised him as he pretended that he didn't notice me watching. The twitch at the corner of his mouth gave him away. Hawk wasn't capable of murder, was he? I found it difficult to comprehend, even though I didn't know a whole lot about him.

"Emmett's over there." Jane indicated a table where he sat alone drinking some glowing blue concoction.

"You ready?" I asked.

"As ready as I'll ever be."

I followed her to the table.

Emmett rose when he spotted her. "How did I get so lucky to be joined by the two most lovely women in here tonight?"

"Oh," Jane threw a dismissive wave and smoothed her black dress. Flustered, she didn't say anything else.

"Can I get you a drink?" he asked.

"I think I'll just have a chardonnay tonight." She looked at me. "Char?"

"Vodka soda with lime, please."

He clapped his hands. "Great. I'll be back shortly."

"I can feel those drums in my gut." Jane gripped her stomach.

"Are you sure that's not just your nerves?" I asked.

"Could be. I drank so much water this afternoon I feel like I'm about to burst. I'll be right back." She hustled out of the dining room in the direction of the nearest toilet.

Heath wandered over from the bar and removed the unlit cigarette from his mouth. "We still friends?" He smiled broadly and cocked his left eyebrow at me.

"Why wouldn't we be friends?" Unless, of course, he was a murderer. Had he heard he'd vaulted to the top of my suspect list?

"After that scuffle this morning with Miss Ophelia, I wondered if perhaps I was guilty by association."

Perhaps he was just plain guilty.

I indicated an open chair. "Only Ophelia is responsible for her behavior. We all are responsible for our own behavior."

"I agree." He sipped his whiskey. "I haven't seen her yet tonight. I actually haven't seen anyone since breakfast."

"You mean you've been holed up in your suite?"

"Nah, I've been roaming around trying to keep myself occupied. I haven't seen Ophelia, Percy, or Victor."

A tingle crawled up the back of my neck. "I hope they're all okay. Ophelia was staying with me because she got that threatening note, but after this morning I think she knew she wasn't welcome."

"I'm sure they're fine." He took another sip.

Why was he so calm? Why was he so certain? "Heath, you got one of those threatening notes too."

"Sure did."

"Why didn't you report it?"

"I'm sure I did." He tapped his fingers on the edge of the table.

Was he tapping to the beat or from nerves?

"I don't believe so. In fact, I'm almost positive Xavier said the ones who reported getting them following Alexander's death were Ophelia, Percy, and Victor."

"Izzat so? Hmm." He sipped his whiskey and held up his glass. "What do you think of this song?"

His change of topic left me momentarily confused. "Oh, uh, I like it. It's fun. Kind of reminds me of that Disney movie. *The Princess and the Frog.*"

"For some people, that movie and beads for boobs is all they know about my city." He swirled his glass over his head. "Look at this place. It's a caricature of N'awlins." He clenched and unclenched his jaw before taking another sip of whiskey and slamming the glass onto the table.

I jumped a little and then shifted in my chair, "Well, uh, you know, they try to make it fun, but I'm sure it's far from culturally sensitive. You should have seen the cruise to Yokohama. They had a blond guy doing ninja demonstrations."

"Ain't that somethin'." His tone was dark and his stare intense as he traced his finger around the rim of his glass.

I scanned the room. Pike and Irving were on opposite sides of each other watching for trouble. Emmett was still fighting to give Hawk his order at the bar. There was no sign of Jane or Xavier. And no sign of the other members of Canailles Nous.

Despite being in a room full of people, I suddenly felt unsafe.

"You know, uh, I'm going to go check on something. Will you let Jane know I'll be back in a little bit?"

"Sure will." He didn't raise his gaze to look at me.

I hustled out of the room and into the elevator, pushing the button to go down to the eighth floor. Santorini. It was only one level, but the stairwell felt like a less safe option. As the elevator doors opened, I hesitated. Even though I wanted to make sure she was alive, I didn't particularly want to knock on Ophelia's door. She'd called Xavier, and now he wasn't at the event. What if they were in her room together? I wasn't sure I could take seeing them together again in another intimate setting.

I headed for Victor's room instead, but just as I went to rap on the door, it opened.

"Oh!" Luke squealed in surprise. "Charlotte, you startled me." He wore a purple feather boa and a black-and-white striped suit with tails.

"Likewise!"

He called over his shoulder. "Babe, it's Charlotte." He turned back to me. "What's up?"

No need to tell them I was worried they'd been murdered. Might kill the party vibe.

"I just came to see what was keeping you guys."

Victor came up behind him. "Hello, *cher*. Might you be willing to settle a disagreement between myself and Crocodile Dundee here?"

"I can try."

Victor waved his hand in front of Luke's outfit. "Tell me, does this scream voodoo priest or Beetlejuice?"

"Oh, uh, I—"

"Come now, Charlotte. Friends don't lie to each other."

I took in Luke's puppy dog eyes. He blinked at me several times in what I could only take as an attempt to play coquette. If so, he was so bad at flirting, it was a miracle he'd landed Victor.

"Sorry, Luke, I'm going to have to side with Victor on

this one."

Luke's shoulders slumped, and Victor pumped his fist in victory.

"However!" I continued. "I think under the circumstances he can get away with it."

Luke's face brightened.

"I was just at the party, and I saw many people in costumes that weren't exactly right. I don't think anyone will notice."

"See, sweetheart?" Luke kissed Victor on the cheek. "I told you it would be fine. Besides, I own this place, remember?"

Technically, he owned the ship and each of the units were owned individually, but it seemed unnecessary to argue the point.

Victor closed the door and ushered Luke down the hall. "Hurry. I told Fee we'd grab her thirty minutes ago."

"You were the one taking so long." Luke knocked on the door across the hall.

I held my breath until Ophelia opened the door and shuffled out of her room. "Bout time you guys showed up. I like to make an entrance, but this is ridiculous." She cast a glance my way and threw a look of disdain. "Charlotte."

"You look lovely, Ophelia."

She smoothed her little black dress. "Thank you." With that, she flipped her long, dark hair over her shoulder and linked her arm through Victor's.

She wasn't with Xavier. So where was he?

I waited a beat for them to step onto the elevator before

heading for Percy's room. It was hard to remember how beautiful I'd once thought Ophelia was. She was forever marred in my mind by her ugly attitude.

I knocked on Percy's door. No response. My pulse quickened. Where was Percy?

And then another thought. A terrible thought.

Was he lying unconscious inside? Or worse, was he lying dead?

Chapter Twenty-Eight

I KNOCKED HARDER on Percy's door. "Percy! Percy, can you hear me?"

From within the suite, there were some sounds of life. Footsteps became louder as they presumably came closer.

From behind the door, Percy's low voice rumbled, "Hold your horses. I'm coming."

Relief washed over me. It was a good sign that he was alive.

He opened the door. "Oh, Charlotte. I didn't expect it to be you."

"Who did you expect it to be?"

He rubbed his beard. "I thought it might be Fee. She was bugging me earlier to go to the dinner, but I wasn't feeling up for it."

"She just left with Victor and Luke."

"Ah." He looked at me for a moment. "Can I help you with something?"

"Oh, uh, no. I was just concerned. Heath had said he hadn't seen you since breakfast and, well, with everything that's happened, I was concerned."

"Sounds like you were concerned." He chuckled. "That's

thoughtful of you, but as you can see, I'm just fine." He glanced over his shoulder. "Would you like to come in for a drink?"

Not really. "Oh, I need to get back upstairs."

"Come on. Just one drink. I make a mean Sazerac." He swung the door all the way open.

"Okay, just one, though. I haven't eaten much today and I'm kind of a lightweight."

"Sure thing." He ushered me inside.

The unit assigned to Percy was stark. White on white on white. I found myself wondering if it was the owners' style choice or pure lack of imagination.

"It's very...clean in here." I eased onto one of two white leather sofas facing each other.

Percy rattled about in the kitchen, clinking glasses and clanging various cocktail-making tools. "Yeah, definitely not my style. I prefer worn leather and art that requires more than just a drop of paint."

On the wall hung a giant canvas, empty except for one green dot in the center.

The glossy white coffee table in front of me was bare, except for the book lying face down. He set down a coaster and a cut crystal glass in front of me. The amber liquid was topped with an orange peel.

I took a sip. "This is so good. Did you work as a bartender in a previous life?"

"Just for my parents. They taught me young so they could keep drinking and fighting without having to stop to make another round. Their love of Sazerac was just about the only thing they agreed on." He winced. A touchy subject for sure.

Had that been where he'd developed his role as peacekeeper?

He sipped from his own glass and ran his fingers through his hair. Despite the tousling, the pompadour stayed in place. I'd have to remember to ask what styling products he used.

"Still reading *A Tale of Two Cities*, I see. How are you liking it?"

"It's my third time reading it. Every time I do, I catch something I missed the previous times."

"I get it. I've read it a couple times. One year at the library I ran a Dickens book club where we read a different book each month, culminating in *A Christmas Carol* in December."

"That's cool."

"You know, it's funny, Ophelia quoted *A Tale of Two Cities* the other day."

"Did she? What did she say?"

"'It was the best of times; it was the worst of times.'"

A laugh rumbled in his chest. "Figures. That's the first line of the book. I've been trying to get her to read it, but that's probably as far as she got." He sipped his drink. "Nobody ever remembers the rest of that line. *It was the age of wisdom, it was the age of foolishness, it was the epoch of belief, it was the epoch of incredulity, it was the season of light, it was the season of darkness, it was the spring of hope, it was the winter of despair, we had everything before us, we had nothing before us.* Now that's how you start a novel."

"And timeless," I added.

"It is. That's what I love about Dickens. His prose may be flowery for the modern era, but the truths he wrote stand the test of time."

"What's your favorite quote?"

"It changes based on what I'm reading and my mood. Last time it was *not knowing how he lost himself, or how he recovered himself, he may never feel certain of not losing himself again.* This reading, what's stuck with me is *A wonderful fact to reflect upon, that every human creature is constituted to be that profound secret and mystery to every other.*"

"Both good ones. The first is pretty self-explanatory, but how do you interpret the second one?"

He leaned back, laid his arm across the back of the sofa, and crossed his right leg. "A lot of people focus on what was happening in that scene, but I believe it speaks to a bigger theme in the book. Sydney Carton loves Lucie in a way she can't receive or return, and he knows he is not enough for her, so instead he commits himself to a life of sacrifice for her. She marries Charles Darnay, with whom she's very much in love in a way she never was with Carton. She cares for him, but she can never love him the way she loves Darnay, so he suffers in silence for loving her. So much of our lives, our thoughts, our dreams, our passions, our longing goes unknown. How many people die having never shared the deepest parts of themselves with those they love? We fool ourselves into believing we know each other, but within each of us is someone we fear is unlovable, and so we carry on with the masquerade."

"You've got quite a poetic soul."

"You mean for a tattooed musician who spends half his life scrambling for crumbs?"

"No judgment. Just an observation."

He shook his head. "There's always judgment." He swigged the last of his drink and tipped his glass toward mine. "Ready for another?"

"No, still sipping."

He got up from the couch and headed toward the kitchen. "How did Fee seem tonight? Did she ask about me?"

I glanced at him busily making his drink, his gaze cast downward. He was concentrating harder than necessary for the task.

Oh. Oh boy.

"She seemed okay. I think she's ready to get off this ship."

"Yeah. Me too."

How had I not seen it before? Percy was in love with Ophelia. She was the Lucie to his Sydney Carton. Did that make Alexander St. Jacques, Charles Darnay in this scenario?

Alexander had everything Percy wanted: The career, the money, and Ophelia's love. He got Percy a job working as a production assistant at a reality TV court show, and he set up the reunion tour. Was that what Percy was alluding to when he said scrambling for crumbs? The crumbs Alexander had thrown his way?

It was one thing to feel like someone had thrown you ʼ the curb for a better opportunity. It was a whole other tʰ to feel disrespected, to feel like you were being given a handout. I knew well what it felt like to be on the receiving end of pity, and it didn't feel good. In fact, it was one of my least favorite things to experience.

Add in unrequited love, and a motive for murder began to materialize before my very eyes.

That still didn't explain why someone would kill Webster.

The room had gone silent. I glanced up at Percy to find him watching me. Were my thoughts being telegraphed by my facial expressions?

"Do you mind if I use your restroom?"

He jerked his chin. "Sure. It's down the hall."

The unit was a two-bedroom, with two full bathrooms and a powder room. As I passed one of the bedrooms, I spotted a piece of paper on the floor near the bed.

I glanced over my shoulder. I wasn't in Percy's line of sight.

Tiptoeing into the room, I squatted down to snatch the paper.

Oh no.

It was a copied photo of Webster with a target superimposed over his face, just like the threatening notes delivered to Alexander, Ophelia, Victor, Heath (supposedly, although I'd yet to see it with my own eyes), and…Percy. Everyone ⸺ceived one except Webster.

⸺new why. It was here, in Percy's suite. But Percy ⸺ well. That made no sense unless—

⸺e only one without a threatening note."

He finished my thought as if he could hear them in my head.

The room felt as if it had dropped sixty degrees in an instant.

Chapter Twenty-Nine

I HADN'T SEEN it coming. Not really. Any time a thought had entered my mind, I'd brushed it away. Nothing about Percy's demeanor had shouted killer.

A picture of the minimalist artwork in the other room floated to the surface of my mind.

It was a pea. That green dot in the center of the canvas was a pea. Staring at it had caused something to keep in the deep recesses of my brain. The pea had been trying to reveal itself, but I kept suppressing it.

Vengeance and retribution. The email sent to Emmett four months earlier luring him onto the cruise had suggested that if Emmett were looking for vengeance and retribution, he could find it onboard with Alexander and Canailles Nous. It mentioned seeing the article in which Emmett had claimed a Rougarou connection to the St. Jacques family.

Vengeance and retribution.

It was part of a quote from *A Tale of Two Cities*.

Vengeance and retribution require a long time, it is the rule. How long had Percy been planning this?

I swiveled on my knees to see him looming in the doorway.

David and Goliath.

Titanic and the iceberg.

Physically, I stood no chance against him. Gone was the soft, warm, teddy bear exterior. In its place was Mount Everest, a.k.a. *Chomolungma*. Icy. Imposing. Deadly.

All the spit evaporated in my mouth. My heart fluttered about a hundred and twenty beats per minute. I could have sworn I heard a spring boing as my overwrought nervous system sent a flood of cortisol and adrenaline through my body.

"Aren't you going to say something?" His gruff question held a note of offense, almost like he was disappointed I wasn't showering him with accolades for having pulled off two murders without anyone suspecting him.

Was there training for this kind of thing? A class that taught how to deescalate a situation where you'd discovered the person across the room was guilty of murder? I'd look into it if I got out of here alive.

I glanced at the bedside table where one of the glass paperweights propped up three books covered in white paper.

It was already an established fact they made one heck of a weapon.

"Don't even think about it," Percy growled. "Come on now, Charlotte. Ask your questions. I know you're *dying* of curiosity."

"Why?" My raspy voice didn't signal strength, only fear and timidity.

"Why Alex or why Webb?"

"I know why Alexander. Vengeance and retribution."

red. "Very good. Anyone who spent more than ...tes with Alex knows the answer to why he had to die. He was a narcissist of the highest order. He used his friends like stepping stools and left us in the gutter."

"But he got you that job—"

His bitter laugh echoed off the white walls of the bedroom. "A production assistant on trash TV? You've got to be kidding. I'd been playing to sold-out crowds. Riding in limos and private planes. All the wine, women, and song I could handle. And I can handle a lot. Then, practically overnight, it all went away. People stopped returning my calls. My bank account dried up. I became a nobody."

"I'm sorry. I can imagine how difficult that was."

He continued like he hadn't heard me. "I begged Alex to bring me along with him, but he acted like he had no say on who played with him on the first solo project. Not true, of course. I told him my mother had been diagnosed with early onset Alzheimer's, and I needed the money. He called one of his new friends and got me the job on *Kangaroo Kourt*. They tried to get that older Kardashian to be the judge, but even she had the sense to turn it down. We got stuck with Milt MacAvoy, New Orleans's sleeziest divorce attorney. The man has no moral compass, and they had him passing judgment on other people's lives?"

The irony of a murderer bemoaning someone else's lack of morals wasn't lost on me. He was on a roll, though, and his rant was buying me time to either come up with an escape plan or get rescued.

"And Ophelia?"

His gaze cut to mine. "What about her?"

"Alexander left her heartbroken as well. That must have made you angry, considering your feelings for her."

His face, already flushed with anger, turned purple. "How could he cheat on her? The woman is perfection."

I stifled my urge to object to that characterization. "She's very beautiful." That was at least true.

"He didn't deserve her, but of course, I couldn't tell her that. She was heartbroken."

Curiosity got the better of me. "Percy, why now? Why this cruise? You had years to get vengeance and retribution."

He chuckled. "You know, it's kind of funny."

I suspected I wouldn't find it funny, but I gave him what I hoped was an encouraging smile. "In what way?"

"I was sitting around on set one day, scrolling on my phone because Milt was stinking up the bathroom after lunch, and I came across the article about what happened to Emmett's wife. He was all worked up about the Rougarou. Unhinged, really. I was about to scroll away but then I saw the name St. Jacques. I had no idea Alex was a fraud—well, not in that way, at least—so I thought, if this guy believes Alex is a Rougarou and killed his wife, I could stir the pot a bit and he might be willing to take care of Alex without me even having to get my hands dirty. I couldn't bank on that, though."

"How did you get the gun onboard? Security screens everyone's luggage."

"I have a storage area in my bass case. I strapped a bunch of metal objects to obscure the shape of the gun. I kept the arate with the rest of my instrument accessories. I [sp]eak it to you, Charlotte, but the security on this ship is actually pretty lax, all things considered."

Considering the poisonous fish that had made its way onto the voyage to Yokohama, he wasn't totally wrong.

"So, how did you do it? You got him to meet you outside before the performance?"

He grinned. "You wouldn't believe how many things had to be just right. I needed to get Emmett to leave the event so he wouldn't have an alibi."

"Another email?"

"Laxative in his cocktail."

"Eww."

He shrugged. "Effective. Then I texted Alex that I had some important news about that song we'd been working on together."

"I didn't know you were working on a song with him. Heath told me he was also working on a song with Alexander."

"Did he now? That's Alex. Always trying to make you feel like you were special, when in reality he was an opportunist. The truth was, I worked on the song, and he was going to take all the credit, as usual. Did you know I alone wrote 'Lamoreaux?'"

"I didn't."

"Of course, because everyone thought Alex wrote it and he never corrected them. He put all of us on the credits, but when he was interviewed, he talked about it like it was his idea entirely. You know it means the lover, right?"

I nodded. *Keep talking, buddy.*

"He thought it was about him, like the reliable narcissist he was, and it was—he just didn't understand I'd written it to mock him. Anyway, back to the night in question."

He seemed to be enjoying letting me in on his secrets, knowing I wouldn't be able to tell anyone else if I was twenty thousand leagues under the sea.

"I didn't even have to confront Alex. He saw me, and before he could say something snide, I shot him in the heart. Silver bullet under the light of a full moon. It was epic. Artistic. Of course, the bullet wasn't really silver. I tried to make silver bullets, but it turns out those aren't super accurate, so I ended up with nickel-plated brass. Still looked silver. And the etched ROUGAROU on the side was a nice touch, don'tcha think? I got an engraver tool at the local craft store for twenty-two bucks."

"So why put the gun in Ophelia's drawer instead of Emmett's?"

"First, he took longer in the bathroom than I'd expected, and I didn't want to hold on to it longer than necessary. Second, while I was waiting for him to come out of his room, it occurred to me a guilty person wouldn't hide the weapon in their own drawer—they'd hide it in the drawer of the person they wanted to frame."

I tilted my head. "Okay, and that would mean not hiding it in *your* drawer but in Emmett's. What does that have to do with Ophelia?"

He tapped his temple. "Ah, see that's why I'm so many steps ahead of you. I wanted people to believe Emmett was the guilty one and he was trying to frame Ophelia. Which makes sense, of course, because she made no bones about how much she despised Alex."

"But if you care about Ophelia the way I think you do, why would you put her in jeopardy? Frankly, I thought Heath was a much more likely suspect. Why didn't you put it in his drawer?"

His condescending chuckle grated my nerves. "Oh, Charlotte. You really don't get it, do you? I knew Ophelia would be cleared. That left all sorts of people as viable suspects, including Heath but especially Emmett Guidry."

"Including you."

He shrugged. "Sure, but why would anyone suspect me? I had more to lose by Alexander's death than I had to gain as far as anyone knew. I'm the peacekeeper. The gentle giant. The thinker not the brute."

"So the peacekeeping thing was all an act?"

"Of course not. I hate conflict. I tried to keep the group together, just like I fought my whole childhood to keep my parents together. Everyone has to figure out their role in life. That was mine. But when push came to shove, I decided I would use that perception to keep the heat off me and focused elsewhere."

When he said it like that, it made sense. And it wasn't that I didn't understand his hatred of Alexander.

"What about Webster?" I held up the flyer. "What did he do to deserve what happened to him?"

Percy's expression softened. "I'm sorry about that."

I almost believed him. "Why did they go that way?"

He rubbed the back of his neck. "Webb was a good man." His voice lowered nearly to a whisper. "Too good."

"What does that even mean?"

"It means he was starting to put things together and was going to go to the authorities."

"How did he figure out it was you?"

He squinted and wagged his finger at me. "I know what you're trying to do. You're stalling. It won't work."

"I really do want to know. Like I've said time and again, and as you yourself have said, finding a motive to kill Alexander was as easy as shooting fish in a barrel." Immediately, I regretted using that particular idiom. "So to speak. But I've been racking my brain trying to understand what someone might have against Webster. Unless, of course, it was a crazed fan."

"That's where the flyers came in handy. They were my plan C. If Alex's death couldn't be pinned on Emmett or one of the members of Canailles Nous—myself excluded, of course—the crazed fan was as good a theory as any, and once Webb was dead, it became my preferred theory. I figured by the time Mesnier and his Keystone Kops were done going over the passenger guest list and the staff with a fine-tooth comb, we'd be in Haiti and I'd disappear with the wind. Maybe shuffle off to one of the smaller islands in the Caribbean and live out my days with my toes in the sand and a cocktail in my hand." His eyes lit up. "Hey! That's not bad. I gotta remember that for a song."

Probably wasn't a good time to mention that the Zac Brown Band, Kenny Chesney, and Van Halen (among others) had already beaten him to it, not to mention every beach town tchotchke shop.

"I'm guessing Webster reached out to you wanting to talk? Asked you to meet him in the captain's lounge?"

"How do you know I didn't lure him there?"

"Because of this." I held up the paper. "If you had invited him there to kill him, you would have brought this and put it somewhere near his body. You didn't go there intending to kill him, did you?"

A flicker of regret passed across his face. "He was more than my friend. He was family. He messaged me. Dumb for him, great for me."

"In what way?"

"The group has always used an encrypted texting app because of Alex's paranoia that someone might try to hack into our conversations. I'm not even sure that's possible, but that's Alex for you. Was Alex, I mean. Anyway, it's not like text messages, so I was able to delete the messages on both sides. No evidence we ever agreed to meet."

"What did the message say?"

"He needed to talk about something important. Part of me wondered if it was about what happened to Alex, but I'd covered my tracks so well, I didn't think it could be."

"And it was?"

"Webster said he found a message from Alex the night he died, and he'd been trying to figure out what it meant. It said *I'll be there in a minute, just need to meet with percussion real quick.* At the time he got it, Webb was confused because he's the drummer, and there is no other percussion. The message made no sense. And then I guess he was trying to message Heath, and when he went to type my name, it autocorrected to percussion."

"Ohhhh."

"Yeah. Now it wasn't *need to meet with percussion*, it was *need to meet with Percy*. Right before he was shot."

"Exposed by autocorrect."

"Ain't that somethin'? So he says he knows I met with Alex, and I'd better come clean or he was going to Mesnier. I couldn't have that."

"So you bonked him on the head with a lotus flower glass paperweight."

"I just grabbed the closest, heaviest thing I could find."

"Are you aware the lotus flower represents enlightenment and purity? A tad ironic."

"I didn't exactly have time to think through any metaphors my murder weapon of choice might have. Not like with Alex. That was poetry, pure and simple."

"So now what?" I touched my lower lip and found it trembling.

His leering smile sent shivers down my spine. "You know. Can't have any loose ends."

If I was going to survive this interaction, I needed to project a level of confidence. His demeanor indicated he was taking power from my fear. I couldn't have that. I cleared my throat, jutted my chin, and pushed enough air from my lungs for my next words to send the message that I still had fight in me. "You'll never get away with this."

He gave a perplexed smile. "How do you figure? I basically already have."

I stumbled to my feet, still holding the paper. "You haven't. We're at sea. Until the ship docks and you step onto dry land *not* in handcuffs, you haven't gotten away with anything. Xavier is onto you. He just hasn't tipped his hand yet. And if you hurt me, he won't stop until he sees you behind bars for the rest of your life."

Even though Percy already took up the bulk of the doorway, when he crossed his arms against his broad chest and widened his stance, he engulfed it even more. "No one knows you're here. I could say you knocked, and I must not have heard you because I was sleeping." He jerked his thumb over his shoulder. "I've got a balcony with your name on it. By the time they even realize you're overboard, I'll be packing my suitcase and headed down the gangplank in Port-au-Prince."

"That's not true."

"What do you mean that's not true? I'm making it true. You'll be shark bait in about five minutes."

"I mean that no one knows I'm here. Lots of people do. I told Heath I was going to check on you." Lie. "And I told him to tell Jane." Sort of a lie. "She'll tell Xavier when she can't find me. And then I ran into Victor, Luke, and Ophelia in the hallway and let them know I was going to check on you." One hundred percent fabrication.

"If that's the case, then I'd better get to it."

Chapter Thirty

PERCY MOVED TOWARD me, malicious intent radiating off his broad shoulders. At the last moment, I ducked under his outstretched arms, and he toppled onto the bed like a felled sequoia.

I'd just made it to the doorway when something knocked my knees from behind, causing me to stumble to the floor. He dragged me backward by my feet and threw me onto the bed. He stood over me, calculating his next move.

Whatever it was, it wasn't good.

He was unrecognizable as the man I'd originally encountered in the alley behind the club on Bourbon Street. The peacemaker. The fixer. The gentle giant.

The teddy bear had morphed into a mauling grizzly.

His eyes blazed. His features had hardened. It was like he'd transformed from a person to a monster.

Maybe there wasn't such a thing as a Rougarou. Maybe the transformation of man into a monster was more about what happened internally rather than externally. Maybe the monster lurking inside him was his real persona, and the man he'd presented himself to be had been the mask.

Maybe the stories of men turning into beasts had been

the only way those who'd known them could rationalize their behavior. Jekyll and Hyde. Wendigo.

Rougarou.

Percy flung himself onto me, using the entirety of his weight to pin me down. The only sound was his breath heavy in my ear and my gasps beneath his large frame.

His stiff hair grazed my face as he maneuvered his body into position to restrain me.

Sandalwood and a touch of sweet tobacco. It was his styling cream. I'd smelled it in the stairwell.

The housekeeping staff had smelled it in the captain's lounge the morning Webster's body was discovered.

"Stop moving," he grunted.

I wriggled beneath him, flailing my arms. My hand whacked against the nightstand. My fingertips brushed something smooth and cool. Glass. The paperweight.

I shimmied toward the nightstand, reaching my hand as I did so. Closer. Closer.

He attempted to wrestle me into submission. "Hold still." He pushed down my right arm.

The angle and pressure sent a sharp pain through my shoulder and down my arm. "Ahhhh!"

He covered my mouth with his hand, and I bit him. This time we both screamed.

"Owoooooowwww!" A piercing howl came from somewhere other than the bedroom and from someone—or something—other than Percy and me.

"What the—"

He lifted his hand just enough for me to take a breath.

"Help!"

He slapped his hand down harder on my mouth.

Once again, from somewhere on the other side of the bedroom wall, came another howl. "Owooooooooooo!"

Percy jerked his head toward the direction of the howl. He'd shifted enough of his body weight for me to almost reach the paperweight. I lunged the rest of the way, gripping it with my left hand and swung it against his head.

There was a crack as glass met skull. He slumped onto me, heavier than before. His eyes were closed, and blood began to stream from the wound.

"Owooooooo!"

I wiggled and twisted, trying to squirm out from underneath him, but he was a dead weight. Every move required more lung capacity than I had with him crushing my chest and sent searing pain through my body.

"Helllp!" I coughed. "Ow!" The pain in my clavicle was excruciating.

"Owooooooo!"

Percy began to moan.

I stared up at the ceiling. I was going to suffocate under the weight. Someone would find us like this. Humiliating.

My tombstone would read:

HERE LIES CHARLOTTE MCLAUGHLIN
SHE FIGURED IT OUT THE HARD WAY

A large banging sound near the front door was followed by an even larger bang.

"Charlotte!"

"Jane?" I squeaked.

"Charlotte! Where are you?"

"In. Here."

I heard the ruckus but couldn't turn my head to see who'd entered the room.

Jane's worried face hovered above me. "Oh, my gawd. Are you okay?"

"Percy did it," I managed to eke out.

She closed her eyes and shook her head with a wry smile. "Yeah, I kind of figured."

"Charlotte." Xavier came into view.

"Can somebody. Please. Get. Him. Off me!"

Pike and Irving rolled a mumbling Percy until I was able to scramble out from beneath him.

Irving placed two fingers on his neck. "I've got a pulse."

Xavier leaned toward Pike. "Can you retrieve Dr. Fraser, *s'il vous plaît?*"

Pike nodded, pushing past a white-faced Emmett as he left the room.

I held Emmett's gaze for a moment, hoping to convey my apology for suspecting him of murder. He gave a forgiving and grateful smile in return.

I let my head hang between my knees, trying to catch my breath. Jane climbed over Percy's hulking form, pushed Irving out of the way, and wrapped her arms around me.

"I'm so glad you're okay. *Are* you okay?"

She released me and began squeezing various parts of my body. She got to my right shoulder and the squeeze elicited a voluntary "yeow."

"I think her arm is broken!"

She squeezed again.

"Yeooww!"

"I'm sorry!"

"Owooooooo!"

The room stilled.

"What was that?" Xavier asked.

"It sounded like a…it can't be." Irving shook his head.

"I'll tell you what that sounds like. I'm not afraid to say it." Emmett's expression was solemn. "It's a wolf."

"You mean—" Jane's tone was hushed.

"A Rougarou."

"I don't know if it's a Rougarou, but whatever it is, that howl saved my life."

⚓

"Your shoulder's broken," Dr. Ian Fraser declared after examining my X-rays. "Technically, your proximal humerus is broken."

"Nothing about this is funny."

He wagged his finger. "Ah, I see what you did there! I enjoy medical puns. So, there's good news and bad news."

"I'll take the good news first for a change."

"The good news is, you don't need a cast, nor do you need surgery."

"That is good news." Jane patted my leg. "See, it's not so bad."

"He's not done. What's the bad news?"

weeks in a sling. No arm movement, little to no physical activity that might lead to further injury. I can't cast it because of the location of the break, so it's imperative you protect it and keep it immobile, or you'll end up needing surgery, and that's a twelve-week recovery at minimum."

I groaned. "I'd almost prefer a cast."

Jane's face brightened. "Hey, you'll be good as new for the holiday cruise to Monte Carlo. I can see you now, spinning that roulette wheel."

Ian and I exchanged amused expressions.

"She doesn't gamble," I said. "Jane, we don't spin the roulette wheel, the casino croupier does."

"You know what I mean."

"I'm going to get you some pain medication." Ian left Jane and I alone in the exam room.

Jane's smile morphed from a broad smile to tears.

"Hey. Hey. I'm okay. It's just a tiny crack in my bones. No biggie. It will heal."

"When we first got inside Percy's room and I saw the blood, I thought for sure you were gone."

"I cracked him pretty good with the paperweight, and you know how head wounds bleed. What I still don't understand is how you knew to come find me. How did you figure out that it was Percy?"

"Vengeance and retribution."

I nodded. "Same. Vengeance and retribution. This is why reading is so important."

"I'm not sure the American Library Association can use that in their next ad campaign, but it's true. When I got back to the table, Emmett was there with our drinks, and you were gone. Heath said you went to go check on something, and at first, I thought nothing of it. After a while, I remembered I was supposed to ask Emmett about the email. He let me read it, and I sat there trying to pinpoint what it was about the wording that was trying to jar something loose in my brain. I just couldn't get to it."

"That's how it's been for me since Irving mentioned it. It only clicked when I was in Percy's living room and the book was on the coffee table. We started talking about his favorite quotes. It came to me like a flash of lightning when I found the threatening note intended for Webster that never got delivered."

"I asked Emmett if there was something about the phrasing that seemed familiar to him, but as you know, he thinks *A Tale of Two Cities* is overrated, so I think he's only read it once. Ophelia, Victor, and Luke showed up and I asked about Percy. Ophelia said something like *oh he's probably in his room reading that book still.* Emmett asked what he was reading, and she told him. Like you said, lightning bolt."

"How did you find Xavier? He wasn't at the party."

"That's the best part."

"I thought he was with Ophelia, but she left her room alone."

Jane narrowed her gaze. "Why did you think that?"

I waved my hand. "No matter. Why's that the best part?"

"He'd been in the library trying to figure out where the phrase had come from. When Irving relayed the contents of the email, it rang a bell with him also. Right as I realized where I'd read the phrase, Xavier burst into the dining room waving the book in the air like a wild man."

"I can't even picture him like that."

"It was a sight. Not only was he more animated than I'd ever seen him, but he was also wading through a sea of voodoo priests to get to us. He panicked when he saw that you and Percy weren't at the table. Ophelia said they'd run into you in the hallway downstairs near Percy's room."

There was a tap on the exam room door. Ian returned holding a sling and a pill bottle.

"Only take these if you need them. Anything you don't need, either return to me or dump them overboard. The last thing we need is someone getting ahold of these who shouldn't be taking them."

"Trust me, I have no desire to become addicted to pain pills, and I wouldn't want to be responsible for anyone else overdosing or abusing them."

He gingerly fitted me into the sling. "Remember. This is twenty-four hours a day for the next six weeks. Only take it off to shower."

"Can I take her back to the room?" Jane asked. "The sun will be coming up in about five hours, and if I'm exhausted, I know she is too."

He nodded. "Let me know right away if you have any ill effects from the painkillers or the pain gets worse. It may increase over the next forty-eight hours or so, but then it should begin to decrease, especially with the pain meds. I want to reiterate: if you don't feel you need them, you can get away with good old-fashioned over-the-counter acetaminophen or ibuprofen."

I started climbing off the exam table, and the room began to spin. I lost my balance and felt myself falling. Jane and Ian rushed to stabilize me.

"Honestly, Char, sometimes I think you're a bigger danger to your own well-being than anyone."

Perhaps there was something to that.

Chapter Thirty-One

PAIN CAN DO strange things to a person. It can envelop them until they become unrecognizable as their former selves. It can infect them, transforming their blood into venom, replacing their mortal desires into an appetite for destruction of themselves and those around them. Little by little, it morphs a person from man or woman to beast. Monster. The vestiges of their humanity are stripped away—love, understanding, forgiveness, compassion—and are replaced by selfishness, deceit, spite, vindictiveness.

A desire for vengeance and retribution.

Over the course of the voyage from New Orleans to the Caribbean, I'd watched as Ophelia's extraordinary beauty had faded into nastiness. Alexander's talent had been eclipsed by his self-absorption and greed. Percy's kind demeanor vanished in an instant as his inner demons possessed him. Not literally, I didn't think. But might as well have been. As I'd stared into his eyes, I'd been unable to glimpse even an ounce of the man I'd met behind that club on Bourbon Street just a week prior.

A chilly gust of wind caused me to pull tight the blanket I'd bundled around myself. Or perhaps it was the remembrance of his malevolent glare.

It was five thirty in the morning, and I was leaning against the railing of the deck atop the *Thalassophile of the Seas* waiting for the sun to rise. Kalispera in Greek meant good afternoon or evening. In the nearly twelve months I'd been a full-time resident on the ship, I'd never gone up to see the sun rise, only set.

The ship had been scheduled to dock in Port-au-Prince, but due to a sudden outbreak of unrest in the area and the fact we had a murderer on board in need of being sent back to the United States, it had been diverted to San Juan, Puerto Rico.

I'd come to embrace change, for the most part. Someone—not Faulkner or Dickens, probably Darwin or Oprah—once said we must evolve or die. Not an exact quote but the gist. Gabe's favorite quote on the topic had been by personal development guru John Maxwell who said "Change is inevitable. Growth is optional."

My life had drastically changed over the past year. My husband had died. His affair had been revealed. I learned he had a son.

Jane and I moved onboard the *Thalassophile of the Seas*. Our relationship had evolved by the sheer nature of the change in our living circumstances. We hadn't lived together since we were kids, and suddenly we'd been thrust into being in the same space twenty-four hours a day, seven days a week.

I felt pretty good for the most part about how I'd navigated all those changes. Not that I hadn't made mistakes, but mistakes were how a person learned. I'd learned a whole lot about myself. I'd learned I had more resilience than even I had given myself credit for. I'd learned I wasn't content living in a bubble and that trying new things, visiting new places, eating new foods were what made me feel truly alive for the first time.

I'd also deepened my connection with my sister. We'd faced obstacles and overcome them together. You couldn't endure what we had the past twelve months and not develop an iron clad bond.

Our relationship had changed.

I had changed.

The ship skirted the northern coast of the island toward the port, and the inky sky above me began to slowly lighten. Behind us to the west, the waning gibbous moon was dipping into the water just as the sun was beginning to breach the horizon to the east ahead of me.

"Do you mind if I join you?"

"Xavier!" I jumped, causing pain to rip through my shoulder. "Ow." I pulled my arm close to my body.

"Are you all right? I did not mean to startle you."

"I'm okay, I just didn't know anyone else was up here."

"Is that a, no? About joining you, I mean."

"No. I mean, of course you can join me. What are you doing up this early?"

"We are going to be docking soon, and making sure this happens in a secure way is part of my duties. I noticed an alert of movement up here, which is unusual for this time of day."

"My sleep schedule is messed up. The pain pills make me sleep long and heavy, and then I end up passing out in the afternoon and waking up in the middle of the night."

"How long have you been up here?"

"Not long." I toyed with the fringe on my blanket. "I thought perhaps you might be getting ready to say goodbye to Ophelia." I didn't have the nerve to look him in the eye as I said it.

"Why would you think that?"

"Because, you know…"

I stole a glance. His face was masked in confusion.

"I do not."

"Please don't make me spell it out."

"You are going to have to do so, because I have no idea what you are saying. Are you implying I have some sort of personal connection with her?"

"Come on. You know I saw you."

His brow furrowed. "You saw me. You saw me doing what?"

Was he playing dumb, or was he actually clueless?

"I saw you and Ophelia. Together." I weighted the last word with implication.

"I am not sure what you believe you witnessed, but we have never been *together*."

"After the pirate party. I came to help clean up, and you were huddled in the corner, kissing, I think, and—"

He threw his head back in raucous laughter.

"What's so funny?"

He exhaled so forcefully his nostrils flared and wheezed.

He shook his head. "Oh, Charlotte. For one so observant, you completely misread that situation."

Could I have gotten it wrong? "I saw you. As soon as I turned the lights on, you moved away from her like you'd been caught in the act."

Unlike those I'd become accustomed to since Gabe's death, the dampened smile he gave me wasn't laden with pity. His eyes sparkled with amusement but also kindness and care. It was like they were trying to convey something else, but I didn't dare attempt to interpret it for fear of disappointment.

"Yes, I was startled, but not because I was in the middle of a romantic interlude with Ophelia. I had been helping her look for her lost diamond earring, and it was easier to do so without overhead lights so that my flashlight could reflect off the diamond. We had just located it and were examining it when the lights came on." His expression was earnest.

My cheeks warmed; such an accusation I'd just made! "I suspect Ophelia may have purposely lost her earring just so you would help her."

"That may be true, I do not know, but what I do know is, I was not in any sort of romantic embrace with her, and I certainly did not kiss her."

"Okay. I believe you. Not that you need to justify anything to me."

"Charlotte."

I whipped around and nodded at the horizon. "Check it out."

"Charlotte."

"Shh. Just watch."

He grunted but moved next to me to face the sunrise.

We stared silently as the sky began to illuminate with pink and orange. The sun's orb began as a tiny sliver and grew until it floated on top of the water's surface like a fireball bobbing in the ocean.

"*The sun himself is weak when he first rises and gathers strength and courage as the day gets on.*"

I turned to face him. "Who said that?"

"Charles Dickens. *The Old Curiosity Shop*."

"That story doesn't exactly have a happy ending."

"Endings—both happy and unhappy—are made in how we interpret the events of our lives."

"Another Dickens quote?"

"Mesnier." He grinned. "My father. Heavily influenced by Aristotle."

"It rings true."

He scanned my face. "Are you happy?"

"What's that other quote about happy endings and if you're not happy, it's not the end?"

He gave a bemused smile. "I do not know this one."

I slapped my palm on the railing. "I know what it is. *Everything will be okay in the end, and if it's not okay, then it's not the end.*"

"Hmm. I suppose that could be true."

I turned back toward the sunrise. "It has to be."

"What was that? I could not catch your words in the wind."

I shook my head. "Nothing."

"Charlotte," he repeated.

"Yes?"

"Please look at me."

Something about the way he spoke sent chills down my arms that had nothing to do with the Caribbean breeze. As I turned toward him again, the glow of daybreak cast a warmth across his face. It was a kind face. Kind eyes with crow's feet at the corners that indicated a life of laughter. He'd barely shown that part of himself to me—the laughter, not the kindness. He'd shown plenty of kindness, almost to the point I wondered sometimes if he actually liked me or if he just tolerated me out of the goodness of his heart, pity, or the fact I was a guest and it was his job to keep me happy and safe.

That's not what I saw in his gaze at that moment, though. The kindness was still present, but there was something else. It kind of looked like affection. Interest. Perhaps even a hint of…desire.

I blinked up at him, trying to wrap my brain around what I was reading in his body language and his expression.

His gaze was intense in a way he'd never looked at me before. He searched my face. My breath caught in a way I'd only read about in romance novels or seen in movies.

It wasn't that I hadn't wanted him to look at me that way. On the contrary, I had hoped at some point I might see ˙˙ ҽves that he viewed me not just as a pain in his neck or ˙ ⁿdle, but as a woman. A woman he wanted n with whom he wanted to be close. To

I'd barely allowed myself the thought before his lips were on mine. They were warm but salty from the sea air. Soft but urgent. Gentle but not passive.

He pulled his mouth away from me, and I had to restrain mine from following.

My lips parted in a combination of surprise and breathlessness. Words failed me.

His smile was confident. He knew how he'd affected me.

"I needed to know."

"Know what?"

"If it was my imagination."

I shivered. "And?"

His smile broadened. He had a dimple on his left cheek I'd never noticed before.

That was the only answer I received.

Mr. and Mrs. Weintraub flung open the door with gusto and walked onto the sundeck, now fully bathed in early morning tropical light. They wore matching terrycloth track suits in banana yellow. Mr. Weintraub's head was wrapped like a mummy. Mrs. Weintraub sported a black baseball cap bejeweled with the word BOSS in rhinestones. I believed it.

She dragged a reluctant Mr. Weintraub by the arm. "Come on, Arty, doctor said you need to stay active while you're recovering." She caught sight of Xavier and me. "Oh! Good morning, you two. I hope we didn't...interrupt anything."

"Not at all," I said.

I sensed Xavier looking at me, but he didn't argue the point. What was there to say?

"Good morning, Madame Weintraub, Monsieur Weintraub. Are you looking forward to exploring Puerto Rico?"

"Oh yes. It's a lovely place with so much history. We're headed to old San Juan right after breakfast."

"Very well." Xavier turned to me. "Perhaps we could continue this conversation later?"

I nodded and smiled. "Sure thing."

He leaned closer and lowered his voice. "Sunset tonight. Same location."

I would have replied, but my words were once again caught in my throat.

After he left, Mrs. Weintraub shuffled over to me, leaving Mr. Weintraub to fend for himself, peeking through the narrow slits in his bandages.

"Look, I know it's none of my business, but if I were single and ten years younger—"

"Twenty," interrupted Mr. Weintraub. "Twenty-five if we're really being honest." He chuckled, or at least that's what it sounded like beneath the muffle of gauze.

She gave him an affectionate swat in his direction. "Oh, hush. You know you can't keep your hands off me, even after fifty-seven years of marriage."

"True. True."

She returned her attention to me. "I'm just saying, I've seen the way he looks at you, and I think there's something there."

"I'll keep that in mind."

Obsessively. Over and over. Counting down the minutes until sunset.

Chapter Thirty-Two

"THIS IS A cool town." Jane held her sun hat on her head with her left hand as she looked up at the colorful display of umbrellas above us in old San Juan. She held Emmett's hand with her right.

"It is," I agreed. "So much to take in with so little time."

"I must admit I'm still a bit disappointed that we were unable to stop in Haiti. Walking the streets of Port-au-Prince would have been invaluable in the crafting of my book," Emmett said.

"It's understandable, though," Jane said. "Until the local authorities get control of the situation there, it's not safe for tourists."

Emmett's mouth pulled downward, probably offended at being called a tourist. He liked to call himself a global citizen. Unfortunately, the criminal elements that had taken over parts of Haiti would have likely only seen his fair skin and American passport and acted accordingly.

"Five hundred years of history and culture in this place. It's stunning," I said.

"It's the oldest continuously inhabited European city in the United States and its territories. It beat St. Augustine,

Florida, by more than four decades," Emmett said.

"Did you know that, or did you read it in a brochure?" Jane pulled down on his hand, bringing him closer to her.

He gave a sheepish shrug. "I read so many things, it's hard to remember."

"Ha. This from the man who can recall the exact moment he first read Faulkner."

"How do you forget reading *As I Lay Dying* while picnicking outside Rowan Oak?"

"I wish I could forget reading it." Her eyes grew wide in recognition of what she'd just said. "I mean..."

He stopped and took a step back to look at her. "You...you don't like Faulkner?"

"I like you," she said feebly.

He shook his head in dramatic disbelief. "But why?"

What was he doing?

"The man can't land a plot to save his life. Stream of consciousness? That's for therapy, not publishing. A run-on sentence of twelve hundred and eighty-eight words? Use some punctuation, for goodness' sake. He made the most mundane things into something absurd and pretentious. He was the king of purple prose. Instead of saying *I went to the bar to have a beer*, he'd turn it into something like, *As I sauntered toward the encapsulation of all that Absalom valued in this enigmatic world where sodbusters laid down their pitchforks to regale each other of their woes over a pint of amber—*"

He held up his hand and chuckled. "All right, all right. Enough. I got it. Not a fan of Faulkner."

She eyed him with pursed lips. "You knew, didn't you?"

"Sweetheart, of course I knew. I graded your essays. You first called him a blowhard and a—oh, what was it? A gasbag who wouldn't know a period from his own—"

"That does sound like me." She laughed. "Agree to disagree?" She held out her hand to shake.

He took it and kissed her palm. "Agree to disagree."

I cleared my throat. "Which brings up my next question. So, Emmett."

"Yes, Charlotte?"

"Have you decided on what comes next for you?"

He gave Jane a sweet smile. "If it's okay with you, I'd like to extend my sabbatical and see where this thing can go."

"I'd like that." She beamed. She turned to look at me. "Is that okay with you?"

"You two lovebirds can do whatever you want. As long as he's not planning to move in."

"I have a nest egg," Emmett said. "I can rent for a bit, see if I want to make anything permanent."

Jane grabbed Emmett by the arm and began walking again. "Char and I have been talking about starting a book club on board. What do you think about that?"

He raised his index finger and opened his mouth.

"And before you even suggest it, this will be a Faulkner-free book club. It'll be good for you to expand your horizons."

He gave her a loving glance. "I'm looking forward to expanding my horizons...with you."

Jane giggled like a schoolgirl. She was young again when

she was with him. He made her happy. And he wasn't a killer, even if he was a bit obsessed with Rougarou.

"Come on, *El Paseo de la Princesa* is this way. The Princess Promenade. Let's go promenade it together." He pulled Jane by the hand.

"Hey, Em, can you give us a minute?" she asked.

He tilted his head. "Of course. Everything okay?"

"Yes, I just wanted to talk to my sister for a minute. We'll catch up."

He smiled and walked ahead.

I scanned her face. "What's up?"

She waved me over to a bench and we sat.

"I just wanted to make sure you're really okay with Emmett coming onboard."

"Why wouldn't I be?"

She looked down her nose in that disappointed librarian way she had. "You haven't always been his biggest fan."

"You're right, but about 90 percent of that was because I suspected him of murdering a man he believed, to be a werewolf. His behavior was definitely cause for concern; don't you think?"

"Even I was starting to wonder, especially after finding out how his wife died and the things he was saying. In his defense, he did hear a howl."

"I can't believe Hawk snuck a husky onboard and was hiding it in a vacant suite. How did he think he could get away with that?"

On his shore leave, Hawk had been informed by his ex-girlfriend that her new apartment didn't allow pets and she could no longer share custody of their four-year-old husky named Fang. He didn't have any place to send the dog, so in a panic he brought him onto the ship. I had to assume there were a lot of people in the cargo loading area who turned a blind eye to the whimpering carrier covered by a blanket that he'd wheeled up the gangplank in New Orleans.

He'd been running to the room every time he got a break to check on Fang, refill his food and water, and replace the potty pads. He'd picked a unit that was owned by a couple who liked to bring their standard poodle onboard and had a faux grass pen for when we were at sea.

So the howling that Emmett had attributed to a possible Rougarou was actually just a lonely doggy begging for someone to come play with him.

"And here I thought I was sneezing because of the gin. Turns out I'm allergic to dogs."

"I thought you might be allergic to Emmett."

"Char, he's a good man."

"I'm teasing."

"I think...I think he's the one."

"You do seem really happy."

"I think we can make each other happy."

"Then I'm really glad for you." I hugged her. "Both of you."

"What about you?" she asked as she released me.

"What about me?"

"I mean, what about you and Xavier?"

"Oh, uh..."

She scanned my face. "What aren't you telling me? You

suddenly look like a stewed tomato."

"We kissed." The words practically burst out of me.

"What? When? How? Tell me everything!"

As I regaled Jane of my romantic interlude with Xavier, her eyes were alight with a joy that I wasn't sure I'd ever seen in her before.

She was in love. Possibly for the first time ever. Her joy was infectious. I wanted that for myself.

There was a song in the movie *White Christmas* about sisters. It was a warning to any man who might contemplate interfering with the special bond between sisters, but there was a caveat for the sisters to not interfere with the other's romantic relationships either.

Jane's and my relationship had been put to the test on this trip. It had been under great duress at times, but it seemed we had come out on the other side stronger for it.

One thing was certain. There was no other bond like that between sisters. It wasn't indestructible and shouldn't ever be taken for granted. It needed to be nurtured.

In my fear of losing her—literally and/or figuratively—I hadn't respected her boundaries. Love didn't look or feel like control, and while I loved my sister deeply, I had let fear for her safety—and fear for what my future would look like—override my love for her. And it nearly cost me the most important person in my life.

"Maybe we can have a double wedding!"

I snapped my attention back to Jane. "Don't you think you're getting a little ahead of yourself?"

"It's called manifestation. I saw a bunch of videos about

it on the TikTok. Come on. Let's catch up to Emmett." She jumped up and pulled me to standing.

"You know it makes you sound old when you call it *the* TikTok." I nudged her as we ambled toward the pathway that skirted the walls of old San Juan.

"I can live with that. I don't mind getting older."

"I know what you mean. In many ways, these are the best years of my life, and it just keeps getting better."

"Our lives."

"Yes. The best days of *our* lives."

The End

If you enjoyed *Frightened to Depths*,
you'll love the next book in…

The Cruising Sisters Mystery

Book 1: *Until Depths Do Us Part*

Book 2: *A Matter of Life and Depths*

Book 3: *Frightened to Depths*

Available now at your favorite online retailer!

Acknowledgments

None of this would have been possible without the nurture and guidance of Dawn Dowdle. You are missed every day.

Thank you to everyone at Tule who brought this series to life, especially my editor Julie, Nan my copyeditor (who probably wonders why I still can't figure out how to use dashes and hyphens after all this time), Kelly, Meghan, Mia, Jaiden, and the wonderful Jane Porter.

Thank you to my friend Dru Ann Love, who supports me and my work and the work of countless other mystery authors through her Dru's Musing blog.

Thank you to Kris and Anjili who have done their best to keep me sane this past year. I love you guys.

I am so blessed to be part of the writing community, and I hope I can give back as much as has been given to me.

To my family and friends who always show up for me, I hope you know how much I appreciate you.

Sydney, Nathan, Zoe, and Parker, I am so proud to be your mom and so grateful to have your love and support.

And of course, to my partner in life, Jeffy J. Having you by my side to hold my hand and catch me when I fall as I learn to fly, has meant more to me than I can possibly express.

About the Author

Kate B Jackson (KB Jackson) is an author of mystery novels for grownups and mystery/adventure novels for kids. She lives in the Pacific NE with her husband and at least one of her four grown children at any given time. Her debut middle grade release is "The Sasquatch of Hawthorne Elementary" (Reycraft Books) about a twelve-year-old boy hired by the most popular girl at his new school to investigate what she saw in the nearby woods. Book one in the Chattertowne Mysteries series, "Secrets Don't Sink," (Level Best Books July 2023) introduces Audrey O'Connell, a small town feature reporter who, when her former boyfriend's body is found floating in the local marina, uncovers the depths to which some will go to keep secrets submerged.

Her debut novel in the Cruising Sisters mystery series, Until Depths Do Us Part (Tule Publishing) will be released Spring 2024.

Thank you for reading

Frightened to Depths

If you enjoyed this book, you can find more from all our great authors at TulePublishing.com, or from your favorite online retailer.

TULE
PUBLISHING

www.ingramcontent.com/pod-product-compliance
Lightning Source LLC
Chambersburg PA
CBHW060904030125
19786CB00007B/93

9 781965 640753